TORSTEN'S HOARD

JOHN J. SPEARMAN

OTHER BOOKS BY THIS AUTHOR

The FitzDuncan Series
FitzDuncan
FitzDuncan's Alchemy
FitzDuncan's Enlightenment
FitzDuncan's Fortune
FitzDuncan's Gambit
FitzDuncan's Hope
FitzDuncan's Inheritance
FitzDuncan's Navy
FitzDuncan's Peril
FitzDuncan's Beginning

Burden Series
Burden

Dexter Falk Series
The Thane's Daughter
The Veil of Shadow

PUBLISHED BY AETHON BOOKS
BY THIS AUTHOR

Orion Spur Series
Misfortune's Favorite
The Scourge of the Scyllans
Fondness for Adversity
Defender's Awakening
Deceptive Betrayal

The Halberd Series
Gallantry in Action
In Harm's Way
True Allegiance
Surrender Demand

The Pike Series
Pike's Potential
Pike's Passage
Pike's Progress
Pike's Purpose

The Perseverance Andrews Series
The Defense of the Commonwealth
The Courage of the Commonwealth
The Resolve of the Commonwealth

Mercenary Navy Series
Rawlins' Redemption
Swiftsure Ascendant
Tenuous Defense

PANTHEON

Major Gods

- Sky and heavens: **Zoryn** (male)
- Earth: **Teryssa** (female)
- Sea: **Marivelle** (female)
- Death: **Thalorix** (male)

Lesser Gods

- Fertility: **Vyran** (male)
- Romance and sexual pleasure: **Lysmera** (female)
- War: **Kravyna** (female)
- Commerce, travel, thievery: **Sylvaris** (male)
- Wisdom: **Eldryne** (female)
- Literature and arts: **Calithra** (female)
- Health and medicine: **Vionelle** (female)
- Smiths and manufacturing: **Korath** (male)
- Luck and fortune: **Serethyn** (female)

CALENDAR

Zorynth: Begins at Winter Solstice, lasts 31 days
Calithran: 30 days
Lysmeran: 30 days
Teryssan: Begins at Vernal Equinox, lasts 31 days.
Vyranth: lasts 30 days
Kravynth: lasts 31 days.
Vionelleth: Begins at Summer Solstice, lasts 31 days.
Sylvarith: lasts 30 days.
Marivelleth: lasts 30 days.
Serethyan: Begins at Autumnal Equinox, lasts 31 days.
Eldrynan: lasts 30 days.
Korathan: lasts 30 days.

1

The tinkle of the bell from the door at the bottom of the steps to my flat woke me. I scrambled out of bed and had only enough time to pull on a shirt before there was a knock at the door. My initial thought was that Catherine was there, but she would have come right in.

"Hello?" I called out.

"Mr. Falk?" came a pleasant-sounding female voice.

"Yes?"

"May I come in?"

"You'll need to give me a minute. I just woke up, and I'm not decent. I must have overslept."

"Not necessarily," she replied. "The sun just rose, but I've been knocking on your door multiple times over the last three days."

I was hopping around, getting my breeches on, fastening them, and tucking in my shirt. The next step was stockings, and then my boots. I raked my hand through my hair in an attempt to look more presentable and opened the door.

"Hello," I said, momentarily taken aback by the woman's appearance.

She strode into the room, and my eyes followed her. Her skin was golden. She had deep brown eyes with long lashes, atop elegant cheekbones. Her hair was a rich brown, captured in a messy bun skewered by a pencil, keeping it mostly off her elegantly long neck. She was wearing the purple robe of a priestess of Eldryne, which moved against her body in a way that hinted at every delightful curve it hid. Upon closer inspection, I saw that the robe was dirty and ragged at the hem.

Despite her garment, this woman was a rare beauty. I must have stared a little bit too much, because she touched her hair self-consciously, as though I might have found fault with her appearance. I snapped out of my daze and broke eye contact to shut the door. When I turned, she sat in my chair in front of the window. I felt the tingle of Sylvaris on my neck quite strongly.

"Yes, I am Dexter Falk," I said. "And you?"

"Fiona Magellan. I am a—"

"Priestess of Eldryne," I said. "Or you wear the robe, at least."

"Yes, I serve the goddess."

"What brings you here so early in the day?"

"I have need of your services, Mr. Falk. Something was stolen from our library in Harkiss, and I need to get it back."

"A book? A scroll?"

"A map."

"Why would someone want an old map?" I asked. "Does it show the location of a hidden treasure?"

"As a matter of fact, Mr. Falk, I believe it does. I was in the process of researching it, and was close to proving that the mythical Hoard of Torsten actually exists."

"Torsten? Torsten?" I muttered to myself. "Wasn't he the guy who supposedly had most of South Gaugan as his empire?"

"That is Torsten."

"I thought that was just a legend, a myth."

"So did everyone except me," she said. "I thought there was a basis in fact behind those stories, and I set out to prove it. The more I learned, the more convinced I became that the tales of Torsten were based on actual events. The map was one of the last pieces of evidence. I am fairly certain that it provides clues to find his treasure."

"Who would have known about the map?"

"That's the strangest thing, Mr. Falk. Only three people know what I was doing, and they are all priestesses of Eldryne. All have submitted to formal questioning by members of the order and have denied spreading the information. As you know, certain priestesses of Eldryne can detect falsehood. All three told the truth."

"And you want to hire me to find the map?"

"Or the Hoard, Mr. Falk."

The back of my neck fairly itched; Sylvaris was connected to me so tautly. It was clear to me that I was meant to assist this woman. His interest in this matter was evident.

"Are you aware of my rates, Miss Magellan?"

"Oh. About that—I have a letter for you from your Archpriest," she said, reaching into a fold in her robe and producing a folded piece of paper.

Dear Dexter,

This delightful young lady was passing through Meropan on her way to find you. The god we both serve alerted me to her presence, and he wishes for you to answer her call. One of my acolytes will find her and give her this missive.

If the Eldrynes ever asked another one of the orders for assistance, it happened so long ago as to be before history was recorded. I can share with you that the god we both serve is eager for you to take part. He desperately would like to have Eldryne in his debt.

There will be no compensation for you of a pecuniary sort. I have a suspicion that you are comfortably well off by now, and what Sylvaris has provided, he can certainly ask you to use on his behalf. Just to be safe, you should probably take a letter of credit with you when you leave Tallesin with Miss Magellan. From the little I know, you will probably travel overseas.

This is the second letter I've written you in less than a year. Neither brought news that you would welcome wholeheartedly. Perhaps the next epistle will.

Azar

"I see," I said as I folded the letter and put it away.

The tingle on the back of my neck had not eased a bit. Indeed, it felt as though a fisherman's hook had lodged there and was pulling me. This was no ordinary job. The god of merchants, travelers, and thieves wanted Eldryne's favor. For what purpose? Mine not to determine. All I needed to know was that he was giving me a clear indication of how he wished me to proceed.

Fiona was watching me with her deep brown eyes, her head tilted as though she was analyzing an ancient text in a dead language. A stray lock of hair had escaped the mound held by her pencil and framed her jawline. I'd been blessed to share the love of two strikingly attractive women in the last year, Agatha and Catherine, but neither possessed the sheer beauty that radiated from Fiona Magellan. I yanked my gaze away before she caught me staring again.

"Ahem, my archpriest has asked me to assist you in this matter, so I will be happy to join you in your search. Please tell me everything you know regarding the map and its disappearance—even the details that seem unimportant."

"There will be plenty of time for that on the journey to Harkiss," she said, rising from my chair. "We should get started immediately."

"Hold on, Miss Magellan," I said. "I need to pack. I need to arrange passage for us on a boat. My archpriest suggested I obtain a letter of credit from my bank in order to obtain funds wherever we end up, and if the sun just came up, the banks won't open for hours."

"Oh. Very well. I am eager to begin. May I wait here?"

"I would prefer it if you returned to the temple of Eldryne. That is where you have been staying, isn't it?"

"Yes."

"Do you know the name of the ship that brought you here? Perhaps they would be willing to take us back."

"I walked."

"From Harkiss?"

"Yes. It took twenty-seven days."

"Why didn't you sail? You would have arrived weeks earlier."

"I knew you would not be here. The goddess told me that you would not return until the new moon of Teryssan. That was three days ago."

"Let me spend the day preparing for the journey, Miss Magellan. I will come by the temple this evening to confirm that we will be able to leave tomorrow."

"Would you like to dine at the temple?"

"If you would like me to."

"Actually, the food in the temple is terrible," she said. "I would prefer to eat almost anywhere else."

"Miss Magellan, do you have any other clothes besides your robes?"

"A cloak. Why?"

"If I am going to help you recover this map, it might be beneficial for you to blend in with the general public. In my experience, priestly robes draw quite a bit of attention; they do not hold up well on the road and are awkward to move in."

"I do not own anything else."

"Then we may need to delay while we have some clothing made for you."

"Are you sure that is necessary?"

"Yes. Haven't you ever noticed that when a member of your order appears, people stop talking?"

"I suppose they do," she said, tilting her head the other direction. "I always assumed it was reverence for wisdom. Or perhaps they are simply thinking. Silence is best for contemplation."

"Silence is detrimental to gaining the type of information that will lead us to the map, Miss Magellan. We want people to speak freely around us—the more, the better."

"Very well," she said after considering this for three full heartbeats. "I will wear common clothes, but you will need to buy them. I have no money for such things. And I will look ridiculous."

"I beg to differ, Miss Magellan. You could probably wear a potato sack and look beautiful."

Her cheeks colored. She frowned. She tucked the loose strand of hair behind her ear.

"When you say things like that, it distracts me," she said. "I don't know whether I like it."

"Then I shall have to be more careful with my tongue, though Sylvaris knows that will be difficult."

"Sylvaris?" she said, studying my face. "Ah, yes. You are god-touched. I remember now. Is he present now?"

"He is," I admitted, "and he is vastly entertained."

"Why? Am I making you uncomfortable? Your face is redder than when I arrived."

"I think that is part of the reason," I said.

"Why do I make you uncomfortable, Mr. Falk?"

"Miss Magellan, you are quite beautiful. It is common for men to become awkward in the presence of a woman so pretty."

She blinked once, twice, three times, like an owl. Her cheeks then turned a shade of red under their golden glow, and the flush crept down her neck. She did not simper or flutter her eyelashes; she merely stared at me, looking me directly in the eyes.

"I fail to see how my appearance should be a detriment to completing the task that lies before us," she said, tilting her head again, causing the strand of hair to fall along her cheek again. "Unless you would find it such a distraction as to impair your abilities. If that is the case, I should find another agent of Sylvaris with whom to work, although you were the only one the goddess instructed me to locate."

"I will do my best to remain focused on the task ahead of us, Miss Magellan."

"Very well. Shall we address the matter of clothing?"

"It is so early, the seamstresses have not opened."

"Seamstress—that implies they will make the clothes. How long will that take?"

"A couple of days."

"Unacceptable, Mr. Falk. Perhaps when we reach Harkiss, I will reconsider the matter, but I have already agreed to wait to leave on the morrow. Visit your bankers, arrange for our passage, and collect me at the temple of Eldryne this evening," she said.

She stood and headed for the door. The fold of her robe hooked the edge of the small table next to the chair where she had been sitting. The inkpot on it would have spilled all over her robes if I had not lunged and grabbed it. As it was, the ink slopped over my hand.

"Oh," she said. "It seems you are distracting me as well, Mr. Falk. I become very clumsy when I am … confused."

2

I found a rag and tried to wipe the ink from my hand, but it would leave a black stain that only time would remove. Fiona watched me the whole time. If she had not been there, I would have cursed a blue streak.

"I'm sorry, Mr. Falk," she said when she saw that the ink would not come off my skin. "I will try to focus better when I am around you."

"Do I distract you, Miss Magellan?"

"I'm afraid you do, Mr. Falk. You are not what I expected."

"And what did you expect?"

"Someone older, smaller, less virile, more untrustworthy in appearance."

"Well, Miss Magellan, I am sorry I am such a disappointment."

"Oh. You mistake my meaning, sir. I am delighted to find you as you are. It is simply that I did not expect … you."

I stared at this golden-skinned priestess who spoke without any pretense whatsoever. It was disarming. The tingle on my neck was undiminished. Sylvaris was, I think, entertained by this woman and by how she kept me off balance.

"I suppose that was meant as a compliment? If so, I'm flattered. Most people expect someone like me to be either a silver-tongued charmer or a greasy fellow that one should never turn his back on. You seem to have imagined something of a combination of the two."

She tilted her head, and another strand of her chestnut hair dropped down. Her lovely face was now perfectly framed. Her gaze was steady and direct.

"You are much more … vital … than I expected. As I said, it is distracting."

"I'm sorry, but I am what I am. Will it be a problem?"

"Perhaps. We shall see. Are there others like you to whom I could turn?"

"Not that I am aware of."

"I see. Well, we shall have to make the best of it, then. Now, you said you have errands to attend to. Please do what you must, and I will see you when you come to take me to dinner this evening."

With that, she let herself out. I shook my head in silent wonderment. What a beautiful, odd creature she was! I tossed the rag into the fireplace. There was no use in it any longer, as the ink had ruined it. I tried to wash my hand with strong soap but knew that I would succeed only partially. When I finished, having achieved the results I expected, I decided I would head to my favorite inn for breakfast.

I grabbed a money pouch, making sure I had enough guilders inside to convince a sailing master to take us to Harkiss. After I finished eating, I would visit the waterfront. Harkiss was not a popular destination. Beyond hosting the Order of Eldryne, there wasn't much to the town. It was on the western coast, on a thumb of land that extended into the vast Entassa Ocean.

The banks would be open after that, and I could obtain a letter of credit. I had a funny feeling that this would be an expensive venture. From the little Fiona had told me, I suspected we would be traveling to the continent of South Gaugan before we were through. It would be difficult to find someone in Harkiss or any other city nearby who would make the trip across the Entassa. Most trade to North and South Gaugan went across the narrower Tiburn Sea to the east.

The Entassa was wider, deeper, and known for strong currents. A quick crossing of it took a month, compared to a week (or less, with Marivelle's favor, as I had experienced) for the Tiburn. It might prove to be easier for us to travel east from Harkiss, back to Tallesin, across the isthmus, and then sail on the Tiburn. The time it would take would be roughly the same.

I pondered this as I walked to the Broken Wheel, my favorite of the inns near my flat. Garrett, the proprietor, was almost a friend. We traded favors back and forth.

"Well, look what the cat dragged in!" he exclaimed when he saw me.

"I've been away," I answered with a shrug.

His mention of the word "cat" gave me a twinge of guilt. I'd just had a tearful farewell the night before, and I should be feeling pretty low right now, except I wasn't. From how strongly Sylvaris had tugged at me earlier during Fiona's visit, I suspected he was playing a part in my resilience. The challenge Fiona laid before me also helped my attitude. Still, before I disappeared again for who knows how long, I resolved to write Catherine a letter before I left.

"Again," he said. "I reckon you haven't spent more than three months in the city in the last year."

"You might be right," I acknowledged. "Any fruit in the porridge this morning?"

"You are in luck, my friend. The first strawberries just hit the market yesterday, and I bought as many as I could afford."

"That sounds wonderful. A bowl, please, and coffee if it's fresh. I had an unexpectedly early start to the day and am still out of sorts."

"The coffee has just brewed, so you're doubly lucky this morning."

"I'll share that luck with you if you can tell me of anyone who would be willing to give me passage to Harkiss. Pay you three times for one meal."

"Well, well, well," Garrett said. "Isn't that interesting? Would this have anything to do with an absolute stunner of an Eldryne in rather tatty robes? The one who has been lurking in the neighborhood for the last couple of days, asking about one Dexter Falk?"

"It would. I take it she's not very subtle."

"Subtle as a sledgehammer, that one. Not one for small talk, neither. But, my heavens! What a lovely! What does she want with you?"

"Garrett, my friend, why don't you let me inspect your kitchen and look at your books, so I can see everything about your business?"

"Point taken, Dex, point taken. None of my beeswax," he said as he retrieved a bowl of porridge and poured a mug of coffee. "Still, the only reason to want to go to Harkiss is the Eldrynes, and there's one here, looking for you. Not much of a co-inky-dink. But, as it just so happens, I do think I know of someone who might take you to Harkiss—Billy Rodhe. He's got bills to pay and no cash."

"How much does he owe?"

"Sixty-five."

"Guilders?" I asked incredulously.

Garrett nodded.

"How in the world did he get so far under?"

"At the end of the Serethyan, he got caught in a bad storm. His boat needed repair—a lot of work. He took it to the yard and had them fix her up. Just before they finished, the woman Billy had been with found where he hid his money, took it, and scampered. He had no way to pay. They've been wrangling back and forth ever since. They won't give him his boat without the money, and without the boat, Billy has no way to ever pay them back. They're fixing to sell the boat any day now. You pay off his debt, and he'll take you wherever you want to go, including Harkiss. He's a good man, Dexter. He deserves better."

"But sixty-five guilders is a lot of money," I protested.

"You're welcome to ask around, but I doubt you'll find any takers," Garrett said.

"Good point," I said. "And the priestess is in a danged hurry to get back. What the heck? It's only money, right? How do I find Billy?"

"That's a bit more difficult," Garrett said, scratching his head as he thought. "He's been staying here and there. His landlord booted him when he couldn't pay the rent. I can put the word out and ask him to find you. He won't waste any time, believe me."

"Garrett, my friend, here are three quadrans for the porridge, the strawberries, the coffee, and the information. Are we square?"

"We are, Dexter. I'll get someone to find Billy. Expect him today. You'll probably also need to provision him. He has no credit on the docks right now."

It was still too early for the bank, so I returned to my flat. I spent the next two hours writing Catherine to tell her that I would be leaving immediately. It occurred to me that she might already know if Portia, the Archpriestess of Marivelle, had told her it was coming. I wasted three sheets of paper trying to come up with the right words to say. In the end, I kept it simple, telling her I was already being called away, that I treasured the time we spent together, and hoped her future was as bright as it appeared to be.

I was just finishing when I heard the bell at my door ring. Heavy footsteps pounded up the stairs to my flat. A sharp rap on the door and, "Mr. Falk?"

"Billy Rodhe?" I called back.

"Yes, sir."

"C'mon in."

The door swung open to reveal a barrel-chested man, nervously twisting a cap in his hands. He looked a bit haggard, which was to be expected based on what Garrett had told me of his circumstances. He stepped inside exactly one pace and stopped.

"Mr. Falk? Garrett said you might be the answer to my prayers. Passage to Harkiss?"

"Aye. Two passengers—me, and a priestess of Eldryne. She's in a hurry and wants to leave tomorrow. I understand your boat is in the yard. Do you think she's ready to sail?"

"Between now and the outgoing tide tomorrow, she will be."

"How much will you need beyond the sixty-five you owe the yard? Any other debts you need to clear before you leave the city?"

"I don't have no provisions, sir. And I don't have no crew. Another five guilders will see to both."

"How about I give you ten more, and you don't cut any corners on either the provisions or the crew?"

"Thankee, sir."

"Of course, you'll probably need to sail in ballast back to Tallesin. Not much chance of cargo in Harkiss. I'll give you twenty-five for that, making an even hundred."

"Sir, ya don have to," he protested.

"Let's just say you're catching me in an odd mood, Billy," I said. "Garrett told me what happened to you, and I'm going to try to change your luck. All I ask is that you make good use of this chance, and if, in the future, you hear of someone who could use a hand, try to help them out. Agreed?"

"Yessir."

I counted out a hundred guilders and swept them into an empty pouch. I handed it to Billy. He insisted on shaking my hand vigorously.

"Thankee, sir. It'll be the best voyage to Harkiss ever, I swear. And I'll never need no help again. Next time you're in the city, you check up on me. You'll see."

"I'm sure I will. Now, go get your boat, and make sure we're ready to leave on the tide tomorrow. What time will that be?"

"Just past eight, sir."

"I'm sure we'll be early," I said as I ushered him out the door.

I'd wasted enough time trying to write Catherine that the bank I used was open. I sealed the letter and wrote her name on the envelope, and the name of her father's business. For a quadrans, I could find a boy who would run it over.

The bank asked a lot of questions before giving me what I wanted. I had more than enough money deposited with them, but I liked that they were so careful. In the end, I left with a letter of credit worth two thousand guilders, sealed in a waxed envelope to protect it against accidental moisture.

When I finished with the bank, I went to the stable where I kept Rufus. I let the owner know that I would be gone, and paid for three months of board, including regular exercise. It bothered me that I would be leaving him behind for so long, after he'd spent a couple of months at the temple of Sylvaris in Dropan without me. I didn't think it was fair to him.

On the way back, I stopped by a food cart. With spring having arrived, the vendors were back on the streets. I bought a skewer of roasted goat and vegetables.

Passing an apothecary, I decided to stop in. I had a vague hunch that Fiona was unaccustomed to sea travel and might experience seasickness. I purchased some ginger tea and peppermint oil, which would help if that happened.

3

I returned to my flat and pondered what to pack and whether to use saddlebags or a valise. My guess was that we would be sailing for the most part, until we reached South Gaugan (when that time came, if it did). I retrieved a valise and stowed both the nice clothing Catherine purchased for me, as well as some rougher, sturdier things that would hold up well aboard a ship.

I pulled my favorite chair around so I could look outside at the market square. It was a fine spring day, and before I sat, I opened all the windows in my flat to get rid of the musty smell from being away so long. Of course, this excursion promised to be a lengthy one. The flat would be just as stale-smelling when I returned. I could only hope the weather would still be warm enough to air it out.

I sat and watched the people and tried to feel guilty about how quickly my heart had closed the chapter on Catherine. Just last night, I had been broken-hearted, but today I was already looking forward to the challenge Fiona had brought me. I felt a mental nudge from Sylvaris then. He never communicated with me in words, but I sensed he was trying to tell me that this is the way things were meant to happen, and that I should accept that I was a part of something greater than myself.

As the shadows grew longer, I stirred myself to set off for the temple of Eldryne. It stood on a quiet square near the courts of the magistrates. Temples of Eldryne tended to be modest and small, and this was no exception.

When I arrived, Fiona was waiting at the front door, a tiny satchel at her feet. She was still in her purple robe, but her hair was more tidily arranged, now held with a comb of what looked to be tortoise shell. As I approached, she picked up her bag.

"Mr. Falk, you are prompt."

I wanted to say something witty and charming, complimenting her on her beauty, but sensed it would not register properly with Fiona.

"Thank you. I try to be," is what I ended up replying.

"Where will we dine?"

"There is an inn nearby with excellent food," I said. "It is frequented by solicitors and members of the magistracy, so your robes will generate little interest."

"Very well. I will pay for my own meal," she said.

"I am afraid I cannot permit that, Miss Magellan. Good manners say otherwise. I will be delighted to pay for both of us. May I take your bag?"

"If you insist."

"I do. May I ask what it contains?"

"My things. It will save time in the morning if I spend the night at your flat."

"I have only the one bed."

"We will share."

I stared at her a moment. Share the bed … with this golden-skinned vision … she could not mean… She must be naïve. My neck tingled, and I sensed Sylvaris's great amusement.

"Very well. Do you steal the blankets?"

"Blankets are communal property in shared sleeping arrangements, Mr. Falk. It would be ill-mannered for me to do so."

"Then let us proceed to dinner," I said.

We went around the corner to the Lantern. Fiona walked beside me, her robe swaying just enough to hint at the figure beneath it. This close to the temple of Eldryne, her robes garnered little attention, except for their tattered appearance.

The innkeeper ushered us to a quiet corner of the dining room. The room smelled of tonight's meal—roast spring lamb. I helped Fiona with her seat, which was something she was unprepared for.

"Why did you do that? I am not *that* clumsy. I am perfectly capable of seating myself."

"I have no doubt, Miss Magellan. But where I come from, a man shows respect for his female companion by making small gestures such as this, even though she is not necessarily in need of any assistance whatsoever."

"Why do you respect me?"

"You are a priestess of Eldryne. That automatically earns my respect and encourages me to act with the utmost courtesy toward you."

"In Harkiss, my fellow servants of Eldryne are indifferent to such things. During my journey, and while in Tallesin, I have found that most men stare at me or make lewd remarks when they think I cannot hear."

"They stare at you because you are uncommonly beautiful, Miss Magellan. Nevertheless, both the staring and the remarks are rude and discourteous."

"In Harkiss, respect is earned through learning and accomplishments, not physical appearance."

"That is probably so, but are there some of your fellow servants you find more pleasing to look at than others?"

"Well … yes."

"You, Miss Magellan, are very pleasing to look at," I said. "I say this not to curry favor with you, since I doubt you think it is a compliment, but as a statement of fact."

"You speak the truth. I am not god-touched in that way like some of my fellow servants of Eldryne, but I can recognize blatant falsehood. In that spirit, I will tell you that I am enjoying the way you look at me. Even though I find it … unsettling … it excites me. Your physical appearance is also pleasing for me to observe. I did not expect to feel any of this, and I will admit to being confused by my reactions."

"Miss Magellan, you are the most direct person I have ever met," I said. "It is … refreshing."

"Is it refreshing or off-putting?"

"Both."

"I know of no other way to behave. I have been at the temple in Harkiss for fourteen years since I was brought there from my village. Life at the temple is very different from what I have seen on my journey, and from what I remember from when I was a girl, but it is what I know best."

"So, you have no experience with flirting?"

"Flirting? Behaving as though attracted to someone, to determine if there is mutual interest, or for one's personal amusement?"

"Yes."

"Flirting can be disingenuous. Is it not more efficient to state one's interest clearly?"

I smiled. How could I not?

"It can also be fun," I said. "And it is a way for many people to learn the intentions of someone they find attractive without risking complete rejection, which can be painful."

"I will consider what you have said. For now, I will be direct. I find your appearance and your bearing highly pleasing, Mr. Falk. You are, what most people would consider objectively, handsome. Your shoulders are broad, you appear to be strong, you move with graceful efficiency, and your voice carries a resonance that I find pleasant. You are not what I expected to find, and I am curious to know more about you. I find that I enjoy the time I spend with you."

I could not help it; my pulse quickened. At the same time, I noticed Sylvaris was paying attention to our interaction. He was not merely entertained; the feeling I was sensing was one of delight. I set my wine glass down carefully, lest my suddenly shaky hand betray me. At that moment, the serving girl brought our dinner, saving me from saying something stupid.

The food was delightful. Accompanied by new potatoes and early peas, the inn added just enough rosemary and garlic to enhance the flavor of the lamb without overwhelming it. Fiona ate with the same efficiency I was beginning to see in all her actions—small bites, chewed thoroughly. Conversation ceased for a time.

"I am glad I insisted on dining elsewhere," she said after she finished the last bite of the strawberries and cream we had for dessert and daintily wiped the corner of her mouth with her napkin. "My fellow servants of Eldryne are terrible cooks. It is the same even in Harkiss."

I had already settled the bill with our host, and I took her comment as a cue to leave. I stood and came to assist her with her chair. By the time I made it around the table, she had already stood.

"Were you coming to assist me in standing up? Even though I needed no help?"

"Yes. Again, common courtesy. And I will carry your bag, if you allow it."

"I brought it with me all the way from Harkiss," she said. "I am perfectly capable of carrying it to your flat."

"It's not that, Miss Magellan," I said. "I would be pleased if you would allow me to do this for you."

"If you insist, although I do not see the point."

"Thank you," I said as she handed it to me.

It weighed almost nothing. I wondered what it contained. Fiona had certainly traveled light if this was all she brought from Harkiss.

We walked through the city streets. The lamplighters had been out. Fiona walked by my side, and her hand occasionally brushed mine. I found myself unexpectedly thrilled at these random touches. Sylvaris was still a nagging presence, and he was seemingly delighted with this woman.

"You are staring at me again," she remarked.

"I am. Forgive me."

"There is nothing to forgive. I have decided I like the way you look at me. You are clearly enjoying my company, which makes me feel unexpectedly rewarded. Is this vanity, I wonder?"

"No, it is humanity," I replied. "You are uncommonly lovely, and I cannot help but react to that. In addition, your mind works in ways that I find refreshing, which further whets my curiosity."

"Do you find my behavior strange, Mr. Falk?"

"The word strange can carry with it negative connotations," I said. "And so far, I have not observed anything negative about you. You are simply quite different from any woman I have met."

"You have not spent time with many servants of Eldryne, then."

"That is true."

We reached the door to the stairs to my flat. The bell tinkled when we opened it. I allowed Fiona to precede me up the steps in the dark. When we reached the top, I paused.

"Please allow me to go first, Miss Magellan. I know my way around the furniture and will light a candle quickly to prevent you from running into anything."

"That is sensible," she said.

I went in and found where I kept a taper. Working quickly by feel, I unraveled the end of the wick. I was about to strike my flint when Fiona bumped into me from behind, her soft breasts lodging against my back.

"Oh!" she gasped. "Sorry. It seemed silly to wait outside when I could follow your footsteps."

"No harm done, Miss Magellan," I said, then tried to strike the flint with suddenly shaky hands.

It took several tries before a spark lodged in the fibers I'd untwined. I blew on it gently, and it took flame. When I turned to light the candles, Fiona was still just behind me, and my shoulder lodged between her breasts.

"I'm sorry," I said.

"It is my fault. I should have stepped away."

I shuffled to the side and went to light candles. Fiona stayed where she was, observing me. When I had lit two candles, I blew out the taper and went to pick up her bag from where I had dropped it. Collecting one of the candles, I started for my bedroom, Fiona right behind me.

"The bed is here," I said. "It is yours. I will sleep in the chair."

"Why? That will be uncomfortable. We begin our journey back to Harkiss tomorrow. You will need to be rested. Your bed is big enough for two. We discussed this. Or are you still afraid I will steal the blankets? May I remind you that your god is the patron of thieves, not mine."

I could not help but burst into laughter. Fiona made a joke. It was unexpected. In the light of the candle, I could see her smile, happy that her jest had landed.

"You've convinced me, Miss Magellan. Which side would you prefer?"

"I will take the window," she said.

She withdrew the comb from her hair and shook it out to let it tumble down her shoulders. Without any warning, she drew her robe over her head. Underneath, she was wearing only a thin shift that revealed as much as it hid.

"You are staring again, Mr. Falk."

"I apologize. I find I cannot help myself."

"Then I will get beneath the covers to eliminate further distraction."

4

I t took me a while to fall asleep. I was very conscious of the person in bed with me. Fiona had no such difficulty.

She woke me, getting out of bed when the sun rose. By the time I opened my eyes, she had already put her robe back on. She then sat on the edge of the bed to watch me dress.

"You have many scars, Mr. Falk," she said. "You must find yourself in fights many times. Is the plethora of wounds due to a lack of skill, or the number of altercations?"

"I am considered skilled by most," I replied with a shrug. "What I do for a living is help people recover items that were lost or taken from them. The people who took those items usually have no desire to surrender them. It tends to lead to a number of ... altercations ... and I am often outnumbered."

She nodded and rose from the bed, crossing to the window. As she stood there, she gathered her hair up in a loose knot and skewered it with a pencil, her comb back in her small bag. I paused while she did this. She really was exquisitely beautiful, and seemingly completely unaware of this.

"We should go, Mr. Falk."

"Miss Magellan, after sharing my bed, would it be possible to ease into a less formal manner of address? I would prefer it if you called me Dexter, or Dex, as my friends do. And we have a couple of hours yet before we need to arrive at the boat. The tide does not turn until eight, and I reckon it is barely six. Besides, I have something I want you to do that will take a few minutes."

"What is that, Dexter?" she said, saying my name as though tasting a new dish and trying to determine whether she liked it.

"Have you ever sailed on the open sea before, Miss Magellan?"

"I have not. And if you insist on using first names, please use mine."

"Thank you, Fiona. The reason I ask the question is that the motion of the waves can make people sick to their stomachs until they grow accustomed to it. There are remedies that I purchased yesterday. One of them is ginger tea. If you will give me a few minutes, I will kindle a fire in the stove and make you some."

"You speak of seasickness. I have read of this. Ginger tea is supposed to help?"

"Yes. It calms the stomach. I also have some peppermint oil for you to spread on your upper lip once we board. The scent also helps with the queasy feeling."

"That was very thoughtful of you, Mr.—Dexter. Yes, we can delay while you prepare tea. Will you have some as well?"

"Only to keep you company, Fiona. I am not typically prone to seasickness, but ginger tea is pleasant, and I will gladly share a cup."

I went to the kitchen and quickly kindled a fire in the stove, building it only big enough to bring the kettle to a boil. While we waited, Fiona took my chair that was facing out the window and watched as the first trickle of pedestrians began in the square below. When the kettle began to sing, I poured two cups and mixed in the powder I'd purchased. While waiting for it to cool to a reasonable temperature, I took care to bank the fire in the stove.

"This is quite refreshing," Fiona commented after taking her first sip. "And it has medicinal properties as well? I did not know, but I will look into it when we return to Harkiss."

"I have more, as you will probably need a few additional cups before your body adjusts to the motion."

"How long does it take most people?"

"Two or three days. It can be quite unpleasant. Your stomach may still feel upset, but the tea and peppermint oil will lessen the symptoms and alleviate the worst of it."

With the tea consumed and the fire on its way out, I took both our bags, and we headed to the Broken Wheel to break our fast. Garrett served us porridge with strawberries. He was a bit intimidated by Fiona's purple robes of Eldryne and did not attempt to engage in his usual banter. That was probably for the best.

Finished, we headed to the docks and went to the end of one of the piers. I stood and looked around to see if I could spy Billy Rodhe. It took a moment, and he actually spotted me first. His boat was three quays down, and I saw him waving his arm. There were two other men aboard with him.

"Welcome aboard the *Hazel Olivia*," he said, "though when we return from Harkiss, I plan to ask Marivelle if I can change her name."

"Why do you need to ask the goddess?" Fiona inquired.

"Because it's bad luck elsewise."

"I do not think the goddess of the seas would care that much," Fiona said.

"But she does," I interrupted to prevent Billy from needing to answer. "It is something particular to Marivelle."

"Why do you need to change the name?" she asked.

"Because she's named after me wife and me mother," Billy said, "and me wife ran off with all my money a few months back and left me in a world of hurt. I don't want her name on my boat."

"Let's stow our bags," I said, taking Fiona by the arm before she could ask Billy more uncomfortable questions.

I took us to the hatch and climbed down the ladder first. I waited at the bottom in case Fiona got tangled in her long robe. She did, the tattered hem getting caught on a splinter, pulling the robe up well past her knees, revealing two lengths of golden-colored skin that were perfectly shaped.

"Stop!" I said, my mouth unexpectedly dry.

I climbed up a few rungs behind her and leaned forward to free the garment. It required me to press up against her back, and I felt the warm softness of her. My fingers didn't want to work properly, and it took me a couple of fumbles before I unsnagged her robe.

"You are breathing rather heavily, Dexter. Was it that difficult?"

By all that's holy, if this woman knew how to flirt, she would flay me alive! But there was no innuendo in her comment, merely an observation. I cleared my throat and stepped down and away from the ladder.

"Your robe is a bit impractical for the tight confines of such a small vessel, Fiona," I said, ignoring her remark. "Perhaps we should find a length of rope to gather it up so you do not continue to catch the hem on things."

"That makes sense," she said, grabbing a handful of her robe and pulling it up, revealing her flawless calves again.

Below deck, the *Hazel Olivia* was cramped but tidy. Here in the stern, we were in the cabin. There was a small galley area and five hammocks hanging from hooks. On the forward bulkhead was a hatch that would reveal the hold when opened. I set our bags down in the corner.

"Are these our quarters?" she asked.

"Yes."

"Where are the beds?"

"On a boat that rolls and lifts with the waves, you would find yourself tossed on the deck if you tried to sleep in a bed. We will use these hammocks."

"They look impossible to sleep in."

"Because they are stowed," I explained.

I took one and unhooked an end, stretching it across to the waiting hook on the other side of the tiny cabin area. When it was fastened, I climbed into it. In the dim light, I could see Fiona looking at me, assessing it.

"It will take some getting used to, I suppose," she said. "Why are there five? There are only the two of us."

"Because all of us will sleep here. Billy and his two crew members need to sleep occasionally."

"Oh."

"The rest of the ship," I said, gesturing at the forward bulkhead, "is for cargo."

"But there is no cargo."

"Not this trip," I said, "but most boat owners make their living from delivering goods, not people. I offered Billy a fairly substantial amount of money to take us to Harkiss, to offset the fact that there is no cargo."

"That is not true, Mr. Falk," Fiona said sternly. "You are lying. I don't have the truth sense my god-touched sisters and brothers in Eldryne do, but I can spot most lies."

"You are correct, Fiona, and I apologize. The truth is more embarrassing to Mr. Rodhe, which is why I fibbed," I admitted, and then proceeded to tell her exactly what Billy's predicament had been, and how I helped him.

"That was compassionate, Dexter. Why would you lie about such a thing?"

"Because I did not want you to think poorly of Billy," I said, keeping my voice low. "Some men break when the world kicks them too hard. Billy was close to that point. From what a man I trust told me, none of his ill fortune was deserved."

"I think no less of Mr. Rodhe for knowing this. You should always tell me the truth, Dexter."

I nodded, feeling her steady brown eyes on me. The light from the hatch above bathed her in an almost ethereal light. I could not help but notice that her robe, still disarranged from earlier, was clinging to the curves of her upper body. She caught me looking again, and I noted a slight smile as I yanked my eyes away.

"I will try."

"I like that you are trying, as you are also trying not to stare at me."

"But you just caught me again."

"Staring, not lying. I find I do not mind the staring. Lying is far more offensive."

"I will strive for complete honesty with you, Fiona."

"Good. Your stares carry honest weight. Perhaps that is why they do not bother me as much," she said with a faint smile that made me feel a small glow.

Just then, Sylvaris reminded me that he was paying attention to our interaction, and he was clearly entertained. In my adventure with Catherine, the archpriestess of Marivelle had told us that Sylvaris and Lysmera were both playing small roles in resolving matters. Sylvaris was clearly invested in the challenge Fiona brought to me. I wondered if Lysmera was also a member of this intrigue.

"Cast off, boys! The tide's turning," we heard Billy call from above.

"We are leaving now?" Fiona asked.

"Yes. Let's go on deck so you can see Tallesin from the water. I may tug you out of their way from time to time. Please excuse me in advance."

I followed her up the ladder, finding it impossible not to gaze at her shapely posterior. Closing my eyes, I shook my head and wanted to laugh. Sylvaris did too.

The mainsail was up, and a light wind was pushing us gently to the harbor mouth. I pulled Fiona out of the way of the two crewmen as they bustled about, tending to the lines. Fiona moved to the starboard rail and watched as the city slipped by. I noticed her shiver in the cool breeze.

"Are you cold?"

"A little."

"Do you have a cloak in your bag?"

"Yes. It takes up most of the room in it."

"I will get it for you."

I scurried down the ladder and retrieved her cloak. There wasn't much else in it. A toothstick, her tortoise shell comb, and another shift. While I was down there, I also found the small vial of peppermint oil. Returning to the deck, I wrapped the cloak around her, surprising her slightly.

"Things are smooth, here in the harbor," I said. "When we enter the open ocean, the boat will begin to move much more. If the ginger tea wears off, please let me know. It will need to be cold, but it will help. And here is the peppermint oil."

"I rub the oil on my lip?"

"Your upper lip, then breathe through your nose."

"You are thoughtful and considerate, Dexter. I suppose you have treated Agatha and Catherine this way."

"How do you—?" I started to ask, as I had not mentioned them to her.

"Eldryne's temple keeps records of people who have served the gods in various ways. Your name was included twice, which is why I was sent to you. Your ... companions ... were also noted, and even though you and Catherine had not yet returned to Tallesin, it was known that you freed a servant of Marivelle's from captivity. Did some of your scars come during those efforts?"

"They did."

"Please tell me what happened. The accounts in the library were very dry. I expect the story you can tell will be more interesting."

5

I began telling her about how Ugarte had hired me to find his missing shipment of spices. By the time I reached the point of meeting Agatha and the rainstorm, we reached the harbor mouth. I could tell Fiona was feeling uncomfortable with the increased motion of the boat.

"Let me fix you some more ginger tea," I said. "I'll be right back."

I hurried down and found the powder. From a freshwater cask, I filled a mug of water and stirred the ginger powder in. I carried it back to the deck and handed it to Fiona, who was looking quite pale.

"Thank you. I hope this helps, as I am feeling unwell."

"It will help if you focus on the horizon," I said. "And breathe through your nose."

"I have not applied the peppermint oil yet."

"Allow me?"

Fiona nodded and handed the small bottle to me. She held onto the ship's rail with one hand and clutched the mug of cold ginger tea with the other. I unstopped the bottle and put some of the oil on my finger. Stepping around slightly, I rubbed it on her upper lip.

"Please continue with your story. It will distract me from what my stomach is doing," she said.

I picked up the narrative where I'd left off, washing up in the cold rain. When I reached the point in the story where Agatha and I first made love, I attempted to gloss over it. Fiona stopped me.

"The two of you had sex?" she asked.

"Yes."

"Did you enjoy it?"

"It was more important to me that she enjoy it, given her previous experience during her marriage, but, yes, I enjoyed it very much."

"Did you love her?"

"At that point, I cared for her very much," I said. "It grew into love."

"And Catherine? Did you love her?"

"Yes. There is a part of my heart that still loves both of them. I was extremely sad to leave Agatha, but the god I serve made it clear to me that my destiny was not with her. The night before I met you, I had just said farewell to Catherine. Meeting you has helped me avoid feeling the sadness I should have from that parting."

"I have never felt love," she said. "There was a boy with black hair and dark eyes, back in my village. He dared to kiss me, then ran away. I left the next day for Harkiss. Is it like what is described in the Lysmeran novels that the younger acolytes are forbidden from reading?"

"I have never read one of them, so I would not know."

"They describe passionate embraces, breathlessness, bodies sliding together," she said. "I have read a few. The better ones make me feel … unsettled."

"Did you find the sensation pleasant?"

"Yes," she whispered, as though confessing a secret.

"That is what the author intended."

"I suspected as much. Did you take Agatha, the way they describe, and ravish her?"

I could not help but laugh. The tingle on my neck from Sylvaris indicated he found this exchange highly amusing. My laughter caused Fiona to look distressed.

"I'm sorry, Fiona. I am not laughing at you. My laughter is directed at what you might have read. In the case of my first time with Agatha, she initiated things. From what she experienced during her marriage, it could only be that way. I would never force myself upon a woman, under any circumstances, and especially given what she suffered at the hands of her husband."

"The novels I have read mention only men's blazing passion and female surrender."

"Then there is much they fail to include," I said. "There is humor, awkwardness, tears and tenderness, and it can be messy at times. Sometimes it is slow and languid, and at others, like a summer thunderstorm, furious and quick."

"Please resume your story," she said.

I did as she asked, picking up the tale with how I followed the bandits to Eudus. Looking over, I noticed Fiona had gone pale, her golden skin now a sickly shade of yellow. She was going to be sick.

"Let's go to the other side, Fiona," I said, taking her arm and pulling her away from the rail.

We had been on the upwind rail. When she heaved, as seemed imminent, I didn't want the contents of her stomach to blow back on us, so I dragged us to the other side. She came with me, leaning more heavily on my arm with each step. The last two paces were a quick lurch, and we made it just in time.

Fiona bent over the rail, her whole body heaving. I wrapped one arm around her hips, well below her twitching stomach, and tried to gather her hair in the other to prevent it from getting in the way. I could smell the strawberries we'd eaten earlier and the ginger tea. When the spasms passed, she remained bent over the rail.

"This is unpleasant," she said.

"If you can straighten up, I will get a wet rag for your face."

She forced herself halfway up with a groan, then bent forward again, as her stomach contracted twice more. It took another couple of minutes before she tried to stand up. When she did, I hurried below and found a clean rag that I soaked in fresh water.

She was still standing where I left her when I returned. I leaned forward and examined her face, daubing with the cloth to remove stray bits around her mouth. When I finished, I put the clean part of the rag in her hand.

I could still feel Sylvaris's presence. He was highly amused. I suppose he would be—talking about love-making one minute and dealing with vomit the next. Even I could see the humor in the juxtaposition.

"Please finish the story."

"I will, as long as you concentrate on the horizon."

We passed the rest of the day on the leeward rail, moving from one side of the boat to the other when we changed tack. In between Fiona's bouts of sickness, I told her the story of Agatha, and then of Catherine. Billy and his two mates, whose names I learned from overhearing were Harv and Tommy, kept their distance. They cast an occasional sympathetic look toward Fiona. I suspected that if I had been the one feeling sick, they would have made fun of me instead.

As you would expect, Fiona was uninterested in food the rest of the day. She meekly drank the water and ginger tea I provided her, acknowledging that the tea was better hot, as we were able to serve it when Billy fired up the galley for dinner.

When the sun went down, I guided her below and helped her into her hammock. The poor woman was worn out. I placed a bucket on the floor beneath her in case she needed it. She nodded at my instruction, then closed her eyes.

"Mr. Falk?" Billy called softly from above.

"Aye, Billy," I said as I came back up on deck.

"How's the priestess?"

"Sleeping, I think. Best thing for her."

"That it is. We made good progress today, Mr. Falk. We'll make Harkiss in seven days for sure."

"How does it feel to have your boat back?"

"Ah, Mr. Falk, can't thank you enough for your generosity. Was able to get Tommy and Harv back, too. They been crewin' for me the last coupla years. I couldn't pay 'em, so they were lookin' elsewhere but didn't pick up with nobody, and we're happy to be back together."

"If you want to thank anyone, thank Garrett at the Broken Wheel. He's the one who gave me your name, told me you hit a rough patch through no fault of your own."

"Sir?" Harv asked, "the priestess—she's an Eldryne?"

"I'm no 'sir' Harv. And Billy, you can stop with the 'Mr. Falk,' too. My name's Dexter—Dex to my friends. And on a boat this small, we'll all be friends before too long. Yes, she's an Eldryne."

"Din't know the Eldrynes grew up 'em like that. She's a stunner but seems a little … off. They all like that?"

"I don't think they're all as attractive. As a matter of fact, I can tell you from my own limited experience, they're not. As far as her personality, I don't think it's too unusual for an Eldryne. They're better with books than people."

"I woulda worked harder at my schoolin' if all Eldrynes looked like her," Tommy said. "D'you think Eldryne minds that we cuss around her priestess? I been tryin' not ta, but…"

"I think Eldryne is smart enough to know how sailors communicate," I said. "How could she hold it against you? If you were in one of Eldryne's libraries, she would expect you to mind your tongue, but Miss Magellan is aboard a boat. Certain things are to be expected."

"That's good," Harv said. "Cause we been tryin' to be good, but some things aren't so easy to change."

"Don't worry about it," I said. "I doubt Miss Magellan is offended. She probably views it as a regular facet of shipboard life—which it is. I'm going to turn in—keep an eye on her."

"G'night," came in a ragged chorus.

I went down the ladder. The shuttered lantern hanging from the beam provided just enough light that I could see Fiona, her hammock gently swaying. She'd shifted in her sleep. Her cloak had fallen away, and her robe had ridden up, exposing the smooth line of her thigh. I tugged it down to cover her.

In the morning, her voice woke me. She was asking Billy if he would light the galley fire to warm some water for her ginger tea.

"It's much better hot," she whispered, "and, I believe, more effective. My stomach is still mildly upset, but a mug of hot ginger tea might see me through."

"Of course, miss. If you'll give me a few minutes, I'll let you know when the water is ready."

I heard her pad over next to me and open my valise. I guessed that she was looking for the ginger powder, but I thought I would have a little fun with her. I pretended to remain asleep.

"Who's a little sneak thief?" I growled when I reckoned she was elbow-deep in my bag.

She shrieked and jumped up, elbowing me hard in the ribs. The impact spilled me onto the deck. I landed on my head. It seemed the joke was on me.

"I'm so sorry, Mr. Falk!" she gasped. "You gave me such a fright. I was just looking for the ginger powder and the peppermint oil."

All I could do was chuckle softly to myself.

"That will teach me to surprise you," I said, rubbing my sore noggin.

"I didn't want to wake you," she said quickly. "You took such care of me yesterday, and I've been such a burden, I—"

"You have not been a burden, Fiona. I've been seasick myself before, and I know how unpleasant it is. As far as the ginger powder and the peppermint oil, they're right there on top. I would have been happy to get them for you, but since you are the one who needs them, why don't you put them in your bag?"

"I'll do that. Are you all right? You hit the deck rather hard."

"I'll be fine, Fiona. It's my own fault for trying to scare you."

"Well, you succeeded. I nearly jumped out of my own skin."

6

Fiona was better that day, but still not hungry. She did nibble on some hardtack soaked in her ginger tea a few times and kept it down. One curious thing was that she preferred to have me apply the peppermint oil to her lip.

She would hand me the vial, tilt her face up and wait patiently for me to finish. Each time I did, I felt Sylvaris's amusement. I was now convinced that Fiona and I were pieces in a much larger game that the gods were playing. I knew Eldryne and Sylvaris were involved, and probably Lysmera.

As much as the stories about the legendary Hoard of Torsten revolved around the fabulous store of gold and jewels, it was also supposed to contain religious artifacts. What those were and which god they belonged to varied depending on the version of the story, but I had heard of a magical hammer that belonged to Korath, a lute that was Calithra's, and a spear associated with Kravyna. I wondered if they were all working toward the same end, or if this was some sort of contest between them.

Thinking about it made my neck tingle. It was unusual to have Sylvaris remain in such close contact with me for days in a row. Thinking back, the last time was probably back when I first arrived at the seat of his order in Meropan. He gave me no indication whether I was correct in my belief that I was merely a piece in a much larger game, but then he wouldn't.

"You're thinking very hard right now, aren't you, Dexter?" Fiona asked.

"Hmm? Oh, yes, I suppose."

"I could tell from the furrow over the bridge of your nose. What is troubling you?"

"Sylvaris is keenly interested in what we are doing," I said. "I wonder what it is about the map, and the possibility of finding the Hoard—a possibility that may not exist—that intrigues him so."

"I am fairly certain that the Hoard does exist," Fiona said. "I was on the verge of being able to prove it *and* determine how to find it when the map was stolen."

"If we can't recover the map, could you still find the location?"

"No. The map was created on vellum—sheepskin—and is actually a palimpsest."

"What is a palimpsest?"

"It is a piece of sheepskin parchment that was inscribed, but the original writing was then scraped off, and the sheet was used again. It is a specialty of mine, deciphering what was in the earlier layer. The ink is gone, but the impression of the nib remains. In the case of the map, what one can see, although quite faded by age, is an old map of the continent of South Gaugan. But what was originally written concerned only a portion of the continent and contained references to astronomical positions."

"If you had those references, would you be able—"

"That is the problem," she said. "The map was taken before I completed writing them all down. Another problem is that the stars move over time. Very, very slowly, but over a thousand years, it makes a difference. I was waiting to have all the coordinates before I went to the astronomers. Then we would need to estimate how old the original was."

Color had returned to Fiona's face. The ginger tea was helping, as was being outside and focusing on the horizon. We kept forward, leaving the stern of the boat to Billy and his mates.

"How old do you think the original is?"

"At least nine hundred years. Torsten's empire, such as it was, collapsed after his death, just before the long Twilight."

"Such as it was? Torsten's empire was—"

"If it were truly an empire, it would have lasted beyond his death," she said. "Instead, all the legends indicate that it dissolved as soon as Torsten died. That tells me that Torsten was more of a warlord than an emperor. He forced many cities to pay tribute to him, but he did not establish the sort of bureaucracy needed to sustain things over time."

It was interesting how Fiona's personality emerged as we discussed this. The blinking owl, unsure of herself in social situations, was replaced by someone confident in her knowledge, and hinted at a passion within her. The breeze tugged at the twin strands of hair that had escaped her pencil and framed her face.

"You're staring again."

"I'm sorry. I was—"

"Do not lie to me, Dexter. You are not sorry in the least. You enjoy staring at me. I find I do not mind, as long as you can keep up your end of the conversation."

"Then I will endeavor to uphold my end. So, Torsten was a warlord?"

"Yes, which makes sense regarding the legend of the Hoard. After conquering these cities, he would have taken their greatest treasures. The greatest of these would be artifacts with ties to the divine. History shows us that most warlords are mistrustful of the people who serve them. It makes sense that he would establish a secret hiding place for the greatest of the treasures. His problem then would be one of maintaining the secret. For that reason, I do not think the Hoard is the masses of gold and jewels that the stories say. Chests of gold would require men to transport them—men who would know the location."

"Unless he killed them all," I said. "The legends say that Torsten was unconcerned with shedding blood."

"Except he would need his guards to kill those people, and in begging for mercy, more than one would have offered up the knowledge of the location, which then meant Torsten would have needed to kill the guards, and so on. There would be no way a mistrustful man would ever feel confident his secret survived. If, instead, the Hoard holds only these religious items, Torsten would have a much better chance of keeping the location hidden."

"Would he have hidden them himself?"

"I doubt it. He could never have sneaked away alone. He sent a trusted confederate to do it, and when that person returned and wrote down the location, Torsten would have killed him."

"And you think that the palimpsest is—"

"The map the confederate created to show Torsten how to find the artifacts," she said. "He would not have made it easy for anyone to understand, hence the astronomical coordinates. It would have required someone with specific knowledge to decipher the clues."

"Would Torsten have known how to do it?"

"What an excellent question!" she said.

Her praise, along with her look of delight, gave me a surprisingly warm glow. It was a feeling I remembered from my days at Meropan, when my masters praised me for solving a particularly difficult problem. It had been a great motivator back then and served the same purpose now. I wanted to see that look on her face again.

"Torsten would not have been able to read the map," she said. "He was a warlord, not particularly educated. He would have had people in his employ who could read it, and when and if he decided to visit his treasures, he would have had them lead him to it."

"And then killed them."

"Most likely," she said with a firm nod of her head.

The movement of her head and the breeze dislodged the lock of hair hanging down closest to me. Without thinking, I reached over and tucked it behind her ear, the tips of my fingers trailing lightly over her temple. Fiona went very still, and her eyes fixed on mine, giving me that owl-like blink.

"You touched me," she said quietly. "On purpose."

"I did," I replied. "I could not help myself. Your expression is so animated, talking about these things, and your hair was in the way. I wanted to see you without its distraction."

"Do it again," she said. "This side."

She turned her face to me so I could do the same on her right side. Her eyes closed while my fingertips brushed her skin. When she opened them, she smiled.

"Is that what the Lysmeran novels call a 'caress?' I enjoyed it. You have a gentle touch for someone with so many scars. Is that what attracted Agatha and Catherine to you?"

"You would need to ask them."

"What drew you to them?"

"Their strength. Their drive. Their perseverance. And, to be honest, both are quite attractive women."

"I know you find me physically appealing from the way you stare. Do you think I am strong like them?"

"You walked from Harkiss to Tallesin to find me. That was no easy journey, through weather that must have been quite unpleasant at times. Yes, you are strong."

"Thank you, Dexter," she said, smiling more with her eyes than her mouth. "In the temple, they call me diligent, thorough. When the Archpriestess is in a generous mood, she has used the term 'brilliant.' But no one has ever called me strong. It pleases me more than perhaps it should that you think so."

"Diligence and thoroughness are signs of strength of mind and of purpose. Walking for a month through the rains of spring shows both of those, plus a physical strength."

"And yet now, with my stomach still in knots, I do not feel very strong. Yesterday, I was helpless."

"I have been seasick. Even Billy and his mates have probably felt it at some point. It affects everyone with equal vigor."

We stayed at the rail as the sun climbed. The wind off the water was still chilly, and she kept her cloak wrapped around her with one hand, while the other grasped the rail. Her appetite returned slowly. She nibbled on some pieces of hardtack softened in her tea throughout the day.

We engaged in small talk. Fiona asked me many questions about the stories I told her of my adventures with Agatha and Catherine. To deflect, I asked her about her life before she went to the temple.

"It was a village of nearly a thousand people, not far from the border of Chiftel, where you said you come from. My father ran the shop that sold small necessary items, like needles, thread, buttons, pins, fancy ribbons, dyes, and even small mirrors, but they were expensive. I was the third child and the second daughter. From the beginning, I was always interested in books. By the time I was ten years old, I had read every book in the village that anyone would lend me. When I was thirteen, a priestess of Eldryne came through. Some of the townspeople suggested she speak to me. She came to the shop and started asking me questions about the books I'd read. When she finished, she asked my father if she could take me to Harkiss."

"How did you feel about that?"

When she told me that they had more books than I could ever read in my lifetime, I was interested. My life at home was comfortable, but I was bored. I hate to admit that, as it was no one's fault—certainly not my parents—but it is the truth."

"And your parents agreed to send you away?"

"We discussed it. I was both fearful and excited. I was not close to the other children my age in the village. They preferred playing games and acting like children, while I preferred books. I did not relish leaving my family, but the priestess painted a very intriguing picture of what my life would be like in the temple. We decided it was something I should do."

"Have you been back since?"

"No, but I send my parents a letter once a year to let them know I am doing well. They reply and tell me about my brother and sister—both married now, and with children. I must confess, their lives seem very small to me."

"In what way?"

"The scope of their existence is the village. Mine is the whole world, dating back hundreds of years."

"Even though you have never left the temple."

"Until now," she said, nodding her head. "I am learning that the world as it is can be very different from what is written in books."

"Given that your last experience with the world at large was when you were thirteen, I'm sure it is."

"Hmm. That is an interesting perspective," she said. "I suppose in many ways I was still that girl when I left Harkiss, but I have been learning throughout my journey."

7

"Do you think our search for the Hoard will have ripples that will extend further than we can see?" she asked, changing the subject.

Sylvaris was alerted by her inquiry. I felt the tingle on my neck sharpen. It reinforced my belief that there was much more involved in our search than we knew.

"Ripples, Fiona? Based on the intense interest Sylvaris is displaying so far, I suspect those ripples might be like waves large enough to travel the width of the Entassa. There might be consequences that extend far beyond the recovery of the map itself."

"Eldryne's interest is scholarly, I presume," she said. "Why is Sylvaris so invested?"

"I suspect it is personal for him—as personal as it can be for a god. He wants Eldryne in his debt. For what reason, I don't know, and I won't waste my time wondering. But if the Hoard does hold divine relics, nearly half the pantheon is watching over our shoulders. Even more important, we are in a race to find it."

"A race?"

"The map did not get up and walk out of the library of its own accord, Fiona. Someone took it, and they took it for a reason. That means knowledge of what it is has spread beyond Harkiss. Someone wants one or all of those relics. They may have divine patronage as well. They have had the map for a month, so they have a bit of a lead on us, except they do not have you and your knowledge and ability."

"You credit me too much, Dexter. I have never chased down thieves, or fought bandits, or persuaded corrupt officials to release prisoners. Those are your gifts."

"But without knowing how to decipher what the palimpsest hides, those abilities are meaningless. And do not account yourself lacking, Fiona. You trudged through twenty-seven days of mud and spring rain because Eldryne told you I would be waiting and that you needed my assistance. There is a certain amount of steel in you."

"It was for the goddess."

"Did you never think of giving up? Did it never seem to you to be a ridiculous journey?"

"Well … it wasn't pleasant, but it was for the goddess. She was most specific—the new moon of Teryssan, your flat in Tallesin, your name, and even the ink stain."

"Did you spill the ink on purpose then?"

"I did not!" Fiona answered emphatically. "It was an accident because you are … distracting."

I remembered Portia, the archpriestess of Marivelle, admitting to Catherine that Lysmera had given Catherine a nudge toward me. Given Fiona's lack of experience in the world outside the temple of Eldryne, it seemed to me that Lysmera might be pushing Fiona with both hands. For me, it required no effort at all on Lysmera's part. Fiona was objectively beautiful, her mannerisms endearing, and her mind incredibly sharp.

"She said you were the one whose help I needed," Fiona continued. "But she did not warn me that I would find you so … appealing. I did not expect it."

"I suppose the gods who are on our side wanted to make sure we would work closely together," I said.

I could almost hear Sylvaris laughing. The tingle on my neck was so strong, my hand darted to it. Fiona caught the gesture.

"What was that?" she asked. "Were you stung by something?"

"No. It is Sylvaris. He is paying close attention to me, ever since you appeared. It is unusual to maintain such intense interest for so long."

"And he communicates with you, how? Through the back of your neck?"

"That is where I physically feel his presence. When I want to call upon him, there is a sort of place within myself that I know how to find with my mind, but when he is engaged with me, it registers in the back of my neck. There are different sensations depending on circumstances."

"For instance?"

"It tingles when he approves or is amused. When he wishes to warn me of something, it burns. When he is impatient with me, it itches."

"Eldryne sends me dreams. Occasionally, when I have correctly interpreted a problem, she rewards me with certainty. But I get no physical sensation. Other than having Eldryne in his debt, do you have any idea what Sylvaris wants?"

"He loves mischief. If other members of the pantheon are interested in recovering divine relics, he may involve himself just to cause as much chaos and confusion as possible."

Just then, a wave slightly larger than normal lifted the boat. Fiona staggered and lurched into my side, her right hand landing on the center of my chest. Without thinking, my arm wrapped around her shoulders to steady her. She stayed leaning against me, pressed to me. It was the closest contact we'd had.

"Dexter, your heart is beating very strongly," she observed.

"I suppose it is."

"Why? The movement of the boat was nothing serious."

"I suspect it is because you are so close to me," I said.

"Hmm. My heart is also beating quite powerfully. I find I like having your arm wrapped around my shoulders like this. Even though there is no danger, it gives me a sense of security," she said, and settled a fraction more firmly against me, her hand still splayed on my chest.

"Your heart has sped up," she noted. "As mine has."

"Yes," I rasped, my throat suddenly tight. "Because you are choosing to remain pressed against me."

"I am enjoying the feeling of my chest against yours, your arm around my shoulders, and my hand over your heart. I have read in the Lysmeran novels about pulses quickening. May I keep it there a while longer?"

"As long as you like."

It struck me that Fiona had no concept of flirting. Neither did she seem to possess the ability to lie. What she said was what she felt. Sylvaris let me know that he was utterly pleased with himself at this moment.

"I have lain with men before, Dexter," she said quietly. "I was curious if it would be like what I have read. It was not. But standing next to you is different. My skin feels tight. There is a heat below my belly, completely separate from the previous upset. I am very conscious of the places where we are touching, even through clothing. It is a new feeling, and I enjoy it. I enjoy it very much."

We stayed glued together like that for most of the day. Billy and his mates observed but said nothing and gave us our space. Fiona seemed to have conquered her queasiness but still wanted me to rub the peppermint oil on her upper lip.

She ate dinner with us that evening and seemed to be cured. When it came time to turn in, she climbed into the hammock next to mine. In the dim light of the shuttered lantern, I saw her brown eyes gazing at me.

The next four days passed like that. Fiona and I stayed forward on the windward rail. She would use the boat's movement to tuck herself against me, then stay that close.

On the sixth day, she abandoned pretense and slid between me and the ship's rail. I kept one hand on the side of the boat and wrapped the other around her middle. When I did, she pressed herself against me and emitted a small hum of pleasure.

Sylvaris, of course, was entertained by this awkward dance of courtship. I imagined him sitting with his chin on his fist, watching intently, as one might watch the show on a pageant wagon. For the first time, I also had the peculiar sense that Sylvaris was not the only spectator.

"Tell me more about the three people other than you who knew of the potential importance of the map?" I asked.

"The first is the Archpriestess, Septima Thoran. She approved my research because she thought it would be a good exercise of my skills, not because she believed I would find anything. The second is my mentor, Sister Wanda Underhill. She taught me about palimpsests, and I consulted with her about the map. The third is sister Deirdre Roget. She is the astronomer who would help me with calculating the coordinates once we had determined the approximate age of the underlayer. All three voluntarily submitted to formal questioning by sisters with truth-sense. None lied."

"Were you present at the questioning?

"No."

"Do you know what questions they were asked?"

"No."

"Right there is a hole large enough to drive a caravan through."

"But my sisters—"

"At least one of your sisters is working against you … us."

Fiona turned in my arms and stared at me with her enchanting brown eyes, giving me one slow owl-blink. The wind tugged at the two matching strands of hair that framed her elegant cheekbones. Her cheeks were flushing red.

"That cannot be," she said with quiet urgency. "They submitted to questioning. Any lie they told would be detected."

"If they weren't asked the right questions, there would be no need to lie. Who was in charge of questioning them?"

"Sister Dagmar Fleisch, the archpriestess's assistant."

"Then she is one of the loose threads we must tug on first," I said.

"But Sister Dagmar—"

"Is a suspect."

"She has served the Order for more than thirty years. She is as loyal to the archpriestess as anyone can be."

"And if that is the case, then the archpriestess is under suspicion. Whoever controls the questions asked controls what truth is revealed. It is not as simple as inquiring, 'Did you take the map?' One must also ask whether the person knew of others who had an interest in the map, and whether the person had shared information about the map outside the circle of the four of you. In addition, there are a number of ways Sister Dagmar could have phrased the questions so that the respondent could answer truthfully and keep the knowledge of the perpetrator hidden."

"That would be … inefficient. And dishonest. Eldryne despises both."

"Perhaps Sister Dagmar believes she serves Eldryne by keeping a secret? Perhaps the archpriestess sent you to Tallesin on what she believed was a fool's errand to keep you out of the way for a long period. Perhaps Sister Dagmar serves another divinity?"

"These questions are … repulsive to me."

"I know they are," I said quietly, holding her gaze. "You've spent the last fourteen years serving the order, believing that servants of Eldryne would be above such things. But human beings are fallible, Fiona, even priestesses."

"Your argument is unpleasant, but … human beings can be weak. If the questions were phrased carefully, or certain of them omitted, the thief would remain hidden. I dislike the possibility that sister Dagmar or the archpriestess might be involved, but I cannot deny it."

"When we arrive at the temple tomorrow, allow me to conduct the inquiry. Your part was to fetch me from Tallesin. Having done that, adopt the posture that you are stepping back to see what I uncover."

"But that is deceptive. I am intensely interested in what you learn."

"You must pretend to be indifferent, Fiona. Did you ever play games as a girl when you pretended to be something you weren't?"

"Of course. All children do."

"And is there anything wrong or wicked in them doing so?"

"No," she admitted reluctantly.

"There is nothing wrong in engaging in a bit of subterfuge now, especially in pursuit of the greater truth."

"Ah," she said, a smile slowly coming to her lips. "Yes. In pursuit of the greater truth. If that is so, I believe the goddess will permit it."

8

We arrived in Harkiss on the morning tide. Billy dropped us at the single pier and immediately pushed off to wait for the tide to change for the return trip to Tallesin. Fiona assumed I would stay at the temple, but I refused. We went to the city center, and I booked a room at what appeared to be the most prosperous inn, the Golden Quill.

"Why?" she had asked.

"If there is a malevolent actor in the temple, it will be more difficult for them to move against me if I am elsewhere."

"I still have trouble believing that a member of the order is responsible for the theft of the map."

"We shall see."

We entered the inn, and I was pleased to see it looked busy. I paid for the room for a week, not knowing how long it would take for us to uncover the truth. The innkeeper's wife took my coin, but not without casting a loaded glance at Fiona. I wanted to tell her to mind her own business, that Fiona would be staying at the temple, but I kept my mouth shut. After taking my bags to my room, we headed up the hill to the temple of Eldryne.

Upon nearing the building, I felt the presence of Eldryne's numen. It was nowhere near as strong as when Catherine and I had been at the temple of Marivelle in Namo, but Marivelle was a major god, and Eldryne, like Sylvaris, was a minor divinity. A priest at the door recognized Fiona and gestured for us to enter.

"The archpriestess is expecting you," he said. "Follow me."

He led us into the temple, a space no bigger than the temple of Sylvaris in Meropan, and certainly not of the grand scale of Marivelle's edifice in Namo. Fiona walked ahead of me—she'd fetched me, and now she was delivering me. The sensation on my neck was one of rapt interest.

We reached the chamber of the archpriestess. The door was decorated with the sigil of Eldryne, an open book. The priest leading us knocked, then opened the door without waiting for a response.

Septima Thoran rose from behind a desk bare of any documents. She was short and slight, with white hair pulled back in the same sort of messy arrangement Fiona favored. She peered at me intently.

"Well done, Sister Fiona. Thank you for delivering Mr. Falk. You may go."

Fiona looked as though the archpriestess had slapped her hard on the cheek. She'd walked for a month to reach me, through a world that was very different from the cloistered confines of the temple, and even endured seasickness on the return. She was clearly not expecting to be dismissed summarily.

"Excuse me, Your Grace," I said, offering a slight bow—very slight, "but I would prefer if Miss Magellan were to stay."

"You do not make the rules here, Mr. Falk. You are here at my sufferance, and only because sister Fiona's dreams were so insistent and verified by those with truth-sense. Sister Fiona, you may leave. You appear sorely in need of a bath and a new robe."

"Your Grace," I responded before Fiona could react to these new insults, "Miss Magellan is not the only one in need of a bath and refreshment. We came directly from the boat that delivered us here—at great expense, I might add— knowing that my own appearance is somewhat disreputable after not shaving for a week. Perhaps that is what you expect from a servant of Sylvaris, but I pride myself on being a man of manners. I am here because the god I serve most closely has indicated to me that he feels this is an important matter."

"And you look exactly as I would imagine an emissary of the trickster," Thoran said. "I doubt your appearance would be improved by a bath. Your word carries no weight here. Sister Fiona, leave us."

I caught Fiona's eye as she turned to obey. In that brief glance, I tried to convey that I would not let her down. I hoped it registered with her.

Fiona left quietly and politely. The insistence of the archpriestess on dismissing her was either an obvious sign of her participation in the map's disappearance, or an intense dislike regarding my involvement, or both. I would have bet on "both."

"You disagree with my sending Sister Fiona away. I decide who remains in my presence while we are in my temple, Mr. Falk. It baffles me that the goddess I serve would have any interest in summoning you here, but she did. Do whatever it is you came to do, then begone with you."

"You Eldrynes favor direct speech, Your Grace, so I will endeavor to deliver that. My own archpriest is aware of my involvement. In fact, he is more than aware. He ordered me to accompany Miss Magellan to Harkiss. A map found on a palimpsest has gone missing. According to Miss Magellan, only three other people knew of the potential importance of this document—you, Wanda Underhill, and Deirdre Roget. There is now another who knows of the map's disappearance, Dagmar Fleisch. All three were questioned by Miss Fleisch in the presence of those with truth-sense. All three volunteered. All three were determined to be telling the truth."

"Then why are you here, Mr. Falk?"

"Because it is obvious that the questions Miss Fleisch asked allowed the truth to remain concealed. Allow me to question the four of you, and I will learn the truth."

"A minion of Sylvaris, sent to lecture me on truth?" she exclaimed. "Sylvaris? Whose disciples lie as easily as they breathe? You presume too much, Mr. Falk."

"I presume nothing, Your Grace," I said, struggling to remain polite. "Eldryne herself sent visions to Miss Magellan, visions verified by your own truth-sayers, instructing her to walk for twenty-seven days through spring mud to find me and bring me here. My own archpriest—"

"Oh, yes. Azar," Thoran said scornfully.

"My own archpriest is aware of what has happened and ordered me to accompany Miss Magellan back here. Eldryne wants the truth to be found, and Sylvaris is aiding her."

"I know Eldryne's will better than anyone," Thoran thundered, standing up and glaring at me. "And she does not require your involvement in this matter."

"Dislike of the god I serve is one thing, Your Grace," I said, remaining seated. "Concealing your own involvement in the theft of the map is another."

"Mr. Falk, you have worn out your welcome here in my temple," Thoran snarled.

She rang a bell that sat on the corner of her desk. The priest who led us to her chamber came in.

"Remove this man from the temple and see to it he does not darken our doors again," she growled.

"As you wish, Your Grace."

"The map is still here, isn't it, Your Grace?" I said. "The four of you plan to use it for your own ends, don't you?"

"Take him away!"

"I'm leaving, Your Grace, but I'm not going to surrender. You may feel you serve the goddess of wisdom, but my master is the god of cleverness. You are trying to be clever, and you will fail."

I rose slowly and turned my back on her. The priest ushered me to go ahead of him. I walked out of the temple and back into the town.

When I returned to the inn, I asked the innkeeper's wife to have a bath prepared for me. I wanted the salt crust off and to shave. Even more, I wanted time to think. As I had been trudging along the street, it seemed as though Sylvaris was rubbing his hands in glee. He did love chaos and confusion, and what followed from here promised to be full of it.

As I soaked in the tub, I reviewed the interaction with Septima Thoran. The flash of insight I'd had in her chamber returned to me. The map was still on the premises, unless they had deciphered it and headed off to find the Hoard. Thoran, Underhill, and Roget hoped to be able to figure it out without Fiona's involvement. Fleisch was also a part of it now.

Sylvaris was clearly thrilled with what I'd learned and the hornet's nest I'd kicked. Secrets in the house of wisdom and truth? What could be better to the god of mischief?

When I finished my bath, I used some of the still-warm water to scrape the whiskers from my face. When I finished, I examined myself in the mirror that the inn had hanging on the wall. I'd done a good job of shaving, but my scars captured my attention. I normally thought nothing of them, but now they served as a reminder that I had found success in even the most challenging circumstances. A knock on the door disturbed my reverie.

"Who is it?" I asked, quickly wrapping the small towel around my waist as much as I could, only to find it left a sizeable gap.

"Fiona," came a voice, clearly in great distress.

The anguish in her tone made me heedless of my appearance. I rushed to the door and opened it. She stepped inside, threw her arms around my neck, and started to bawl.

I managed to shut the door. When I went to put my arms around her to comfort her, the towel dropped to the floor. I was glad she was distracted or my embarrassment would have been almost unbearable.

I stroked her back, murmuring nonsense sounds, the way I did to Rufus when he'd been frightened. She had obviously bathed, as she smelled sweetly of soap, and her hair was still damp. The tattered robe was her only garment, though. I did not feel the shift underneath.

"She cast me out," Fiona sniffled, after she calmed enough to speak.

"What?"

"She cast me out of the order."

"Who? The archpriestess?"

"Yes."

Fiona was clearly devastated, and I felt awful for her, but a part of me wanted to laugh out loud. For all her supposed wisdom, Septima Thoran was acting stupidly—or at least, not cleverly. She had just confirmed my hunch but done so in a cruel way.

She had severed Fiona from the life she had known for the last fourteen years. Before that, she dismissed her from her office, ordering her to bathe and change as though she were a novice who tracked mud into the sanctuary. She had been petty and mean-spirited. Contrasted with Fiona's innocent and deep-seated belief, Thoran's actions offended me to my core.

The map might still be inside the temple walls. If all four of them were still present, they had not yet solved the mystery of it. Of the four, the key players were Underhill and Roget. If they were missing, then we needed to find them.

Fiona's shoulders were still shaking against my bare chest. I held her close but not tightly, rubbing her back with my left hand and stroking her loose, damp hair with my right. Fiona's world had just been updated, and she needed an anchor. She'd chosen me.

"I have nowhere to go," she moaned. "I don't even own any clothes."

"You will stay with me," I said quietly. "We will buy you clothes. You came to collect me for a reason, and that reason still exists, no matter what Septima Thoran says or does."

"You are naked," she said in wonderment, suddenly registering that fact.

"Yes, I am."

"And you are … aroused. Because of me?"

I blushed furiously and tried to pull back, but she would not let me.

"I do not mind. The view is … pleasant. And your scars are like a map of your past adventures," she said quietly as her finger traced one on my chest. "A map I will learn how to deci—oh, Dexter! What am I going to do?"

She threw her arms around me again and resumed sobbing. I waited for her to calm down again. When she did, I quickly stooped and retrieved the towel.

9

"Fiona," I said as calmly and evenly as I could even though my blood was pounding in my ears, "what we're going to do is this. You will let me get dressed. We will go to the seamstress and get her working on new clothes. Perhaps she might have something that fits that you can wear immediately."

"Yes," she said with a sniffle.

"What we are *not* going to do is give up. Do you understand me? Septima Thoran has just betrayed her own participation in the disappearance of the map. She and the other sisters are probably hoping to use it to their own ends. The first thing we need to learn is whether Underhill and Roget are still present at the temple."

"Why?"

"Because if they are, that means that the map is still there. If it is, I will figure out how to get it."

Fiona looked up at me with her large brown eyes and gave me an owl blink. She was still pressed close, the palm of her hand still on my chest. It was right over my heart now, and I could feel it thump.

"You mean, steal it back," she said, as direct as ever. "From my order, from my archpriestess."

"She cast you out, Fiona. It is no longer your order, at least not until we set things right, and she is no longer your archpriestess. And I prefer to think of it as recovering something that was taken from you. I'm rather good at that sort of thing. Sylvaris thinks so, at any rate."

"You seem very certain," she said, a tiny smile appearing at the corner of her mouth.

"And I am certain that you deserve better than to be tossed aside like pounce after it has dried the ink on a letter," I said firmly.

She nodded and released me. I stepped over to my valise and started pulling out a change of clothes one-handed, clutching the towel almost closed with the other. I picked one of my most respectable outfits.

I needed to drop the towel to dress, and Fiona was watching me closely. My state of arousal dictated that I put on my breeches with my back to her. Perhaps I was reading too much into things, but Fiona looked almost wistful as I finished buttoning up. My shirt and jacket followed, then I sat on the edge of the bed to pull on my boots. The last things I grabbed were my money pouch and my sword.

"Come along, Miss Magellan. It's time to get you some proper clothing."

On our way out, I asked the innkeeper's wife to recommend a seamstress. Again, the woman gave Fiona an up-and-down. I tilted my head, leaning forward to make sure the woman met my gaze.

"Is there a problem, madam?"

"Well, no, sir. It's just … she's a member of the order. They frown on them having relations—"

"Ah. Then let me put your mind at ease, madam. She is a former member of the order, having renounced her service today. We need to get her new clothing to celebrate her new life as a free spirit. In fact, she will be staying in my room for the duration of my stay. I will be happy to give you the extra for her board for the week. How much do I owe you?"

"Oh," the woman said, slightly chastened. "Um, one florin, five for the board. And I apologize, sir. It ain't none of my business. It's just so unusual, you see."

"I'm sure it is," I said, counting out the coins. "And let me throw in an extra florin to make sure it stays none of your business. Agreed?"

"Yes, sir," she said with enthusiastic sincerity as she scooped up the money.

"And the name of the best seamstress in town?"

"Mrs. Cuddy, sir. If you go right out the door, take the first right, and then four doors down, you'll see her sign."

"Thank you very much," I said. "You will see us again for dinner, if not before."

"You lied!' Fiona hissed at me when the front door closed behind us. "I did not renounce the order. They expelled me."

"Po-tay-toe, po-tah-toe," I said. "As she said, it's none of her business, and I was just reminding her of the fact. She will probably talk about us after we've left town, but I hope I will have kept her mouth closed for the duration of our stay."

"I do not feel free. I feel like a page ripped out of a book."

"Then we shall use that page to begin a new edition," I said, "with a different binding—not purple."

The seamstress was exactly where the innkeeper's wife said. A painted wooden sign showed a needle and thread. The door gave a pleasant jangle when we opened it.

The seamstress was a pink-cheeked woman of about fifty. Her dark hair showed strands of silver, and she wore a measuring tape hung from her neck like a badge of office. She stood and greeted us.

"Hello, sir, and, uh, sister?"

"Not anymore," Fiona said, pretending to be cheerful. "I left the order just now."

Fiona's cheeks flamed scarlet. It was the closest thing to a lie she'd told in fourteen years. I hoped Mrs. Cuddy would think Fiona's embarrassment was due to her being involved with me.

"Well, good for you, then," Mrs. Cuddy said with a broad wink to me. "How may I help you? As if it isn't obvious. That robe is a tattered mess, and the color does you no good either. What is it you're looking for?"

"As you can see, Mrs. Cuddy, Miss Magellan is uncommonly beautiful. I was told you are the only person who can do her justice. She needs three dresses—all for everyday use—and traveling clothes. It's a pity we're not on the east coast or I would ask you if you knew what a cortaderia skirt was."

"We're not so far removed from civilization here in Harkiss, Mr.—uh?"

"Falk. Dexter Falk, at your service, madam," I said, giving her a sweeping bow.

"Oh, Mr. Falk, you are a charmer. But, yes, I know what a cortaderia skirt is. Never made one before, but I have the patterns here somewhere."

"You do? Fabulous! Then she will need three of those as well, with blouses, jackets, and, of course, underthings for all. Of the three dresses and skirts, please make two in summer weight."

"Traveling somewhere warm?"

"I believe so. And, Mrs. Cuddy, can you tell me where I might obtain a suitable valise for Miss Magellan? And recommend the best cobbler in town? She will need a pair of riding boots that will also be comfortable to walk in."

"The saddler will be your best bet for a valise. If you go back to the main square and go left. Keep going until you smell the horses and then look for the saddler. When you return, I'll send you to the cobbler I would recommend. May I ask, sir, what sort of budget do we have?"

"It is very kind of you to be concerned, Mrs. Cuddy, but you need not trouble yourself. In fact, if you can get everything made by the day after tomorrow, I will double whatever you wish to charge. As I mentioned when we entered, your clothes need to do her justice. I have one more small request—if you have anything already made that is close to Miss Magellan's size, I would be interested in obtaining that as soon as possible. She has nothing else to wear, you see."

"I may have something," Cuddy said, sticking her little finger in her mouth in thought. "We will need to measure to see what alterations need to be made. If it is workable, I can work to finish it while you visit the cobbler. That will take an hour or so, and if it's not too far off, I can do it."

"Very well. Fiona, I leave you in Mrs. Cuddy's capable hands. Mrs. Cuddy, do not tell Miss Magellan what anything costs."

I felt like laughing once the door closed and I was a few paces away. Acting lah-di-dah like that was not something I did often, but it felt completely appropriate for this situation. Mrs. Cuddy would be left with the impression that I was some rich gadabout who had seduced an innocent member of the order of Eldryne. That suited my purposes just fine.

I found the saddler without difficulty, and they had a valise that would be large enough to hold the clothing I'd just asked Mrs. Cuddy to make. It occurred to me that Fiona probably did not know how to ride, but we would worry about that later. It would be quicker for us to sail from Harkiss to just about anywhere important, and I had enough money on me to bribe a fisherman to take us all the way to Tallesin if necessary. If our search did lead us to the continent of South Gaugan, it would be easier to travel to Lenoa or Dropan and sail across the Tiburn than to try to find passage across the Entassa.

All my glib assurances to Fiona left one important task somewhat unaddressed. I would need to sneak into the temple of Eldryne, find the map, and abscond with it. That would be a daunting task, but from the amount of interest Sylvaris had been showing since Fiona appeared at my door, I had a feeling he might offer some assistance.

Something was clearly amiss with the archpriestess. I wondered if she had been seduced by some outside influence, or if the lure of obtaining the Hoard—whatever it contained—was enough incentive to bend Septima Thoran so dramatically. An outside influence worried me the most because it meant there were other players in the game. I supposed we would find out as things progressed.

When I returned to Mrs. Cuddy's, Fiona was standing on a small riser, in a pair of borrowed slippers that were too big for her feet. What drew my attention most of all was the green velvet dress she was wearing. It suited her golden skin coloring as though it had been dyed especially for her. Mrs. Cuddy was on hands and knees pinning up the hem.

The bodice was trimmed with white lace and showed the upper swell of Fiona's breasts—just enough to be interesting without a hint of scandal. I could see where Mrs. Cuddy had slit the back seam of the dress to let it out slightly. It fit well in the shoulders and accentuated the hips in a pleasing way.

"Ah! There you are, sir. We are in luck. This dress was ordered for the Feast of Zoryn last year but was never picked up. I thought I'd never recover the cost of the fabric, but then here you are. I'll be able to have this ready by the time you're done with the cobbler. Now, if you ask me, Mr. Falk, you should also have the cobbler make Miss Magellan a pair of shoes along with them boots you're thinking of. She has a pretty turn of ankle, she does, and a dress like this lets her show it off."

"You're quite right, Mrs. Cuddy," I said. "You've talked me into it."

Fiona blushed furiously, hearing herself be discussed like a prize horse—a pretty turn of ankle indeed. I could also tell that she'd looked in the mirror at herself in that dress and was perhaps beginning to understand why I stared at her so. I took a seat on a stool by the door, my sword by my side, the valise at my feet, arms and legs crossed as if I owned the world.

"You go change, dear," Mrs. Cuddy said as she got back on her feet. "I'll have this ready in an hour, and we can throw that set of rags away."

Fiona went behind a screen, and I heard the rustling of cloth. Mrs. Cuddy went to a standing desk, made some notations, and did some quick figuring. When she finished, she brought the piece of paper to me.

"If you're serious about paying double to get the pieces the day after tomorrow, I can call in some help," she said in almost a whisper so Fiona would not overhear. "The total, including this piece you just saw, would come to thirty-one guilders, six florins."

"Mrs. Cuddy, you've been so helpful; if you can indeed finish altering that magnificent dress by the time we return from the cobber, why don't we compromise and call it thirty-two guilders even?" I responded, not lowering my voice at all.

Mrs. Cuddy smiled with her whole round face.

"You strike a hard bargain, Mr. Falk, but I'll agree to that."

Fiona appeared, once again in her tattered purple robe, as I was counting the coins into Mrs. Cuddy's hand. The older woman surprisingly crossed to Fiona and hugged her, whispering something in Fiona's ear. I wondered what they had discussed while I was out, but figured Fiona would tell me later.

The cobbler was next, and when Fiona took off her very battered shoes for him to measure her, I learned that even her feet were pretty. He whittled the lasts while we were there and agreed with Mrs. Cuddy that Fiona needed a fine pair of shoes to go along with her new boots. I agreed and offered him the same deal as Mrs. Cuddy—double if he could finish the work in two days. He accepted, then asked me to examine samples of the leather he had available. I made my choices, and he totted up the amount.

As before, I rounded up, offering him ten guilders, which he accepted with a pleased smile. Fiona and I then returned to Mrs. Cuddy's for the green dress. When Fiona emerged after putting it on, I had to agree with Mrs. Cuddy. Fiona's battered walking shoes looked completely wrong, while the dress accentuated her beauty in every other way.

10

"Mrs. Cuddy, we forgot a cloak. Miss Magellan will surely need one. Can you help us?"

"Don't you fret, Mr. Falk. I'll whip one up. Seeing as how you've been so generous, I'll just throw it in."

"Why, thank you, Mrs. Cuddy."

"No, thank you, Mr. Falk. You take good care of Miss Magellan now, will you?"

"I fully intend to, Mrs. Cuddy."

"What was all that about?" Fiona hissed at me once we were a few doors down.

"What? Me playing the part of a wealthy ne'er-do-well who seduces beautiful priestesses away from their calling?"

"Oh? Is that what that was? I'm afraid I told Mrs. Cuddy the truth. I left out the part about the map, of course, but—"

"Why, Miss Magellan! Aren't you the one who told me that telling a half-truth was as bad or worse than a lie?"

"Well, in the last few hours, I learned that my archpriestess is a liar, and there was no one on this earth I trusted more."

Her voice cracked as she uttered this, and she halted. I set the valise down and turned to face her. I clasped her shoulders lightly.

"The sin is hers, not yours. You were true to your goddess. You *are* true to her. Eldryne is the one who sent you to me, not Septima Thoran. It seems clear to me from what happened today that your archpriestess would have prevented it if she could have."

"But you are a thief, and I want you to steal the map for me," she said, tears flowing from her brown eyes.

"I recover things for people, Fiona. After all, what else can you call it when you steal from a thief? In larger terms, I try to set things right. What did you tell Mrs. Cuddy that made her want to hug you?" I asked, trying to distract her.

"I told her … I told her… Actually, I would like to keep that a secret for now. That's not a lie, or a half-truth, is it?"

"No, it's not."

"I will tell you, just not now."

"That's fine. The dress looks beautiful on you, by the way. I'm certain you will catch me staring many more times."

"Mrs. Cuddy said the same—that it made me look even more beautiful and that you would stare."

"Can we return to the inn now? It's almost time for dinner."

"We spent the whole afternoon doing that?"

"Indeed, we did. Time flies when you're having fun."

"That was fun," Fiona admitted. "Mrs. Cuddy was very flattering. She showed me drawings of what you called a cortaderia skirt. It's so I can ride a horse and still look like a lady, isn't it?"

"That's the intention."

"I've never ridden a horse, except a pony when I was little, and the fair came to our village. I don't really remember it, though. Will we need to do a lot of riding?"

"I don't know. It's likely, but probably in the future. Are you feeling better now?"

"Yes."

"Then, here," I said, offering her my handkerchief. "Please wipe your eyes and blow your nose, so Mrs. Nosy Innkeeper's Wife doesn't have anything new to gossip about."

Fiona favored me with a laugh and did as I asked, honking away. She handed it back, and I tucked it in my jacket pocket. I picked up the valise and offered her my arm. She took it, and we returned to the inn.

Mrs. Nosy Innkeeper's Wife did a double-take, seeing Fiona in the dress. I laughed silently as I followed Fiona up the stairs. We stayed only long enough to drop the bag, as I had already smelled dinner when we entered the building.

We took a seat in the dining room, finding it rather full. Fiona drew quite a bit of attention as we crossed to an open table. The dress really did make her look even more stunning.

"Fish or fowl?" the serving girl asked.

"Fowl," we both answered at the same time.

"Be right back," the girl said.

Sure enough, she returned in a couple of minutes with two plates, a basket with a small loaf of warm bread, and a carafe of wine. She plunked everything down somewhat gracelessly, but I don't think Fiona noticed or cared. If I were to guess, I think the fowl was some type of pheasant. It was tasty enough, and Fiona enjoyed it.

"One thing I won't miss is temple food," she said. "Even what we ate on the boat was better, once I could eat again."

"I have a feeling you'll return to the temple," I said. "There's a reason why Eldryne sent you to me. And I mean, you, specifically, to me, specifically. Don't ask me what that reason is, because I don't know yet, but it has to do with the map, and the Hoard, and Septima Thoran and her minions. Sylvaris is part of it, and perhaps other divinities."

"Is Lysmera one of them?"

"I don't know."

"I think she is. From the moment I met you, I have felt strange, but the overall effect has been quite pleasant. I think about you all the time when you are not present. Mrs. Cuddy caught me daydreaming about you. This is new to me."

"Fiona, you have had quite an effect on me as well. The morning you found me was only hours after I said farewell to Catherine. I expected to be extremely sad about that for a length of time, and yet you consumed my thoughts almost immediately."

"Lysmera," she whispered.

"I believe that Lysmera cannot force people to do things they would not do of their own will," I said. "She does work to remove obstacles and impediments and helps speed the process along when she wishes."

"And your feelings about Catherine would have been an impediment, so she removed them?"

"I hate to think of it that way," I said. "My feelings for Catherine are still there, as are my feelings for Agatha, but they no longer oppress me. Lysmera did not remove those feelings; she just made them less urgent, if that makes sense."

"Dexter, I no longer wish to talk about this here. We have finished our meal. May we return to your room?"

"Our room," I said.

"I suppose it is," she said, tilting her head in the way she often did. "May we?"

"Of course."

I followed Fiona up the stairs. The room was as we left it, except a candle had been lit at the washstand. I shut the door after I entered and turned to find Fiona staring at me intently.

"Dexter, I have been thinking about this all afternoon while Mrs. Cuddy measured and pinned and chattered. I have been thinking about how you appeared naked when I arrived this morning, and how the sight of your arousal made me warm. I have been thinking about this since you took care of me while I was seasick," she said as she began unbuttoning her dress. "I want this, Dexter. Do not refuse me."

She finished with the last button, and the dress slid to the floor. The candlelight painted her body in warm amber and shadow. She stepped forward tentatively.

How could a sane man refuse such a gift? I gathered her in my arms, and our lips met for the first time. Her lack of experience showed immediately in how she kissed me. We worked through that and many other things that night.

The same curiosity that drove Fiona to search for hidden clues in pieces of old parchment was present in her exploration of the carnal. We reconnoitered one another quite thoroughly. When at last we lay still, she fell asleep with her head on my shoulder and her leg thrown over mine. I idly stroked her back gently, listening to the small sounds of the night until I joined her in slumber.

As usual, Fiona was up with the sun. She had risen, washed at the basin, and now sat perched on the edge of the bed in her green dress. As I blinked sleep from my eyes, she was peering down at me with a faint smile playing on her lips.

"I have decided that the Lysmeran novels are … inadequate," she said, leaning forward and brushing my lips with a brief kiss. "But I suppose the authors did the best they could to capture the actual sensations in words."

"Good morning to you, too, Fiona," I said with a smile.

"Ah, yes. Good morning. I find myself surprisingly cheerful despite being cast out of the order yesterday."

"Well, if you'll allow me to get up, perhaps we can begin rectifying that."

"You think you can convince the archpriestess to change her mind? I doubt that is possible."

"You are correct, Fiona. When I said we would rectify the situation, I did not mean we would have you reinstated immediately. After we find the map and presumably what it discloses, I believe we will vindicate you, and the order will beg for you to return."

"That makes more sense," she agreed.

"If you would move, I could get up and get dressed, and then we could see if they are serving yet."

"I do find myself particularly hungry this morning. Is that a consequence of our lovemaking last night?"

"It often is."

"Interesting," she said, clearly making a mental note, as she rose from the edge of the bed.

I rolled out from under the covers and began gathering my clothes. Fiona watched me the entire time. It was disconcerting to say the least, but I managed to wash up and get dressed without incident.

We broke our fast downstairs, clearly among the first risers at the inn. While we ate, Fiona had removed her shoe and began brushing her foot along my calf under the table. It took me a moment to realize that she was not doing it to tease. Fiona did not know how. She was doing it because she wanted physical contact, and our hands were busy eating.

"Do you enjoy touching me like that, Fiona?" I whispered.

"Oh!" she gasped, pulling her foot away. "I did not realize … it's just that I find your touch brings me a feeling of comfort and warmth."

"I did not say I minded, Fiona. Just make sure the tablecloth is long enough that Mrs. Nosy Innkeeper's Wife has nothing new to gossip about."

Fiona bent down, assured herself that the tablecloth reached the floor, and resumed running the sole of her foot up and down my calf. I grinned at her, and she blushed with a faint smile. When we finished eating, I stretched my hand across the table, palm up.

"Try holding my hand, and see if it gives you the same feeling," I suggested.

Fiona did and soon withdrew her foot. Her hand clasped mine gently, and she smiled more broadly. When the serving girl took the dishes away, I used that hand to help her up.

"I did not need your assistance to stand," Fiona whispered, "but I did not want to let go of your hand. Is that why you do some of the things you consider mannerly? To give the excuse to touch one another?"

"I had never considered it in that light, Fiona, but there might be some truth to your observation."

"If that is the case, I'm sure I will enjoy it more now and no longer find it annoying. What will we do now?"

"How often do members of the order come into town?"

"All the time. Why?"

"We need to learn whether Wanda Underhill and Deirdre Roget are still here. If they are, then the map is somewhere in the temple. If they have left, then they have succeeded in figuring out how to read the map and are on their way to find whatever it discloses."

"It will be several hours before we can expect anyone to come from the temple," she said. "As I mentioned, the food at the temple is awful. Many come to town to eat."

"In the meantime, let's obtain some paper, and you can draw me a map of the interior of the temple, as well as you can, especially where you think they would hide the map."

"I know exactly where she would keep it. There is a small room next to the chamber where you met her. It is used to house sacred texts. Only the archpriestess and Sister Dagmar have keys."

11

I asked the innkeeper's wife for a sheet of paper. When I told her it was to make some rough sketches, she handed me an old broadsheet with an advertisement for the inn on one side. It was perfect for our needs, and I thanked her kindly. She smiled in return. It seemed as though she was warming up to me.

We returned to the room, and Fiona started recreating the layout of the temple's interior. I watched. The strands of hair on either side of her face came loose, and she stuck the tip of her tongue out of the corner of her mouth when she was concentrating hard.

Her pencil scratched steadily. She was lost in a fog of concentration. Given the opportunity to stare at her without reproach, I indulged myself. As my eyes roved over her form, I found new things to admire along with those features I'd already noted.

"Come take a look," she said after working nonstop for at least an hour.

I stepped up close behind her and held her shoulders lightly. Fiona sighed quietly, straightening up to lean against me gently. She reached up and took my right hand by the index finger.

"Here is the archpriestess's chamber, and her private scriptorium is here," she said, guiding my finger over her drawing. "There are two entrances to her audience chamber. The one by which we entered yesterday, and this one, which leads to her bedchamber. Her bedchamber has another entrance as well, over here."

"I will probably do this at night, so I doubt I'll go that way," I said.

"The scriptorium is always kept locked. I have never been inside of it. The archpriestess has one key that she keeps on a chain around her neck, and Sister Dagmar keeps the other in a locked iron box in a drawer of her desk."

"Don't worry about keys, Fiona."

"Why not? You need a key to get in."

"Some of us find ways to unlock doors without having the proper keys."

"Is that one of the abilities Sylvaris grants you?"

"Yes and no. I have a very good set of lockpicks. Perhaps the skill with which I use them comes from Sylvaris, but I have also had many lessons. In Harkiss, they taught you how to unlock ancient manuscripts. In Meropan, I learned different skills."

"I suppose that makes sense," she said with a brief nod. "Now, you can certainly go in through the main entrance, but there is generally a priest or priestess on duty through the night. Usually, they go to the narthex and sleep, but you cannot be sure of that. The better choice will be to enter through the kitchen. The door to the garden is never locked because the cook is lazy and can't be bothered. From the kitchen, you can make your way through this corridor first, skirting the refectory, and then this passage will lead you back to the corridor that reaches the archpriestess's chamber. It can be confusing, especially at night, but don't worry. I'll be there to guide you."

"No, you won't."

"What do you mean? I'm coming with you."

"Fiona, I do not doubt your courage or desire. But getting into and out of places without being seen is something I can do very well—perfectly, if Sylvaris is with me. It is not one of your many skills and talents. I will need you to be elsewhere."

"Where?"

"On whatever boat I can convince to take us as soon as I show up with the map. Harkiss is too small for us to remain. Although Eldryne is not known for her warrior ways, the temple has enough people that they could apprehend us once they discover the map is gone."

"You want to leave like a thief in the night."

"I explained it to you before, Fiona. We are not stealing the map; we are recovering it in the service of Eldryne."

"Recovering," she said with an owl-like blink. "A nicer word than theft, but it still involves entering a locked room without permission and taking something that does not belong to you."

"If you want to split hairs, Fiona, the map belongs to the temple, and therefore, to Eldryne herself. Who has been a loyal servant to the goddess? And who is pursuing motives that certainly do not appear to be honest and aboveboard? Eldryne sent you the visions to come find me. Septima Thoran would not have permitted it except for the fact that you went to the truth-sayers to verify the veracity of what you saw. If she'd had her way, she would have told you to disregard them."

"She did. That is why I went to the truth-sayers. The dreams were so vivid and held such a sense of urgency that I needed to be sure."

"And how did the archpriestess react when she learned this?"

"She allowed me to go, but looking back, I can tell she was not pleased with me."

"Who suggested that you walk to Tallesin, instead of waiting and taking a boat?"

"She did, but between the seasickness and the walk, I don't know which is worse. I never experienced the height of unpleasantness on the walk that I did while aboard Billy's boat. I'm glad we sailed, though. Even being seasick had a benefit. You entertained me by telling me of your adventures with Agatha and Catherine. I learned more about you."

"Well, clearly, I did not scare you away. I shall have to try harder in the future."

"A joke," she said, then shrugged it off. "You will not allow me to accompany you into the temple when you go?"

"I would prefer it if you would see the sense of my argument and not press the issue."

"I wish to share the risk with you."

"Having you accompany me increases that risk tremendously. I grant that you know the interior of the building intimately, but while you were studying scrolls, I was in Meropan, learning how to move without being noticed. And if they caught us, the consequences for you might be horrible."

"And you intend to do this tomorrow night?"

"Yes. We must wait for Mrs. Cuddy to finish making your clothes and for the cobbler."

"I don't care about those things."

"Fiona, getting the map is only a beginning. You will still need to decipher it. We will need to find an astronomer to help us with the coordinates. Assuming we're successful, then we will need to travel to where they lead. You will need clothing for all of that."

"I understand, Dex. I am not a child. It is more that I am impatient."

"Impatience is a thief's worst enemy."

"I thought you merely *recovered* items for people?" Fiona said innocently. "Now you admit to being a thief?"

"Fiona, are you teasing me?"

"Yes."

"Something new you're trying?"

"Yes. I thought it would be humorous."

"It is. But sometimes girls who tease get punished."

"Punished?" she asked, her eyes wide. "How?"

"Like this," I said, leaning forward, pulling her loose strand of hair away, and kissing below her right ear in a spot I'd discovered the night before.

"Or this," as I placed another kiss on the nape of her neck. She shivered, and a small squeak escaped her.

"Your punishment does not seem too brutal," she said softly.

"Let the punishment fit the crime, I always say."

"Ah. You are teasing me in return. I think I like this game," she said as she turned to face me.

"If it's a game, then it's your turn."

"I would like to repeat some of what I learned last night," she said, draping her arms around my neck. "Continued practice leads to mastery."

She pressed her lips to mine. From a slow, tender beginning, the kiss gradually intensified. Her mouth opened, and her tongue ventured out. Not long after, our clothing managed to disappear, and we stumbled into bed.

"I smell food," Fiona said later, after we both dozed briefly. "Once again, I am hungry. Is this to be expected?"

"It's not unusual," I said. "And it is lunch time."

"We need to get up," she said, bolting upright. "I need to learn if Sister Wanda and Sister Deirdre are in the temple."

I watched as Fiona left the bed and found her dress. The sight of her putting it back on was almost as entertaining as taking it off. She wrapped her hair around her fist and stuck her pencil back through it.

"Come along, lazybones. We have things to do,' she said, and her stomach growled audibly, "and you must feed me."

After I dressed quickly, we descended the stairs. Fiona took my arm when I offered it. She was becoming more used to small courtesies. In the dining room, we took a table in the back corner. The serving girl brought us bowls of lentil soup.

"Three sisters just entered," Fiona whispered a minute later. "The gray-haired one is Sister Lena. The other two are novices. And another two brothers came in, but they are not with the first group. I do not like them very much."

"Would Lena know if Roget and Underhill are in the temple?"

"She would. She is the head of the custodial team. They know where everyone is."

"Do you feel comfortable approaching her, or should I pretend to be a pilgrim?"

"Sister Lena was always friendly to me. Let me try."

"You should tell her that the reason you wish to know is that you hope to have those two sisters intercede on your behalf with the archpriestess."

"That is not exactly true, Dexter."

"Can you make yourself believe it is the truth for five minutes?"

"It is a plausible scenario," Fiona admitted after consideration. "If I did not suspect that Sister Deirdre and Sister Wanda were part of what is taking place, it is logical that I would hope for them to plead with the archpriestess to restore me to the order. Yes, I can believe that for the duration of the conversation, which I expect will be brief."

"I know this is awkward and unpleasant," I said. "But you are a brave woman, Fiona Magellan. You will succeed."

Fiona rose smoothly and crossed to the table where the three women were. She nodded with a small bow of respect and spoke quietly. Even at this distance,

I could see Lena's eyebrows lift in astonishment. News of Fiona's ouster must not have spread.

Fiona gestured in the direction of the temple and then touched her chest in a small pathetic motion, as though she were still reeling from what happened. Lena patted her arm in a kindly way and spoke at some length.

The conversation lasted perhaps five minutes, and Lena seemed to be sympathetic to Fiona's plight. When Fiona returned to the table, she kept her head down, as though she were still morose, but I could see her eyes gleaming. She'd learned what we wanted to know. I also suspected that part of her look of subdued triumph was that she had carried out her ruse successfully.

"Both are still in the temple," she whispered when she returned to the table, still looking downward. "Sister Lena says that Sister Wanda has been spending most of her time in the archpriestess's scriptorium. Sister Lena thinks it would be a bad time to approach Sister Wanda, as she has been short-tempered and angry as of late."

"That is very good news," I said. "It means they are not making progress."

"But, Dexter, Sister Wanda taught me everything about palimpsests. If she is having difficulty, how can I hope to succeed?"

"Because Eldryne chose you for this task. Have faith that she would not have selected you if she planned to abandon you."

"That's interesting," Fiona commented, "being urged to have faith by a follower of Sylvaris. He's considered the most faithless of all the gods, you know."

"I'm aware of his reputation. It is not entirely deserved."

12

That afternoon, I left Fiona in the room to refine her map. She promised to point out things like squeaky door hinges and creaky floorboards. I went to the harbor and waited for the fishermen to come in for the day.

As they pulled in, the usual clamor rose. Captains and fishmongers haggling over prices, the good-natured banter between members of the crews as they hauled baskets of silvery fish up from the holds, and gulls screeching, hoping for a snack. Beyond them, the Entassa stretched endlessly to the horizon.

I needed someone who valued coin over curiosity. He would not be among the first arrivals, who returned to the harbor as soon as they deemed the day a success. My target would be a straggler who stayed out longer because the fish weren't biting for him, but not too long, or the market would already be sated by the time he returned.

A half-hour after most of the boats had pulled in, I saw a likely candidate. I asked one of the fishmongers who it was. He squinted for a moment.

"*Evelyn Claire*, Johnny Greer," he said.

"Looks like he had a tough day," I commented.

"Aye, he's put together a string of 'em. Been on a run o' hard luck."

I handed the man a quadrans for the information and waited for Greer to pull in. His boat looked well-kept, so that wasn't the reason he wasn't bringing in fish. He had only two men in his crew, while the other boats carried four. I assumed Greer was at the wheel, a lean-faced man with a pipe clenched between his teeth. His men brought only three baskets of fish up, none of them full.

"Aw, Johnny, I'm sorry," one of the fishmongers said. "What you got's only good for chum. Mebbe tomorrow, eh?"

A few other merchants came to look at his catch. One finally expressed interest, but I could tell the price he was offering was low. There were no other takers, and with a look of disgust, Greer finally gave in. As I approached, I heard Greer cursing, muttering something about pig slop, and I knew how the man who bought his catch intended to use it.

"Mr. Greer?" I called out. "A word?"

Greer's eyes raked over me. He saw the quality of my clothing and the rapier on my hip. He decided to climb onto the pier to meet me but said nothing.

"Mr. Greer, I would like to talk to you regarding chartering your boat for a trip to Tallesin," I said, keeping my voice low. "I'll pay well, but I expect my coin buys your complete discretion. Are you interested?"

"How much coin? And why the need for secrecy?"

"The coin is twenty-five guilders now, and another twenty-five when we reach Tallesin. And the need for secrecy wouldn't be much of a need if I shared it with you, would it?"

"For fifty guilders, Mister, you can rob the temple itself, and I wouldn't care," Greer said. "When?"

"Tomorrow night, well after midnight."

"How many people?"

"Two."

"Lessee the color of your coin, mister."

"If you don't mind, I'd rather get off the pier so fewer eyes are on us. Why don't you give your boys this, and tell them to go get a pint and have them pour one for you?" I suggested, handing him a florin.

Greer whistled so sharply that it stung my ears. Both of his crew popped up.

"Oy, fellas," Greer said gruffly. "Another crappy day, but things'll turn around. Take this and have them start pourin'. Don't drink it all up 'fore I get there."

He handed the stouter of the two the coin. Both of them looked surprised and delighted. They vaulted over the rail before Greer could change his mind. I waited until they disappeared before opening my money pouch and counting out twenty-five golden guilders.

"Tomorrow night, eh?" he asked.

"Aye. A couple of hours before sunrise, but earlier than your competitors will probably get here. They'll think you headed out for an early start to change your luck."

"Luck needs changin' but mebbe it just did."

"Head on out tomorrow, if you don't mind, just to keep up appearances. I don't want to give anything away before we start."

"You got a deal, Mister—?"

"Falk. Dexter Falk."

"We'll see you tomorrow night in the wee hours, then."

"Yes, you will."

We shook hands, and I climbed onto the pier and headed back into town. No one had been paying any attention to us, which reassured me. I certainly didn't expect trouble in Harkiss anyway.

By the time I returned to the inn, the first diners were arriving. I went to the room and found Fiona sitting by the window. She turned and smiled when I entered.

"I've booked us passage back to Tallesin on the *Evelyn Claire*," I said. "Did you finish making notes on the map?"

"I did, an hour ago. Then the time just seemed to drag."

"Well, I saw people beginning to assemble for the dinner hour. Shall we?"

"Yes, please."

The food at this inn was excellent, even though the service was indifferent to the point of rudeness. I didn't let our cranky serving girl ruin my meal. Dinner was a beef roast with root vegetables. Fiona ate with the same measured efficiency I had come to expect.

"So, you picked Greer because he seemed down on his luck?" Fiona asked.

"I did. His ill fortune made him more likely to be interested in my offer. He'll make fifty guilders from a two-week trip. That's more than he would clear in two months, even if the fish were coming his way."

"First Billy, and now him," she commented. "Do you make a habit of helping people who are struggling?"

"Not necessarily. I would like to think I'm as compassionate as the next man, but some people struggle because they simply aren't good at what they do. In Billy's case, and I think in Greer's, they are perfectly competent but are enduring a streak of bad luck. Someone like that, if I can catch them at the right time, can be of great use, and perhaps I can help turn their fortunes around."

"From the stories you told me while I was seasick, I would think that Marivelle is still in your debt. Perhaps you should pray to her on Mr. Greer's behalf."

"You have a kind heart, Fiona. Remind me to do that when we are closer to Tallesin. Mr. Greer is going out fishing again tomorrow, and if his luck turns, he may decide not to take us where we need to go."

"Would you pray to Sylvaris to keep the fish away from him for one more day?"

"No. That would be mean-spirited. I hope you know me well enough by now to know—"

"I was attempting to tease you again," she said, clearly crestfallen that she failed.

"Ah. Well, it is a learned skill, Fiona. As brilliant as you are, I'm sure you will master it in no time."

"I was hoping to earn another punishment, such as this morning's," she said, adding the perfect amount of pout to her lips.

"Oh, now that is a good tease," I said. "I will definitely need to punish you for that one."

Fiona's eyes held mine, performing that slow owl-like blink of hers. The corners of her mouth curled up slightly. She was blushing as well.

"Will the punishment be as … thorough … as it was this morning?"

"Even more so, since you are still teasing me."

Fiona rose, took my hand, and drew me after her. I followed her up the stairs. At the landing, she stopped and turned to me.

"I hope your punishment includes lots of kissing. It is as new to me as most everything else we've done, but kissing seems to be especially important at the beginning and the ending."

"And the middle," I said.

"Yes. Then, too."

She let go of my hand and scampered to our room. But the time I made it through the door and locked it behind me, her dress was already on the floor. I hurried to join her.

Later, we lay there. Her head was on my shoulder, and an arm and a leg were thrown over me. She sighed.

"Dexter, tomorrow night, I will wait on Mr. Greer's boat, but I will not like it."

"It is not a question of your courage, Fiona. It is my trust that I have developed particular skills that you lack—skills that Sylvaris can enhance when he chooses to."

"You have mentioned that before—that he withdraws his assistance from you in the middle of something. That seems … cruel. At the very least, it is dangerous."

"I am convinced it amuses him," I said, stroking her back languidly. "When I reach a point in things where I can manage with my own ability, he pulls away sometimes. Up to now, I have always extricated myself from danger, but many of the scars you seem to delight in fingering came about as a result."

"If you are caught—"

"Then take the *Evelyn Claire* to Tallesin. I will give you the twenty-five guilders I promised to Greer when we reached there. In Tallesin, go to the temple of Sylvaris and ask them to send word to Azar, our archpriest. He will know what to do."

"I will not sail without you."

"Then I suppose I had better not be caught."

"Now you are teasing me," she said with a mock growl. "I shall have to punish you for that."

Sleep came slowly to me when we finished. There was still a slight twinge in my neck. Sylvaris had not left me alone since Fiona arrived at my flat. I wondered what other gods were paying attention. If what Fiona believed was true, Korath, Calithra, and Kravyna had an interest. Eldryne certainly did. I mused a bit, wondering if the goddess of wisdom, known for her even-handed temperament, was angry at her archpriestess.

That pushed me to speculate on why Septima Thoran was acting as she was. Was it in pursuit of personal glory that she would be the one to find the treasure?

Or was she working at the behest of another order, either in hope of reward or under threat of punishment?

Of those two options, a threat seemed more likely. The Eldrynes were notoriously unconcerned with material pleasures. Many people had attempted to bribe those with truth-sense in the past, and all had failed.

My mind was busy chewing on this gristle. I finally settled on personal vanity being Thoran's motive. If another order were threatening the Eldrynes, more resources would be brought to bear on the problem, other than Fiona and me. An archpriestess afflicted with narcissism would be something that Eldryne would want to be handled quietly. It probably annoyed her no end that Sylvaris had involved himself.

I felt a soothing almost-caress on the back of my neck just then. It was as though I were a dog and my master was saying, "Good boy." It could only be Sylvaris.

13

It was raining when we woke in the morning. The clouds were the sort of low, gray overcast that promised to stay for at least a day. We had no need to go out into the weather until later, when we went to pick up Fiona's clothing and boots.

She found a book in the inn's common room—a Lysmeran romance. She delighted in showing it to me. I studied the drawings she'd made of the interior of the temple complex. After lunch, when Fiona grew bored, she started reading one of the bawdier parts of the novel out loud to me, exaggerating the supposed sighs and gasps of the lovers in the text. I decided she needed to be punished for that, which is what she'd been hoping I would do.

After we recovered, I lent her my cloak, and we went to collect her things from Mrs. Cuddy and the cobbler. I got wet on the way to the seamstress, but as promised, she had a cloak made for Fiona. Everything fit wonderfully, and we were off to the cobbler.

I made Fiona throw away the ugly temple shoes that had carried her all the way to Tallesin. They were just about used up anyway. Given the rain and puddles, Fiona wore her new boots out. I carried the purchases, and we returned to the inn to pack them away in her new valise before heading down to dinner.

Fiona did not eat well that evening. The food was good, but she had no appetite, pushing things around on her plate. Our conversation was fitful. I suspected she was worrying about tonight.

I ate quickly, and we left the table. Returning to the room, I made sure everything was packed. I chose my darkest clothing, then went to sit in the chair by the window.

"Come here, Fiona," I said.

"What?" she said, somewhat snippily.

"Sit in my lap and let me hold you until it is time to take you to the *Evelyn Claire*."

She did so, rather grumpily. I wondered at times if some of her emotional development stopped when she reached the temple. It would be something to discuss between us in the future, but not tonight.

After squirming for a time, she finally settled down and relaxed. Not long after, she fell asleep. I sat in the flickering candlelight, holding this exquisite creature in my arms, and reviewed in my head the drawings she'd made of the temple's interior.

When I judged the hour was late enough, I squeezed her shoulders and shook her gently. She woke by degrees. In the guttering candlelight, I saw her eyes blink slowly.

"Is it time?" she asked.

"I think so."

"It is still raining."

"Rain is our friend tonight. It helps people sleep more soundly."

"I still think I should go with you."

"And I *know* that if you do, you will jeopardize everything, Fiona. Do not give in to the temptation. Stay on the boat. And if I am not back by first light, sail to Tallesin without me. Then, when I catch up to you, you may scold me."

"I would prefer to *punish* you … thoroughly."

"I think I would enjoy that much more than a scolding," I said, kissing her forehead.

She rose from my lap, and I followed. We swirled on our cloaks, and I grabbed our bags. There was no worry about leaving the inn—I'd paid for an entire week, and we had days left.

We made our way down the streets and into the street without noise. The streets of Harkiss were dark—no lamps. My sense of direction was always strong, and I led us to the pier without difficulty.

"Ahoy, *Evelyn Claire!*" I called out softly as we neared where I thought the boat was moored.

A shuttered lantern appeared a few seconds later.

"Aye. Mr. Falk?" came a whisper back.

"Yes, and my guest."

Greer opened the shutter on the lantern when he heard our footsteps close. I handed our bags over to him, then he helped Fiona over the side. I turned to walk away.

"Where you goin'?"

"I'll be back in an hour or two, Mr. Greer. If I'm not back by daybreak, leave without me. Do not let Miss Magellan leave the boat to come find me. You have my permission to knock some sense into her with a belaying pin if necessary."

"Dexter!" she hissed.

"I'll be back, don't worry."

I leaned over the ship's rail and touched my lips to hers. Then, with a nod to Greer, I set off down the pier. I quickly slipped into the dark night.

The streets of Harkiss were empty, and none of the windows showed any light. Everyone was happily asleep. My boots splashed softly, and the hood of my cloak clung to my head. Sylvaris was with me. He loved it when I engaged in a bit of larceny.

The temple was at the top of the hill, and I circled around to the garden gate—wide open. I followed the stone path to the kitchen door. As Fiona predicted, it was unlatched. The hinges produced only a faint sigh as I pushed it open. The fire in the stove was banked, giving off only a little heat. Next to it snored one of the cooks, lying on a pallet. I stepped past him without a sound.

Leaving the kitchen, Fiona's drawing lived in my head. I skirted the refectory along the narrow service corridor, keeping my eyes away from the solitary lamp that burned within.

I reached the intersection, turning left, and then staying to the right to avoid the creaky floorboards Fiona warned me about. At the third intersection, I paused to listen—nothing.

Turning right, I entered the main walkway of the cloister. The third arch on the left was the entrance to the chamber where the archpriestess gave us such an unfriendly welcome. The door was locked. Before putting my picks to use, I pressed my ear against it. There was no sound.

The lock was simple but heavy. The sound of it snicking back was the loudest thing I'd heard since entering the temple. I pushed the heavy wooden door back slowly, lifting as I did to prevent any hinge squeak, as I learned back in my youth in Meropan.

The door to the scriptorium was only ten paces away, in an alcove on the right. This lock was so worn as to be nearly useless. It opened easily. I shut the door behind me and felt around gently on the counter in the dark for the lantern Fiona said would be there.

When I found it, my fingers scrabbled for the char cloth I expected would be nearby. Then, two strikes of the flint, the second catching the char cloth, a puff of air for a flame, and then lighting the wick. I had light, and the object of my hunt was easily spotted.

The parchment was on the counter a few feet away. A faded map of the continent of South Gaugan on its surface, but even in the dim light, I could see indentations in the surface that did not match the lines. It matched Fiona's description perfectly and could only be the palimpsest.

There was another parchment a little further down, but it looked new. The lines on the map were mere pencil tracings, not ink. There were other markings on it—letters and numbers. Fiona had said her parchment was perhaps a thousand years old. The one closer to me was clearly the one.

On either side of it were pages of notes on foolscap. I looked up at the shelves and saw dozens of scrolls enclosed in leather tubes. I didn't care about the scrolls; I wanted one of the tubes. I pulled one down and emptied it, then rolled the parchment up and placed it inside. For good measure, I rolled up the pages of notes and put them in as well. Fiona hadn't mentioned it, but I figured it was probably her work, and I didn't want the archpriestess and her cronies to profit from it.

I sealed the tube and tucked it into my waistband. After blowing out the lamp, I made my way back out, locking up behind myself. Again, the snick of the lock on the heavy door to the archpriestess's chamber made the loudest sound of the night. I retraced my steps all the way out.

As I jogged down the temple hill, I felt Sylvaris's glee. He had remained with me the entire time. I half expected him to abandon me in the middle, as this was one of the easiest jobs I'd ever pulled. I certainly had not needed to call on him for assistance. He'd simply been a spectator tonight.

I paused on my way to the waterfront to listen for any pursuit. There was none. It occurred to me that the Eldrynes had probably never been robbed before. Sylvaris seemed to agree with me.

The pier came up more quickly than I anticipated. I saw the faint outline of the shuttered lantern hanging from the *Evelyn Claire*. I slowed to a walk as I approached. There were two shadowy figures I could see.

"Dexter?" Fiona called out quietly.

"Yes. I'm here," I said, noting the glow from the bowl of the pipe of the other figure—Greer.

"Mr. Greer, if you would cast off, we can wait for the tide," I said as I climbed over the rail.

He whistled softly, and his two boys handled the ropes and shoved us away from the quay, then busied themselves with the mainsail. Fiona threw her arms around me. I patted her back reassuringly as we drifted away from the dock.

"Did you—?"

"Of course. You'll have to wait until it's light and the rain stops before I show you."

"Yes, getting it wet would be awful."

"There were also pages of notes next to it on foolscap. I rolled those up and tucked them in as well."

All I can say is that Fiona nearly attacked me with kisses then, to the point where we nearly tumbled.

"Whoa!" I said, wresting my mouth away from hers.

"I've been kicking myself the whole time you've been away," she said. "I never mentioned to you that you should get my notes as well. It's a good thing you're so clever. All that worrying I did was for nothing."

"Well, it seemed like a good idea at the time. I didn't want you to have to recreate your earlier efforts, and I didn't want them to profit from what you'd done."

"What else did you see in the scriptorium?"

I told her about the newer piece of parchment. She pressed me for every detail I could remember. As I related them, the frown on her face grew.

"The letters and numbers were more clear than the map of South Gaugan?" she asked.

"Yes."

"I think they made a copy based on my notes."

"Why would they need a copy?"

"It's possible that Sister Deirdre was unable to figure out the calculations. There are other astronomers elsewhere who might have more success."

"Then we need to find one first."

"And we have the original," Fiona said. "There are other parts of the scripto inferior I had not yet transcribed. I doubt Sister Wanda made much progress while I was away. Even though she taught me, the pupil outstripped the master a few years ago."

"Scripto inferior?" I asked.

"The original writing, before it was scraped."

"We still have the advantage then."

"We do, but I do not think they will give up. Your little visit may provoke them into moving more vigorously."

14

"What do you think the scripto inferior that you hadn't identified yet includes?" I asked, slightly proud of myself for using the term she'd just taught me.

"I concentrated on the numbers first. Those would be the basis for the calculations. Again, remember that we are dealing with the appearance of the heavens as of when the original was created, back in Torsten's time. The part I had not yet transcribed was text."

"And you don't think it's as important?"

"I don't know. It could be simply a paean to Torsten, about how he's so wonderful and great, ruler of so many cities, conqueror of so many peoples, etc."

"That would be no help at all."

"Agreed, but hidden in that praise poetry might be clever instructions, like, 'subtract three from every fifth number.' It wouldn't be that obvious, of course. You would need to know that you were looking for something like that. Torsten wanted the location to remain a secret, and this is one of the ways they did things."

We were tucked under the small canvas awning that Greer had erected over the cockpit. The shuttered lantern swung slightly with the boat's movement, playing across Fiona's golden skin. She was wearing one of the traveling dresses we'd just purchased. It was practical, but the way it hugged her body reminded me why I kept getting caught staring.

"Hidden instructions in praise poetry? It sounds like the kind of thing Sylvaris might employ, requiring cleverness to solve the puzzle."

"Exactly," she said, giving me a slow blink with the long-lashed eyes. "Torsten, or whoever wrote the underlayer, knew this map would be seen by others at some point, so he buried a hint that the casual onlooker would not notice. When I have finished identifying the rest of the document, we will probably be able to find that clue."

"How?"

"It will be in a line that seems slightly awkward or presents a non sequitur—something that doesn't quite follow the narrative."

The *Evelyn Claire* pitched slightly more than normal, and Fiona lurched into me. Instinctively, I wrapped my arms around her to steady her. She remained pressed against my chest, her right hand splayed over my heart.

We stayed like that for quite a while, until the sky started to lighten with the gray of false dawn. The rain eased to a gentle patter on the canvas overhead. Without a word, Greer and his two crewmen began moving.

"Tide's turned," Greer said when I turned my head to him. "Folks'll think we went out early to change our luck."

That reminded me of Fiona's suggestion. I silently composed a prayer to Marivelle in my head, asking her to reward Greer with good catches when he returned to Harkiss. I didn't know whether Marivelle still considered herself in my debt at all—probably not—but a prayer on Greer's behalf wouldn't hurt.

The movement of the boat increased as they left the harbor. We sat down on a small bench under the windward rail to avoid toppling. I looked at Fiona, worried about the rise and fall and how it might be affecting her.

"Mr. Greer made me some ginger tea while we waited for you. You may apply the peppermint oil if you like," she said, handing him the small glass bottle.

"Do you feel you need it?"

"I enjoy the feeling of you putting it on, and the smell is very pleasant."

I unstopped the bottle and put some oil on the tip of my finger. Fiona tilted her head up, her eyes closed, as she waited for me to rub it on. As I traced her upper lip, I noticed her breath caught slightly.

For a time, we watched as the gray-green Entassa slid beside us. The low gray cloud layer showed signs of breaking up. Harkiss was now just a dim smudge to the west.

The weather cleared as the day wore on and stayed fair all the way to Tallesin. Greer dropped us at a quay, and I paid him the other twenty-five guilders. He took it with a nod of thanks, then the boys shoved the *Evelyn Claire* off, and Fiona and I headed to my flat.

It was late afternoon on a fine spring day, and the city was bustling. Upon arrival at my flat, I hurriedly unpacked our dirty clothes and took them downstairs to the milliner's shop. Philomena, one of the girls who worked there, did my laundry for me and kept my flat spotless. When she saw Fiona's things mixed with mine, she raised an eyebrow.

"Come upstairs and meet her whenever you like, Philomena. Fiona is a wonderful young lady—extremely intelligent and learned."

"I wouldn't want to interrupt anything, Mr. Falk."

"Nonsense. She might be working on a project she has, but she would probably welcome seeing a face other than mine. Besides, she will need a hat for the summer sun. Perhaps you can entice her downstairs and have her pick one out."

I returned upstairs to find Fiona had finally opened the leather tube and withdrawn the parchment. She had been frustrated by the conditions on the *Evelyn Claire,* which forced her to wait. The document was spread open on the table, which she had dragged closer to the window. She'd weighted down the corners with odds and ends—salt and pepper shakers, a trivet, and an actual paperweight.

I watched her silently. The tip of her tongue was poking out of the corner of her mouth in concentration. She danced between the parchment and the foolscap to the side, observing, then writing down quick notes in pencil.

"The angle of the light is *perfect* right now," she said quietly when she noticed I'd returned. "The archpriestess would not allow me to take the parchment out of the main scriptorium. The archpriestess and Sister Wanda feared that the strength of the sun would damage the vellum. Lamp light is not as revealing as natural sunlight. I will not leave the piece out in the sun too long, but I am seeing the scripto inferior very clearly right now."

"And your earlier notes?"

"All correct, but what I can see much more clearly now is the paean to Torsten. I am hurrying to capture as much of it as I can while the angle of the light is so perfect."

I stayed in the background, watching as Fiona would hop back and forth between the parchment and her notes. She continued for the better part of an hour before stepping back with a sigh. Removing the weights she'd placed down, she rolled the vellum up and returned it to the leather tube. As she did, her stomach gave a loud rumble I could hear across the room.

"I think it's time I feed you."

"Please. I find I'm starving all of a sudden."

We went to the Broken Wheel, and Garrett ushered us to a table. I could tell that Fiona's face was radiant with excitement. After our meal came, I asked her about what she'd found.

"Well, the good news—the best news—is that natural light is revealing the lettering of the praise poem much more clearly than I was able to see before. I was able to double-check all the astronomical figures, and my notes were correct."

"The way you say that implies that there is something not so good," I commented.

"Nothing I didn't know or suspect before," she said. "The language is in an archaic form of Mykenan—pre-twilight. There are very few scholars in the world who can translate it. There were none at the temple—this I know. We will need to find someone who can do it. If we do, he or she will also be able to give us a solid idea of how old the underlayer is. That will be of great use when we find an astronomer who can work out the calculations of star positions."

"Tomorrow, we will call upon Ned Wilbur, the head priest at the temple of Sylvaris," I suggested. "He probably won't know anyone who can translate archaic Mykenan, but he might know someone who can point us in the right direction."

"And an astronomer."

"I suspect an astronomer will be easier to find. I know they don't grow on trees, but I would imagine there are more of them than experts in ancient tongues."

Fiona giggled—a new sound to my ears. I raised my eyebrow in response. She blushed.

"The mental image of astronomers growing on trees," she said. "I was imagining one with a stem sticking out of a bald head."

For all the strangeness of the past weeks, her long walk to find me, her seasickness, and then her expulsion from her order, she could still appreciate a bit of whimsy. It was one of the many reasons I was finding myself drawn to her. It had been so unexpected, and she was so different from anyone else I'd known, it baffled me when I thought about it.

"Perhaps there's a grove nearby," I suggested.

"I like it when you joke with me, Dexter. The temple was not a place for jokes. Perhaps, when this is over, and I am restored to the order, I can work to change that."

Fiona's excitement over what she was able to see bubbled up as we ate. She described how the angle of the sun and the strength of its light revealed the faint indentations in the vellum. She could hardly wait until tomorrow, when the afternoon sun would return.

"The praise poem is longer than I thought," she said. "Forty-two lines. I was working quickly, so I will need to check that I copied everything accurately. Of course, I still have no idea what it says. The system of lettering is entirely different from any modern language. The shape of the letters was originally determined by pressing a flat-edged stylus into wet clay, then modified as time passed until the twilight, when men forgot how to read and write for several hundred years. When written language reemerged, few of the letters looked anything like what had been before."

"What caused the twilight?" I asked. "I know of it, but only that it ended. How did it begin?"

"There are many different theories," she said. "Of course, North and South Langjord were illiterate at the time, populated with primitive peoples whose written language was pictograms."

"Pictograms?"

"Little drawings instead of words. Written language was mostly confined to the southern half of North Gaugan and the northern half of South Gaugan. Different theories exist for why language was forgotten."

"Such as?"

"Some people believe it was a plague sent by the gods because mankind had forgotten to show due reverence. I don't think that is the case. The theory I trust is that a tribe of barbarians from North Gaugan swept down and conquered everyone, to the point of near-total destruction. They were illiterate, and during the early days of their rule, reading and writing were unimportant."

"What changed to bring literacy back?"

"I think it had to do with taxes and tribute," Fiona said. "If you are the ruler, you want to know who has paid and how much, and who has not. Especially in an age without money, where taxes were paid in grain or goods, you need a system of recording the information that can be interpreted the same whether it is in a province or the capital. Scribes had value once again. Writing materials needed to be reinvented or scavenged. That is where palimpsests come in—the vellum was too valuable to throw away. They scraped it off and used it again. In the case of this piece, a notation of astronomical readings and a poem in praise of a long-dead warlord was deemed expendable. They never knew what it meant."

It was interesting watching Fiona discuss this. A part of her personality came alive. We stayed until the grumpy serving girl cleared her throat for the fourth time, and we realized we were the last patrons. As we left, I apologized to her and to Garrett for keeping them overlong.

15

"Are you still worried that I will steal the covers?" she asked as we entered the bedroom in my flat.

"No. It's remarkable how much things have changed since that first night. Most, for the better," I said.

"I would agree. And I am happy to have a bed to share with you, Dexter Falk, rather than a hammock by your side."

Fiona stood there, every inch of her golden skin on display, her clothes and underthings neatly folded on the chair. She smiled and slid under the covers, then made a play of tugging all the blankets to her side. I quickly stripped and jumped in to defend my claim to them.

Fiona let out a squeak as we wrestled for control of the blankets, and we tumbled together in a tangle of limbs. Somehow, she ended up on top of me, her hair freed from its messy bun, enclosing us in our own private world. She moved her hands up to pin mine above my head.

"I surrender!" I admitted.

"I win!" she exclaimed with a cackle of triumph.

"No, I do," I said, as I lifted my head so our lips would meet, and the blankets we'd been tussling over were soon kicked out of the way.

Once again, Fiona was up with the sun. I convinced her to slow things down a bit by offering to prepare us a hot bath. She agreed, as we both felt salt-encrusted after our journey from Harkiss. That bought me some time to wake up as I found the tub, removed the cobwebs from it, kindled a fire in the stove, and started fetching water from the fountain in the square in front of my flat.

I allowed her to go first, as the tub would barely hold a single person, but I volunteered to scrub all her hard-to-reach places (and some that were readily accessible to my roaming hands). When she was finished, I dried her with a towel, then took my turn in the cooling water. As I was drying myself, my stomach gurgled.

"Let's nab two birds with the same snare," I suggested. "The temple of Sylvaris will be serving breakfast soon, and we need to talk with Ned Wilbur anyway."

Fiona agreed, and after tossing the used bathwater out of the kitchen window, I dressed, and we headed out. I offered my arm to her, but Fiona took my hand instead, entwining our fingers together. It made me realize that, for all her knowledge, I was her first love. She'd never experienced these sorts of feelings before, and I felt a sudden weight of responsibility.

We reached the temple, and the novice priest at the front door sent an acolyte to tell Ned we were there. Both of them were new to the temple since my last visit. Of course, I'd been away for months, so it wasn't surprising.

When the acolyte returned to take us inside, we went to the refectory, where breakfast was being served. I immediately smelled strawberries and was happy they were still in season. Ned Wilbur separated from the group he was with and came to greet us.

"Ned Wilbur, Fiona Magellan," I said, introducing them.

Fiona gave him a slight curtsy, acknowledging his status as the head priest of the temple. He smiled, not used to such deference. He took us to the head of the table.

"Porridge with strawberries, coffee or tea if you want it," he said. "Please sit. Are you the Sister Fiona who walked twenty-seven days to find Dexter?"

"I am that person, but I am no longer a member of the Order of Eldryne."

"Pish posh," Ned replied. "Sister Fiona, Eldryne did not cast you out. Septima Thoran did, and when you and Dexter are successful, she will face her own reckoning. You still regard yourself in service to the goddess?"

"I … I suppose I am."

"Then to me, you are Sister Fiona, regardless of whatever temporary insanity has possessed your archpriestess, and you are most welcome here, even if you did come in with Dexter."

We filled our bowls from the steaming cauldron and helped ourselves to as many strawberries as we wanted. An acolyte came and poured coffee for us. Fiona ate with her usual precise movements and kept her head down. I realized her status as a defrocked member of her order was making her self-conscious.

"Fiona, you look uncomfortable," Ned noted. "Would you be more at ease if we moved to my office?"

"That is not necessary," she said quietly.

"But I feel guilty that you are ill-at-ease. Remember, Sylvaris is not picky. He is the god of merchants, travelers, and thieves, and is not ashamed to rub shoulders with people from all walks of life."

"Eldryne prefers the studious and diligent," Fiona answered. "And shuns those who are not."

"Eldryne forgets that sometimes the only way to learn something is the hard way, and I expect she will be reminded of that in the months to come," Wilbur said.

He spooned some strawberries into his porridge and stirred it absent-mindedly, looking at Fiona with a calm and slightly amused expression. Fiona sat up straight, wearing one of her new outfits that Mrs. Cuddy had made. She looked directly at Ned and gave him an owl-blink with her long-lashed eyelids.

"Forgive me, Father Ned, but you act as though you know something," she said.

"I know many things," he said with a small chuckle. "Most of it is useless knowledge, but there are a few tidbits germane to your current situation. This is neither the time nor the place to go into detail, as Dexter suggested earlier. Rest assured, Fiona, you are among friends, and you owe me no more respect than you would give Dexter, and I hope that is as little as possible."

"You tease one another," Fiona noted.

"Of course," Ned answered.

"Oh. I am a novice in the skill of teasing, but Dexter is teaching me. He punishes me when I do it correctly."

It took a moment for Ned to process what Fiona had said, then he burst out laughing. Fiona fought it, but the corners of her mouth turned up in a faint smile. I, of course, turned bright red.

"Well played, Fiona. Well played," Ned said, still laughing. "I've never seen Dexter blush before, and you turned him an interesting shade of puce. You are welcome at my table any time, and you do not need to drag Dexter along. We might have much more fun without him. Now, eat up. We have much to discuss. The strawberries are wonderful this year."

"Although porridge is no measure of culinary skill, at the temple of Eldryne, it would be watery or burnt, and the strawberries would be either unripe or past their prime," Fiona remarked.

Ned barked with laughter again. His joviality drew the others' attention at the long table. Even though they sat at a distance, trying to give us space, they could not help but wonder why the head priest was laughing so much. Ned merely shook his head and waved at them, telling them to pay him no mind.

"Fiona, my dear, we are no great masters of the kitchen arts, but we do believe in eating as well as we can. I hope we will see you at many more meals while you are in Tallesin."

"You say that, implying we will not be here long," she noted.

"And that is why we must finish eating and repair to my study," Ned said, pushing his empty bowl away. "Dexter, you know the way. Come when you are finished."

Fiona and I finished not long after. The entire time after Ned left us, I noticed she was paying quiet attention to the acolytes and novices down the table from us. Their conversation was boisterous. From her expression, I think she was beginning to realize the holy orders were not all like what she'd experienced the last fourteen years in Harkiss. I hoped she found it a pleasant revelation, and not something that caused discomfort.

When she finished, I offered my arm. She took my hand, again entwining our fingers. We went to Ned's study.

"Come in, come in," he said, bustling from behind his messy desk. "Dexter, shut the door. I know some, but not all. I just received a letter from our archpriest yesterday. Let me tell you what he shared with me, and you can fill in the blanks."

"You have a palimpsest," Ned began once we sat down, "that Dexter 'recovered' from the temple of Eldryne in Harkiss."

"That is known here already?" Fiona asked.

"It is known to me, and the two of you. I doubt anyone else is aware. It is certainly known in Harkiss. I do not know what they plan to do about it."

"Your archpriest knows and communicated with you by letter?" Fiona inquired.

"Azar, the archpriest, is connected with Sylvaris with an incredibly close bond. Sylvaris knew that Dexter took the document, so Azar then knew."

"Sylvaris has been, literally, a pain in my neck since Fiona arrived," I commented.

"I am unsurprised to hear that, Dex. Reading between the lines of what Azar sent me, the two of you are in the middle of a significant upset within the pantheon. All started, young lady, by your discovery of the underlayer of the palimpsest in question."

"What sort of upset within the pantheon?" I asked.

"The kind Sylvaris *loves*," Ned replied, rubbing his hands together in glee. "Gods are taking sides. Let me reverse course briefly and tell you what Azar shared with me. You, Fiona, found the underlayer on a piece of undistinguished vellum. One of your colleagues brought it to the attention of your archpriestess, believing you found something that might be potentially of great value."

"Sister Wanda," Fiona breathed, "but she always expressed the greatest doubt that—"

"Part of the archpriestess's design," Ned said. "She felt that as long as you were uncertain, you would keep your mouth shut. She did not want news of your discovery to spread to anyone outside of her and a trusted few."

"Why?"

"That is unclear. When you reported that you had dreams where Eldryne told you to find Dexter, the archpriestess wanted you to disregard them."

"Except I went to the truth-sayers who verified that they were true visions," Fiona said.

"Yes. Now, your colleague had been paying close attention to your work. Did you notice her spending a great deal of time with you?"

"Yes. I thought that was because she doubted it was of any importance and she wanted me to be especially thorough as a result."

"It was so that she would know everything you learned, and then at night she would copy the notes you made."

Fiona looked devastated. Learning that your mentor was working against you—actively betraying you—was a difficult thing to swallow. She squeezed my hand tightly enough to cut off my circulation.

"Eldryne had her own reasons for wanting to keep this discovery quiet, but decided your archpriestess was untrustworthy. Why? We don't know. She turned to Sylvaris for help, which is when you had your dreams."

"But you said the pantheon is somehow involved," I remarked.

"All of the orders spy on one another," Ned said. "It's one of those things we all know and try to pretend isn't taking place. Word spread to some of the other orders that you might have found the key to the location of Torsten's Hoard. That immediately seized the attention of Calithra, Korath, and Kravyna."

"Are their relics part of the Hoard?" Fiona asked.

"Young lady, they *are* the Hoard."

16

"I knew it!" Fiona breathed.

"So, what does that mean?" I asked.

"As I said, Eldryne wanted to keep this quiet and hoped that enlisting the aid of Sylvaris would allow her to wrap this up without a fuss. That all blew up when Kravyna heard about it. She demanded that Eldryne turn the search over to her people. Hearing that, Calithra and Korath are completely opposed to Kravyna taking charge of this and cast their lots with Eldryne and Sylvaris. The problem is that Eldryne is powerless, as is usually the case. She supports you, Sister Fiona, but her archpriestess is working toward her own ends. Eldryne sits and wrings her hands in despair."

"What of the major gods?" Fiona inquired.

"The major gods—Zoryn, Teryssa, Marivelle, and Thalorix—have deemed this matter beneath their notice. More accurately, they have no wish to involve themselves in what they view as a squabble among the lessers. Divine politics, you understand, dating way back to long before the twilight, when the majors counseled the minors against creating these divine artifacts, stating that humans were fallible and could not be trusted with such powerful implements. The other factor is that as long as the disagreement involves only the minor gods, the cosmos remains intact, and human suffering is minimal. If the majors get involved, things escalate."

"Not if they're all in agreement."

"That's the thing, Fiona," Ned remarked, "the majors maintain a delicate balance between themselves. They are harmonious, but only as discordant notes blended together create a more pleasing whole. In the dim and distant past, they have openly opposed one another, with disastrous results."

"What of the other minor gods?" I asked.

"Vyran and Vionelle don't care. Serethyn never takes sides."

"You did not mention Lysmera," Fiona pointed out.

"She has allied herself with Sylvaris in recent months," Ned replied. "Lysmera has always enjoyed a bit of mischief, and Sylvaris has always been her favorite playmate. If she is involved, it will be on his behalf."

Fiona's golden cheeks flushed like ripe apricots. She did not look away from Ned, but her long-lashed owl-blink came twice as she processed what Ned had just shared. For me, I could tell that Sylvaris was immensely entertained by what was shaping up. If Lysmera was his favorite playmate, Kravyna was his favorite foil. And in the middle of this cosmic competition, Dexter Falk and Fiona Magellan were just pieces on a much larger board.

Sylvaris sent me the equivalent of a shrug, as in, "What did you expect?"

"Azar told me you will need to find an expert in archaic Mykenan and a talented astronomer. He recommends a man in Dorul, just south of the city of Namo in North Gaugan. The man's name is Valerian Wouk. He should be able to point you in the direction of a competent astronomer. They're much easier to find."

"May I see the letter from Azar?" I asked.

"Unfortunately, no," Ned replied with a genuinely sad expression. "It includes things you are forbidden to read. On a happier note, there is a caravan leaving for Lenoa tomorrow. A group of priests-militant is returning to Lenoa along with it. They will lend you a tent and bedrolls. Azar added a cryptic note to the letter, suggesting you rent Sara for your companion, who could only be you, Miss Magellan. I do not understand, but presume you will."

"Sara was the mule I rented when I headed to Lenoa to find Ugarte's spices," I said. "She was a very good girl and would be perfect for you, Fiona. One more question—is Septima Thoran working with the Order of Kravyna?"

"According to Azar, it did not start out that way, but he suspects they may have established contact, especially now that you recovered the palimpsest. It's another good reason for you to leave Tallesin tomorrow, especially accompanied by priests-militant."

"That reminds me," I said. "I owe Varak, the head of Kravyna's temple in Lenoa, a practice bout."

At that moment, I imagine Sylvaris having fallen out of his chair and rolling on the floor with laughter. Ned gave me an extremely sour look. Fiona was puzzled.

"Remember when I told you how the temple of Kravyna in Lenoa assisted us in recovering the ships?" This I directed at Fiona.

She blinked slowly, then nodded.

"Varak, their head priest, 'invited' me to engage in a practice bout with him the next time I was in Lenoa. The Kravynans take these things extremely seriously. If I tried to avoid him, it would be considered an insult to him and a terrible stain on my honor. I will have to participate in this contest. With Sylvaris and Kravyna on opposite sides of the current dispute, you could also consider it a proxy battle."

"How dangerous will it be?" she asked.

"I won't die, most likely, unless something goes hideously wrong or Varak breaks all bonds of behavior. The two of us will probably emerge bruised and bloody, but otherwise still functional."

"You speak of this as a friendly game of tiles," she remarked, but a clear look of distress was written on her face.

"It won't resemble anything like that, Miss Magellan," Ned commented. "Dex, I would recommend avoiding Varak, but I also know why you cannot. Who knows? Perhaps you will win his neutrality in what is to come."

"But, Father Ned, Dex is covered with scars. He cannot possibly hope to compete with the head priest of a temple of Kravyna."

"Miss Magellan, Dexter probably has not told you this, because he does not consider it something to boast about, but for every one of those scars, two or three people are dead. He is exceptionally gifted."

"Is this true, Dex?" she asked.

"As Ned mentioned, it's not something I like to discuss."

"I do not mean to pry, only to understand."

"You deserve to know what sort of man you will be accompanying on this journey. I have been doing Sylvaris's work since I left Meropan over ten years ago. Sometimes blades are drawn. With all due modesty, I am skilled. It is not because of my connection to Sylvaris, but it is perhaps one of the reasons he has invested in me so much. What matters is I'm still here, and others who opposed me are not. I'm not a cold-blooded killer, but there is blood on my hands."

"What will happen in your contest with the Kravynan?" she asked.

"He will attempt to demonstrate his physical superiority over me and compel me to submit. I will endeavor to prevent that."

"Do you think you can win?" she asked, concern and a faint sense of excitement showing in her expression.

"The best outcome will be a draw," I said. "That means he does not lose face in front of his people, and I earn his respect."

"Bruised and bloodied," she commented. "It seems ridiculous to me."

"It is how the temple of Kravyna determines merit," Ned said with a shrug.

"Will Varak know of any alliance between the archpriestess and his order?" she asked.

"It's possible," Ned replied. "His order may have sent a pigeon. The most likely places for the two of you to go are Lenoa and Dropan. Both temples might have been alerted."

"Will that make a difference in your … contest?"

"It will increase the importance of it to Varak. He is, in his way and according to the tenets of his order, an honorable man. He will adhere to the rules for such things. If I am able to force a draw and earn his respect, it might remove him and his temple from the list of our potential foes."

"The entire order?"

"No," I said with a rueful laugh, "only the temple in Lenoa. But since we will be there for a few days while we arrange passage to North Gaugan, it would be better not to need to look over our shoulders the entire time."

"What would happen if you lose?"

"If he defeats me, it might mean an end to our quest."

"What if you win?"

"It might anger Varak enough that he orders his people to seize us in order not to lose face."

"Then you must force a draw."

"As I said."

"The caravan leaves at first light tomorrow," Ned reminded us. "It's a small one and not really carrying anything worth the attention of priests-militant, but they need to return to Lenoa, and I figured it would be better to have them escort someone than ride off alone. I've already made arrangements with them."

"You mentioned a tent and bedrolls," I said.

"And don't worry about food. The caravan master has agreed to feed the priests and you in exchange for my waiving the usual donative. I have one more thing to give you and then I must return to my duties," he said as he handed a letter in a sealed and waxed envelope to Fiona. "It's for Valerian Wouk, from Azar. I do not know what it says, but it probably urges him to assist you."

Ned rose and we clasped forearms as we used to do in Meropan. He then took Fiona's hand and brushed it lightly with his lips. She blushed in response.

Outside the temple, the spring sun had chased away the few clouds there had been when we woke. Fiona took my hand again. We were heading to the livery where I would ask about taking the mule Sara to Lenoa.

"He is not what I expected," Fiona commented after a couple of blocks.

"Ned?"

"He reminds me of a kind old uncle from the storybooks."

"Do you expect every Sylvaran to be shifty and cunning?" I asked.

"No," she answered quickly, then laughed and amended, "yes. There is a certain image that is stuck in my mind. You do not match it, nor does he. In fact, none of the Sylvarans I saw today strikes me as that type."

"Well, you are nothing like the usual sister of Eldryne," I said. "I always picture dried-up old biddies with their hair pulled back so tightly it makes them squint."

"We do have a few of those," Fiona admitted with a smile.

"Sadly, I doubt you'll find the shifty, cunning type in any temple of Sylvaris," I said. "I've never encountered one, at any rate."

We reached the livery and the man remembered me, though not by name. As it turned out, Sara was available. Thinking he had an advantage because I requested a specific mount, he attempted to haggle. Sylvaris was still paying attention, and with his ability to persuade lent to me, I put a quick stop to that.

"Why did you want this particular animal?" Fiona asked after we finished and were leading Sara away.

"I rode Sara before, when I met Agatha. She is sure-footed and calm. You said you have no experience in riding, and Sara will take good care of you."

"How can a mule take care of me?"

"She won't start or stop abruptly, which might throw you off balance. She doesn't lurch. She's sweet-tempered for a mule. By the time we reach Lenoa, you'll feel as though you always knew how to ride."

From there, we went to the stable where I kept Rufus. He nickered when he saw me, making me feel even more guilty for leaving him alone as much as I did. The stableman gave me a carrot. I broke it into pieces and asked Fiona to hold her hand out. I adjusted her fingers to tuck them away, then put a piece of carrot on her palm.

"Go ahead," I said. "Offer it to him."

It was clear that Fiona was a bit trepidatious. She gave me one of her owl-blinks. Rufus was very big next to her, and his teeth, I'm sure, looked enormous. She tentatively extended her hand, and Rufus, sensing her unease, picked the bit of carrot up daintily with his lips.

"That tickled!" Fiona gasped as Rufus chomped twice, then gave her the kind of look that said, "More, please."

Fiona fed Rufus the rest of the carrot, and he was as gentle with the last bite as the first. I urged her to pet him, and she reached out to stroke his long snout. After a couple of strokes, Rufus turned his head and licked her hand.

"You've made another new friend, Fiona. Rufus really likes you."

I arranged with the stablemaster to house Sara overnight and told him we would collect both animals at sunup. He agreed without a fuss, and Fiona and I headed back toward my flat. Along the way, I stopped and bought a supply of dried fruit for our journey.

"They agreed to feed us," I said, "but it will be rather plain. These will give us something to look forward to."

17

When we returned, I saw that Philomena had washed our clothing and returned it to us. That reminded me that Fiona would need a hat. Summer was around the corner, and she would need something to keep the sun out of her eyes. We went downstairs to the milliner's and Philomena came over to assist us.

"We'll be doing a lot of traveling in the next couple of weeks, and Miss Magellan needs a hat that will serve her well either riding or aboard ship," I specified.

Philomena's eyes brightened with the quiet delight of a craftswoman who knows her business. She circled Fiona slowly, taking into account her height, her coloring, and her figure. Fiona stood still, enduring Philomena's scrutiny.

"Moderately wide brim for the sun, but not too wide—the wind off the waves would play havoc. Straw, so it doesn't get hot. Leather band for strength, chin cord of strong ribbon. No lining, just the soft band inside," Philomena said. "Please take your hair down. Dexter, find a suitable length of ribbon and tie it back for her."

She darted over to one side of the room and returned with a hat with a shallow crown, while I did as ordered, choosing a light blue piece of ribbon and tying Fiona's hair back in a plait. Fiona tried the hat on, and it cast a soft glow over her golden skin. Fiona studied her reflection in the mirror, giving one of her slow blinks.

"It is … serviceable," she said after a moment. "But the color is too pale. It will attract dust on the way to Lenoa and then seem dirtier than it is."

"Try this one," Philomena said, having already retrieved another candidate while Fiona was assessing the first.

This had a deeper crown and was woven of a reed that was more gray than yellow. The band on the outside was green leather and matched the color of the cortaderia skirt Fiona was wearing. A final selling point, at least for me, was that the maker had affixed a small silver emblem on the right side of the leather band. It was similar to Eldryne's sigil, showing an open book.

Fiona noticed the ornament as well and stared at it briefly. She put the hat on, and Philomena tied the black ribbon under Fiona's chin, which would keep it on even in a stout breeze. Fiona examined herself in the mirror. It framed her face perfectly, in my opinion.

"Does it suit me, Dexter?"

"Remarkably well," I said.

We left the shop and went in search of lunch. Fiona was unfamiliar with food carts, and I vowed to remedy that gap in her experience. We strolled around the market square, sampling different offerings. As we walked, I caught Fiona looking at her reflection in different shop windows, wearing the hat. It was not vanity—it was curiosity.

"You are staring again," she noted. "Is it the hat? Do I look odd?"

"Not odd," I said. "You're beautiful. This is a slightly altered aspect, but no less attractive. If you take the hat off and allow it to rest on your back, held by the ribbon under your chin, you will look like a lady from the southern plains."

"Like Agatha?"

"Like Fiona, raised in a different environment."

Fiona tilted the hat back as I suggested. She turned to look in a window. Our eyes met over her shoulder.

"I see what you mean. I saw a drawing once that I am reminded of. You like the hat."

"I like the woman who wears the hat."

We tried a few different food offerings before Fiona settled on the one she enjoyed the most. It was skewers of meat—goat, I think—with dried fruit in between the chunks of meat, then roasted over a brazier. When we finished, she urged me to return to my flat.

"The afternoon sun is upon us, and the light will be optimal for my further examination."

Fiona wasted no time upon our return. She withdrew the parchment from the tube and weighed it down with the same objects as the day before. She arranged her notes beside it.

"The light is perfect," she said quietly, really speaking to herself.

She put her head close, examining the vellum from the side. Straightening, she would dart sideways to her foolscap and compare it to what she'd just seen, checking to make sure she'd transcribed things accurately. When she reached the previously unseen part of the text, her progress slowed. The whole time, the tip of her tongue peeked from the corner of her mouth.

I was content to watch. There is a kind of beauty exhibited by someone in the midst of engrossing work. Fiona completely ignored me, and I minded not at all.

While she was busy, I went to the other room and pried up a floorboard. I had quite a bit of money stashed away, both invested with banks and also hidden in my flat. I found a small chest with four hundred guilders in it. I dumped them into the false bottom of my valise. The money might be needed to get us to North Gaugan.

Finally, she stopped. She stood and stretched, reaching her hands above her head, and I heard the small pops of vertebrae unkinking in her back. She made a small sound of relief.

"Forty-two lines of text, in three groups of fourteen lines each," she said. "All my earlier work regarding the astronomical figures is verified. We are as ready to see Valerian Wouk as we can be."

"All we need to do is get there and then find him."

"We ride over the isthmus, we find a boat and sail across the Tiburn, we figure out what this map says, then go to South Gaugan and find it," Fiona said. "Until I set off to find you, Dexter, I'd lived in only two places—my village and the temple. Now, in just a few short months, we will have traveled the world."

I smiled at the wonderment in her voice.

"But first we must get through Lenoa, and this man Varak. You said this is a 'practice bout.' What does that mean?"

"We will fight one another with weighted wooden swords," I explained. "Perhaps a small buckler will be included."

"Buckler?"

"A small shield used to deflect an opponent's thrusts or slashes."

"And even with wooden swords, you will be injured?"

"They will have enough heft to break bones. If unskilled or unlucky, a person could even be impaled by one, even though the tip is dull and rounded."

"And there is no way of avoiding it?"

"Kravyna's people take these challenges seriously. It is how Varak became head priest of that temple, by defeating all others in single combat. Someday, a challenger will come who will unseat Varak. Even defeated, as long as he fights with honor and skill, he will remain a valued member of the order."

"And you wish the contest to end in a draw?"

"Yes. That will be the most difficult result; to achieve a draw in such a way that honor and respect are both satisfied, but that wins us freedom to continue."

"Are you afraid?"

"I will not lose, Fiona."

"It sounds ridiculous," she said.

"Because it is," I agreed. "It's completely pointless. I wish I could avoid it, but I cannot. There is no way to get through Lenoa without Varak learning we are there."

"Then nothing more needs to be said. I am hungry. Is it time for dinner?"

"I believe so. Shall we?"

We headed to the Broken Wheel, and Garrett seated us himself. Dinner was a type of fish I'd never tasted before, and it was delightful. Fiona enjoyed it as well. We returned to my flat and finished packing for our trip.

"We won't enjoy the luxury of a bed until we reach Lenoa," she said a little later as she appeared naked in the door of my bedroom. "And once there, this Varak will beat you to a pulp, so I would like to take advantage of this opportunity tonight."

She received no argument from me. I jumped up from my chair. She let out a squeak, and I chased her onto the bed.

Fiona rose while it was still dark. I fumbled and managed to light a candle. We dressed, and then I took our bags, and we headed to the stable. Dawn was just breaking to the east, but people were stirring in the city already. The stable's grooms were already saddling Rufus and Sara. I flipped them each a quadrans, then checked the girths. Finished with that, I tied the handles of our valises together with a set of leather thongs and rested them behind my saddle.

Fiona managed to climb aboard Sara without much difficulty, though I stood by to assist if necessary. She was wearing one of her cortaderia skirts and her new boots, with her hat slung behind her head. She looked the part, at least, but I planned to hold Sara's reins. Soon, I hoped, Fiona would feel confident enough to take them herself.

"I understand why this skirt is designed in this way," she said as we started, "but now I am able to appreciate its practicality."

We reached the caravan while they were still eating breakfast. They allowed us a bowl of porridge, and I gave Fiona a handful of the dried fruit I'd bought the day before to mix in with it. Like the others, we ate standing up.

The priests-militant arrived just as we finished. There were three of them, riding their destriers and leading a pack mule. They introduced themselves as Brothers Pierre, Artur, and Emil. We set off for Lenoa shortly after.

I will not bore you, dear reader, with the description of our trip over the pass. Other than Fiona's bottom being very sore from riding, there were no problems. She did not complain at all, but I could tell she ached. Fortunately, there was no chafing. By the middle of the second day, she felt comfortable enough that I gave her the reins, and she managed without difficulty. Sara was a gentle and sure-footed animal, which I knew from previous experience.

Along the way, we encountered several caravans heading in the opposite direction. A man named Bartlett was leading one, which contained a dozen wagons loaded with spices belonging to Mr. Ugarte. It was in his caravan that I met Agatha, not quite a year earlier.

I had recommended to Ugarte's man in Lenoa, Ferrare, that he hire Bartlett for future shipments. I was glad to see that he had followed my advice. Bartlett was happy to have the business.

"How were things at the temple of Sylvaris?" I asked.

"Last year, things with the temple in Lenoa were so bad," Bartlett commented, "but the new head priest is terrific. It's a pleasure to have professionals in charge again."

"Glad to hear it. The archpriest himself came to Lenoa to straighten everything out. Anders Farrell was hand-picked by him."

"Then he chose well," Bartlett said.

18

I learned that Fiona understood Midonese, though her pronunciation when speaking it was terrible. She needed to repeat herself multiple times before the locals understood. Still, with every conversation, she improved.

Rather than stay at the temple, I booked us a room at what I believed was the nicest inn in the city. We arrived in the late afternoon. I arranged for them to prepare a bath for Fiona, while I walked first to the livery and turned Sara over to them, and then to the temple of Kravyna to inform Varak that I was in the city.

A stout man with a shaved head was at the entrance of the temple of Kravyna. Though he was thick of build, there was not an ounce of fat on him. As I climbed the steps, he shifted to a guard position and lowered his pike menacingly.

"State your business," he growled.

"Here to see Varak."

"He's busy. Come back tomorrow," he answered gruffly.

"He'll see me," I said confidently. "He invited me to come spar with him the next time I was in the city. My name is Dexter Falk. Tell him I'm here."

"Leon!" the guard shouted without moving his head or relaxing his stance. "Tell Varak someone named Dexter Falk is here!"

I heard the clicking of hobnailed sandals on the stone floor inside the temple as someone ran to deliver the message. The guard continued to stare me down. I waited, pretending to be bored, but Sylvaris was displaying keen interest in what was happening.

Footsteps, heavy and sure, sounded from within the temple. Varak appeared a moment later, his gray hair still close-cropped, like the bristles on a brush. His face bore the nearest equivalent to a smile I think he could muster.

"Well, if it isn't the wolf in the story," he said. "My archpriest just sent me a pigeon yesterday, asking me to detain you if you showed up. That why you're here? To give yourself up?"

"No, Varak. We have a previous matter to settle—your lack of manners in addressing my companion at the time."

"Ho, ho," he grunted in what for him passed as a laugh. "When you didn't come to Lenoa right away, I thought the matter was settled."

"No, Varak. It is not. We agreed to a practice bout. The conclusion of the business in which I was engaged when we last met did not enable me to return to Lenoa until now."

"And now you are in the thick of something else that involves my order. You and a woman with golden skin. Why should I not simply follow the instructions of my archpriest and hold you?"

"Because you are a man of honor, Varak, as am I. We fought together, and when we finished, we clasped arms and agreed to settle the matter when I was next in Lenoa. That should take precedence over anything else."

"You have balls the size of melons, Falk. Tomorrow, first light, until the sun rises over the east wall of the arena. That's about two hours. Weighted wasters and bucklers. I believe I said that either I will chastise you for your impudence, or you will teach me to mind my manners. Once we are finished, I will decide what to do about the pigeon."

He extended his right arm, and we clasped forearms. Varak immediately turned and went back inside as soon as we released. I headed back to the inn.

"The water is still warm if you would like to bathe," Fiona said when I entered the room. "Did you meet with Varak?"

"I did," I said as I stripped to get into the tub. "We meet tomorrow at first light on their practice grounds."

"I will accompany you."

"No, you will not. You will go to the temple of Sylvaris and wait for me there," I said firmly. "Varak has already received a pigeon from the head of his order, instructing him to detain us. He mentioned you. If we are both in his temple, it might be a temptation he cannot resist."

"I was planning on watching you, as a great lady observing the fight of her champion in the storybooks I read as a child."

"This is not that kind of story," I said, as I washed quickly.

"It is not like any story I have read before," she admitted. "Fine. I will wait at the temple. You will come to me immediately when you are finished, or I will—"

"You will stay in the temple until I return, even if I need to crawl. Do not expose yourself to risk, Fiona. Your knowledge and your notes give us the advantage. I would not willingly surrender that edge to our rivals."

"Rivals? Not foes?"

"At some point, I hope it is after we succeed, things will settle back down. The alternative is war between the orders. Although the major gods are not involved in the search for the Hoard, they would step in if it became an outright war."

I finished washing and stood. Fiona brought the damp towel she had used and started drying me. Her touch was gentle, and I felt she was attempting to show her concern for me through her actions.

"I will go to the temple as you ask, Dexter. But I will not be happy about it."

"Let's not think about it for a few hours," I suggested. "I'm very hungry, and the food at this inn is excellent."

Fiona was silent during the meal. The food was excellent, but she ate without appetite. When we finished, she took my hand, and we returned to the room. Her beautiful brown eyes were brimming with tears by the time I closed the door.

"I'm scared, Dexter. You've told me that I should not worry, but I can't help it. My life has changed so dramatically since I found you. When the archpriestess cast me out of the order, you told me I was freed. I didn't understand then, but I do now. I was scared. The life I knew was closed to me. But a new life has opened up, one that has taken me outside the temple walls, sailing on the ocean, riding on a mule, with new challenges along the way. And there is the love I feel for you, and the excitement and pleasure we take in one another's company and in our bodies. I did not realize how empty my heart was until you filled it. And now I'm scared that, having shown me what can be, I will lose you."

I crossed the room in three strides and gathered her in my arms. Pulling her close, I kissed the swelling tears from her eyes. I lifted her chin up so our eyes met.

"You will not lose me to Varak," I said. "I swear to you on all that's holy, our adventure will continue."

Fiona searched my face for any sign of falsehood. Her gaze was steady, penetrative. She found only the belief in my heart. She shuddered and pressed her face to my chest, the wet tears on her cheeks dampening my shirt.

"I believe you, but that does not quell my fears. Help me forget them tonight."

I cupped her face and kissed her, tasting the salt of her tears and a trace of the wine we drank at dinner. Her fingers worked the buttons of my shirt with a now-practiced efficiency, so different from her fumbling efforts when we first started exploring one another. Our clothes fell away as we continued to kiss, moving to the bed eventually, taking our time. When at last we lay tangled in the bedclothes, she raised herself up, one leg over mine possessively.

"If you die tomorrow, Dexter Falk, you will be an oath breaker, and I shall be quite cross with you."

Sleep claimed her quickly after that. I remained awake, staring at the ceiling. Though difficult to notice at first, the tingle in my neck was a new feeling. It seemed like reassurance. Whether it was a sign that I need not fear tomorrow's outcome, or acknowledgment that I was doing exactly what Sylvaris wanted, or some combination of the two, I did not know.

Morning came too soon. Fiona woke me with a soft kiss. It was still dark outside. I could see from the light of the candle she had already lit that she was already dressed in a gray-green cortaderia skirt with a matching jacket. With her hair tied back, her hat slung behind her, and her riding boots, she looked more the adventurer than the scholar. My heart gave a small lurch at the sight.

"You will come straight to the temple of Sylvaris when you have finished," she said, stating it firmly and not asking a question.

"I will."

"You are confident," she noted. "I hope not too much. Will Sylvaris help you?"

"No. My skill in combat is my own, not granted by the god."

"And what of Varak? Will Kravyna assist him?"

"I'm sure she will, but he is only a man."

"That does not seem fair."

"I am used to fights that aren't fair," I said as I pulled on my breeches. "This won't be the first, or the worst. Go to the temple now. Take the map and your notes. Tell the head priest what is happening. His name is Anders Farrell, and he is a good man."

"Like Father Ned?"

"Good like Ned, but very different. You will see," I said as I kissed the top of her head.

At the door, she paused and gave me one of her long-lashed owl-blinks, then was gone. I finished dressing hurriedly, strapped my rapier to my waist, and set off for the temple of Kravyna.

The city was quiet. Only the bakers were busy at this hour. When I reached the temple of Kravyna, a different guard was at the door, no less menacing than the one before.

"He is waiting. Come."

He took a torch from a sconce and entered the temple. I followed the disciple through the building to the practice ground in the back. It was a circular space, with sand spread over a stone floor. The area was lit by torches, and I could see a crowd of disciples standing along the edge to watch.

Varak was already there, clad only in a breechclout. It was the custom at the temple of Kravyna to fight nearly naked. The area covered by the small piece of cloth was the only part of the body off-limits to attack. Other than that, there weren't any rules that I knew of.

A disciple handed me a breechclout. I quickly stripped and tied it around my waist. That finished, I took the opportunity to stretch my limbs, as Varak had been doing.

"You came. Right on time," he said.

"I keep my word, as do you," I said.

"Choose," he said, jerking his head at the pair of wasters and bucklers.

The wasters were wooden copies of the short swords the Kravynans favored, weighted with a channel of lead to equal a metal blade. The tip and the edges were rounded to reduce injury, but with enough force, you could punch through a man's chest, and an unchecked slash would break bones.

The buckler was a small, slightly curved shield, about the size of a dinner plate. Made of bronze with a handle in the center, they were used to block opponents' blows but could also be employed as a weapon in their own right. Getting hit in the face with one was an unpleasant experience, as I learned the hard way years before.

It didn't matter which weapons I selected. I knew they would be as nearly identical as possible. If one broke, the contest would halt temporarily until a replacement was issued.

I chose the ones to the right. Varak picked up the others, and we moved to the center of the arena, roughly five paces apart. The sky was just beginning to lighten. Varak raised his wooden blade in salute, and I did the same. Then, without another word, he attacked.

19

I'd seen Varak fight before on the *Emerald Gale* when we freed her from the Molutian pirates. The speed and ferocity of his assault were what I expected, but it still took all my skill to parry. I gave ground until he paused to gather himself.

His attack was that of a bull, an apt analogy considering he was built like one. I had the advantage of reach by a couple of inches, but he outweighed me by at least thirty pounds, all of it solid muscle. There was no question of his stamina. He trained every day and could keep up a fight like this for hours on end.

I would need to be a wolf, agile and quick. To satisfy Varak's honor, however, I could not simply dodge his attacks. I must face them head-on, give ground as I must, and strike when the few opportunities presented themselves.

He came on like a storm, his weighted practice sword whistling through the air. I met it with my buckler, the impact numbing my hand. He followed with a slash that I parried, and my riposte with the rounded end of the wooden short sword caught him square in the ribs. I heard a muffled snap and guessed I had cracked one. He grunted involuntarily with the force of it, as I skipped to the side to dodge his next blow.

He followed me faster than a man of his bulk should be capable of moving. The next exchange was pure fury. If my strike to his ribs had hurt him, it did not show. I gave ground slowly, waiting for another chance to land a blow.

An unexpected pebble under my foot distracted me just enough that he was able to take advantage. His buckler crashed into my face. I both heard and felt the crunch and knew he'd broken my nose.

"First strike to you, first blood to me," Varak commented, backing up a stride.

"First *visible* blood," I said as I spat. "My nose has been broken before, and it will be again, I reckon. Your rib is already quite purple. I'm sure it hurts. Not many people alive can claim they broke one of Varak's ribs."

"And none ever dared to boast about it and live," he said, immediately resuming his attack.

He came in quickly again. I darted inside the arc of his swing, landing an uppercut to his jaw with my sword hand. The blow staggered him back, and as he moved, he tried to hit me again with his buckler. I sensed it coming just in time and dropped to the ground. It clipped the top of my ear as I rolled to the sandy floor, the grit clinging to the sweat that already covered me.

We circled warily. He was the veteran of many, many fights, and knew when he needed to change tactics. His bull charges had enabled him to smash my nose, but I'd broken a rib of his and made his ears ring with my uppercut.

"Calling on your god for assistance, thief?" he taunted.

"Sylvaris has given me many things," I replied, "but my skill at arms is all my own. It's why he loves me so much. Is Kravyna carrying your burden, old man?"

The words left my mouth before I weighed them. They enraged Varak, who came at me with a roar. Blow followed blow, and it was all I could do to meet them with buckler and sword. The shock of the repeated impacts was numbing my arms.

Varak overstepped just a hair, and I took advantage. I stepped forward. His buckler caught me on the back of my head, but mine hit him just below his sternum. Air exploded from his stomach with a grunt as I knocked the wind out of him. I spun away before he could land another blow and allowed him to recover.

Though the only rule of which I was aware prevented striking an opponent's groin, he'd given me a moment after breaking my nose. I'd grant him the same courtesy. He had the grace to acknowledge it with the slightest dip of his head as we circled again.

The disciples of Kravyna watched with intense silence, ringed around the enclosure. They'd all seen Varak fight many practice matches. I doubted they'd ever seen him winded before.

He struck again, going low. The strength of his slash overpowered my parry, and he thumped my right thigh hard enough that I would feel it for days. I'd already aimed a snap kick, going for the darkening spot on his ribs. My foot connected as my right leg collapsed after his blow. I landed face-first on the sand, blood spattering the ground under my still-streaming nose.

I rolled just in time to prevent him from smashing my head open with his waster. Scrambling to my feet, my right leg was fine now, but weak. Once the adrenaline wore off, it would seize up.

Both of us were hurt enough now that we weighed our options carefully, circling slowly. Varak would not give me the satisfaction of rubbing his chest where I'd struck him twice. I would not show him how weak my right leg felt.

He attacked again, with a speed and fury that seemed undiminished from when we began. We traded blows and parries in flurries of wood and bronze. He connected with my left shoulder, numbing the entire arm. I managed to rake the tip of my waster across his broken rib.

He went for my right leg again with a backhand slash, and I smashed my buckler against the side of his face for his trouble. If it had been earlier in the fight, I might have dropped him with that blow. With my left arm still somewhat numb from his strike to my shoulder, it merely staggered him.

We backed away a pace and resumed our circling. There was blood on the sand from my nose, but our footing was still secure. I sensed Varak was about to launch another attack when we heard a shrill whistle. The sun had risen above the east wall.

Varak stepped back and lowered his waster. I did the same. We stood facing one another, both our chests heaving with the exertion and the pain we'd absorbed. I could see the edge of the sunlight behind him. The watching disciples turned and departed.

"I will have to remember my manners around your companions in the future," Varak said quietly.

"And I will curb my impudence in the days to come."

"You fight well, Falk. I did not expect you to last. Most who face me are finished halfway through. Yet here you stand."

"I came to settle a matter of honor, Varak. When we finished, I hoped the two of us could look one another in the eye with mutual respect. Have I gained what I sought?"

"Aye," he said after a long moment. "We have two Vionelles standing by to tend to our wounds. Then you should leave."

"You will not detain me?"

"You kept your word to me, even knowing that I received instruction from my archpriest to hold you. Then you fought well—as skillfully and as staunchly as any I have faced since I won this position. If you promise me that you will not linger in Lenoa, my people will not interfere."

"What did the note say?"

"Only that I was to look for you and a golden-skinned Eldryne and detain you. That was all. There are only so many words that can fit on the scrap of paper a pigeon carries."

"What will you tell your archpriest?"

"I will explain it was a matter of honor. He will understand and accept it. Follow me."

He led me inside to a tiled room and untied his breechclout. I did the same. Some of his disciples came in, carrying buckets of water. They came and dumped them over our heads to rinse away the sweat, blood, and sand. The water was cold enough to make me want to gasp, but I managed to refrain.

When they judged us clean after many buckets of cold dowsing, they left, and two priests of Vionelle entered. Seeing them, I noticed they had been in the crowd watching us, though I had not known they were agents of the goddess of healing. The one who came to me checked my shoulder and thigh first, to make sure no bones were broken. When he finished that examination, he inspected my nose.

"Not too bad," he said. "I'm going to set it. On three. One … two…"

"Yow!" I yelped. "What happened to three?"

"Oops. I forgot," he said with a smirk, then produced a roll of gauze and started stuffing it up my nostrils. "Keep this in for two days. When you remove it, do so gently. It will resume bleeding, but only for a short time. You will hurt for a couple of weeks. I recommend that you get off your feet and stay down the rest of the day."

While he was taking care of me, I saw the other priest tending to Varak. He was cinching Varak's ribs tightly with a broad wrap. Varak was trying to remain impassive, but I could tell it hurt. My priest used a wet cloth to clean up the rest of the blood that dripped from my nose after the buckets of water were dumped on my head. When he finished, a disciple of Varak's handed me my clothes.

I dressed slowly. The ache in my shoulder and thigh grew by the minute, and they refused to move as smoothly as before. Pulling my boots on was especially difficult. I finally finished and strapped my rapier around my waist.

"Well fought, Falk. Don't linger in Lenoa. Three days or less. When you next pass this way, tell me what this is all about. You can buy me a mug or three of ale and share the tale. And if there is a time when we can draw swords against a common foe, I will look forward to it."

"I would rather have you as my ally, Varak, and hope we never meet in anger again. When this is over, I will find my way to you. We can have a contest of ale-drinking and storytelling, and leave the wasters and bucklers to others."

We clasped forearms again. This time, carefully, aware of our injuries. I limped out of the temple and into the street. My right thigh had seized up, and moving it made it throb. My shoulder felt as though he'd driven a spike in it. There was still blood trickling down my throat from the back of my nose.

Despite that, I was smiling. I'd achieved what I sought—a draw—the most difficult outcome. If I'd won, Varak would probably have seized me to counter the loss of face in front of his people. Losing would mean I was unworthy of any clemency. Only a draw enabled me to walk away.

The streets of Lenoa were fully alive now. No one paid attention to a man in conservative clothes limping toward the temple of Sylvaris. Speaking of whom, I felt his satisfaction, almost as though he wished to pat me on the back. Even though my skill in combat was my own and not due to our connection, he was still pleased with me.

20

nders Farrell was lingering on the front steps of the temple when I hobbled up. He looked at my face and winced. When he noticed I was taking the steps one at a time, he came forward to help, but I waved him off.

"Miss Magellan is in the garden," he said, "worried sick about you. You're still alive, so that's to the good, I guess. I see your nose and your leg are injured. Anything else?"

"Shoulder. Just a bruise, like the leg. I'll heal."

"She told me you need to get to Dorul in North Gaugan. The Marivelles have a schooner that is due to leave in the morning for Namo. I'll send a message to them, asking them to give you passage."

"That would be perfect—better than I could have hoped for. Thank you."

"I must say, Dex, if I'd known there were Eldrynes who looked like Miss Magellan, I would have ignored Sylvaris's call and crawled on my hands and knees to Harkiss."

"Have you spoken with her much?"

"We spent most of the morning in conversation. Beautiful and brilliant—rare to get them both in the same person. Pardon me for asking … Catherine?"

"We said our farewells in Tallesin," I replied. "She will help with her father's porcelain business, but we both knew that Sylvaris would continue to use me as he sees fit. Before I had a chance to grieve, Fiona arrived at my door."

"Well, I'd better not keep you from her any longer. She's been pacing back and forth for most of the last hour, beginning when she thought your little contest would end."

Farrell walked with me until I turned to the temple's herb garden. Fiona turned when she heard me open the door. She darted toward me but stopped two paces short. Her brown eyes widened, and she gave me two of the slow owl-blinks I'd come to adore.

"Dexter," she breathed, that single word conveying all the care she had for me. "Your face…"

"He broke my nose. It will heal, but you'll have to put up with the decoration that comes along with it."

"And you're limping."

"My right thigh is probably turning an interesting shade of purple, as is my left shoulder," I said. "Varak had Vionelles waiting when we finished, and one inspected me and fixed my nose."

"And you achieved the outcome you wanted?"

"A draw? Yes. Varak has given us three days' grace to leave Lenoa."

"Anders tells me that there is a ship from the Order of Marivelle leaving tomorrow for Namo."

"He said the same to me. I hope we can obtain passage with them."

"Why wouldn't they allow it?"

"The major gods do not wish to be involved in this tussle over Torsten's Hoard. The Order of Marivelle may refuse to take us. If it is one of the order's ships, the sailing master is probably god-touched and will receive a message directly from the goddess."

"If they do not allow us to sail with them—?"

"We will need to find someone else who is heading that way. I will need to check the map, but Namo is not the only port near Dorul."

"Jenestra is also close."

"Ahem," Anders Farrell cleared his throat behind us.

"Yes, Father Anders?"

"Bad news, I'm afraid. The sailing master aboard the Marivelles' ship apologizes. 'Dexter Falk is known to be a friend of Marivelle, but he is not to be given passage at this time.' That's the message the acolyte brought back."

"Will you please send your people out to see if anyone is heading to either Namo or Jenestra?" I asked. "I would do it myself, but I think I'm going to go lie down for the rest of the day."

"I'll see what we can turn up," he said. "Both are prosperous, busy ports. And if no one is planning on heading that way, you might be able to convince someone to take you for the right price, with the hope they might pick up a load for the return. In the meantime, you do look awful, Dex, if you don't mind my saying so."

"We'll be at the Mary Rose," Fiona said.

She slipped her arm around my waist without asking and helped me stand. I draped my right arm over her shoulders as we started to move. My right leg was not working properly.

"Anders?" I called after him. "You wouldn't happen to have a crutch handy, would you?"

"I can help you," Fiona insisted.

"I can barely walk, my dear. I don't want to—"

"I walked for twenty-seven days to find you, Dexter Falk. I've sailed on the open ocean and lived to tell about it, although there were times when I almost wished to die. I even rode on a mule over the Fullan Pass, which made my butt hurt like nothing I'd ever imagined. I can get you back to the Mary Rose."

"Yes, ma'am," I said.

We moved haltingly. I needed to put more weight on Fiona than I wanted, but she never complained. We did stagger once or twice, but that was my thigh muscle's fault.

"Do you have any willow bark?" she asked the innkeeper when we arrived.

"No, miss."

"Send someone to the apothecary to fetch some. Do you need money?"

"Yes, miss."

"Here are two florins," she said, fishing the coins from the money pouch I'd given her. "Have them buy as much as this will afford."

"Yes, miss."

"Willow bark," I said. "A great idea for my leg and shoulder, not so much for my nose."

"It's for later tonight. By then, your nose should be scabbed over inside," Fiona explained. "Otherwise, you won't get any sleep."

I needed to take the stairs one at a time, moving like an old man. Fiona stayed by my side patiently. When we entered the room, she guided me to the bed. Once there, she stripped off my clothes, wincing and hissing when she saw my thigh and shoulder.

"Varak hits rather hard," I said by way of explanation.

"You look like a tree fell on you."

"That's pretty close to the way it felt."

"What happened to him?"

"I broke one of his ribs, maybe two, knocked his wind out once, and might have loosened a few of his teeth."

She helped me get onto the bed to lie down. She sat next to me, holding my hand and gazing into my eyes intensely. Gently, ever so gently, she kissed my thigh, my shoulder, and the swollen bridge of my nose.

"A kiss to make it better," she said. "My mother used to do that when we skinned our knees and got a cut."

"My mother did, too."

"You kept your promise," she said. "To Varak, and to me. You came back."

"I told you I would."

"Even so, thank you for not dying. When the archpriestess first cast me out, I told you I felt like a page ripped from a book, but you told me I was free. I have discovered that your view of things is more accurate. Freed from the temple, I have learned things I would never have known otherwise—about myself, and about the world. My curiosity extends beyond the world of books now. I am grateful, and wish to continue with you as my guide."

"I'm afraid there is little I'm prepared to show you today, Fiona."

"I am aware. Rest."

As uncomfortable as I was, I did doze off. Fiona brought me lunch and later, dinner. Just after I finished eating the latter, there was a knock on the door. Fiona opened it to reveal an acolyte from the temple of Sylvaris.

"Begging your pardon, Miss Magellan, Mr. Falk," he said. "*Pelican's Piety* sails tomorrow on the tide, bound for Jenestra. She's a three-masted bark. Her captain says you can have the owner's cabin for forty dinars. Says they'll feed you, but if you want anything to drink other than water, you need to bring it."

"When is the turn of the tide?" I asked.

"Around eleven."

"Would you be so kind as to tell the captain we accept, and deliver the money to him?"

"Of course, Mr. Falk."

"Fiona, you know where my money pouch is."

She counted out the coins and handed them to the young man. When she finished, she handed me some of the willow bark that had been delivered while I slept. I looked at it with a slight scowl.

"I know it tastes awful," she said, "but it will help your thigh and shoulder immensely. Your nose has probably long since scabbed over, so you do not need to worry about its blood-thinning properties."

I took it and chewed, grinding it up. The bitter taste made me want to screw up my face with disgust, but I dared not because of the pain in the center of my face. Fiona brought me some water to wash the taste away a bit after I finished chewing it.

"Tomorrow, let's see about buying a case of wine for the journey," I said.

"I will not allow you to spend the entire voyage drunk, no matter how much pain you're in!" Fiona exclaimed.

"I have no intention of doing so. If *Pelican's Piety* is a three-masted bark, she will probably have a crew of about thirty sailors. In charge of them will be at least two officers, plus the captain, who is in charge of everything. The officers usually dine together, and since we will be in the owner's cabin, they will probably include us. The wine will be for the group. Even if they do not invite us to dine with them, I intend to share it as a gesture of goodwill."

"Oh."

"Another thing you never encountered in your reading?"

"You are teasing me. Yes. Like how a 'practice bout' with the head priest of a temple of Kravyna involves bodily harm."

"Some things are only learned by experience," I said smugly.

"You engaged in another contest like that?"

"No, that was the first, but I have a superficial understanding of how some of the other orders conduct themselves."

"There are many things that can be learned from reading," she said defensively.

"I would not argue the point with you. I know you are correct."

"Good. Because I found a Lysmeran novel in the inn's common room while you were sleeping. Reading it gave me an idea of how I might reward you for not dying today. If I understood it correctly, I should manage to avoid aggravating your thigh and your shoulder," she said with a sly smile, as she started to remove her clothing.

When she finished, she pulled away the bedclothes. Moving slowly and carefully, she positioned herself on top of me. She took great delight in proving that there were some extremely useful and enjoyable things that could be learned from books.

21

I still ached in the morning but was not as hobbled. The willow bark, awful as it tasted, did an effective job of reducing the pain. Fiona made me chew some more before we broke our fast. When we finished eating, she asked the innkeeper's wife if they had someone who could accompany us to the harbor and carry our bags. She assured Fiona it would be no problem.

I then asked Fiona if she would take Rufus to the temple of Sylvaris and ask them to keep her until we returned. While she was away doing that, I returned to our room and packed our things. It did not take long, and I was waiting in the common room when she returned, having managed to bring the bags down with me.

The innkeeper saw me, and a boy of about ten or eleven came out and took them. I sent him to deliver them to the *Pelican's Piety*, and gave him a Midonese argent, the equivalent of a Thetlarian florin, for his trouble. When Fiona learned I had brought the bags down, she tsked me for doing so, and I pretended it had not been difficult.

"You should know better by now, Dexter Falk. Do not lie to me."

"Fiona, even in such trivial matters as bringing bags downstairs, a man has his pride. Yes, it hurt more than I expected. No, I probably should not have done it. But the pain was my punishment. Allow me to pretend that I was brave and noble for not complaining about my own stupidity."

Fiona regarded me carefully, her gaze still while she considered what I said. Finally, she gave me one of her long-lashed slow blinks. The corners of her mouth turned up in a smile.

"There are other ways I prefer you to demonstrate your manly pride, Dexter. If you do something foolish like this again, I will berate you publicly. You will suffer a great loss of 'manly pride,' so I would advise you to be more thoughtful in the future."

"Yes, miss," I said with as much humility as I could muster, bowing my head.

We stepped out onto the streets and headed for the harbor. I did not need her support, but I was moving more slowly than usual. Spotting a wineseller, I steered us inside. A hatchet-faced man came to greet us.

"We are about to sail to Jenestra aboard *Pelican's Piety*," I said, "and I would like a case of wine that will travel well that I can share with the officers."

"I believe I have just the thing," the man said, rubbing his hands together. "It's from Malvas, an island near the Kryyders."

"I'm familiar. Dry or sweet?" I asked.

"I have both."

"The dry, then."

"Excellent choice, sir. Now, if I recall correctly, she's leaving soon."

"On the tide."

"I can have someone run it down to the ship. He'll be right on your heels if you're heading that way."

"We are."

"A case will run two dinars."

"That's a fair price," I said, lifting an eyebrow.

"You were expecting to haggle?"

"I prefer not to."

"Judging by your battered appearance, I didn't think so," he said.

"Very well," I said with a chuckle as I fished the gold coins from my pouch. "Thank you."

"My pleasure."

"I understood very little of that," Fiona said when we returned to the street.

"Malvas is an island near the chain of the Kryyder Islands but separated enough that it is not considered one of them. The wine from there has a higher content of alcohol, about double or triple that of regular wine. As a result, it does not suffer as much from being jostled around and is a favorite of seamen all over the world. The sweet version I find cloying. I prefer the dry."

"I suppose that is knowledge I could find in a book," she said, "but not in the old manuscripts I have been studying."

We reached the harbor not long after. The *Pelican's Piety* was easy to spot—one of the larger ships tied up to a quay. The captain saw us coming up the gangway and scurried over to meet us. He was a wiry man, but short. His hair was jet black, and the skin of his face was creased from wind, weather, and sun.

"Mr. Falk? Ma'am? Custer Cole. Yer baggage's already in yer cabin."

"We appreciate you taking us on short notice."

"Owner's cabin'd be empty otherwise, and yer forty dinars means the crew will eat well on the voyage. Ye'll benefit from that as well. If ya don' mind me askin', didja see the wagon what run over ya? Yer nose is still fulla gauze."

"He had a 'practice bout' with the head of the temple of Kravyna yesterday," Fiona said in a tone that was an odd mixture of pride and scorn.

"Varak? An' yer still standin'?"

"Aye, barely."

"How long didja last?"

"The full time."

"Whoa. That puts ya ahead o' everyone else who's tried since he took over. Man's a demon, they say."

"Aye," I replied, as I noticed a man huffing toward the gangway with a case of wine on his shoulder. "We brought a gift for the officers' table, if you'll permit it."

"Malvas? Dry? Much appreciated. With a formidable man like yersef, a beautiful lady, if'n ya don' mind me sayin', and a case o' Malvas, this is shapin' up t'be a sweet voyage."

Cole's grin split his face. I returned the smile but only slightly. The swelling of my nose reminded me not to move my facial muscles much. Fiona stood in one of her traveling skirts, a matching jacket over a white blouse, her hat hanging on her back, and her hair tied with a light blue ribbon that I hadn't seen before.

"We're grateful to be aboard, captain. We'll stay out of your way."

"Don' worry. Quarterdeck's all yours 'n mine. Yer cabin's the starboard side. Meals at noon 'n dusk, 'n we got a good cook. If the lady needs anythin', jes' holler."

He clapped me on my left shoulder, and the pain nearly drove me to my knees. He didn't see it and strode away with a tip of his tricorn hat to Fiona. She noticed what he'd done.

"Is part of your manly pride not yelping when someone hits you where it hurts?"

"He didn't know, Fiona, and he seems like a nice man. I don't want to make him feel bad before we've even cast off."

Fiona merely pursed her lips. She turned to look over the deck of the ship. It was far larger than the *Hazel Olivia*, with three masts to the other's one, and yards that were as long as the other ship's mast was tall.

"This is a big boat," she said.

"She's a ship," I replied. "Upward of a certain size, boats become ships."

"And what size is that?"

"I'm afraid you'd have to ask Captain Cole. My nautical knowledge only extends so far. I can tell you that this is the biggest ship I've sailed on."

"Let's go see the cabin," she said.

We went down the ladder to the main deck and through the door on the left (putting us on the starboard side). By ship standards, the owner's cabin was spacious. I could stand up inside without ducking my head. The bed was big enough to fit both of us, suspended by ropes hung from bolts in the beam overhead.

"You should rest," Fiona said, "after you have some more willow bark. Between carrying the bags downstairs, the walk to the harbor, and the captain's slap on the back, you're looking a bit pale."

"For a little while," I agreed. "But when we leave the harbor, make sure I'm up. I want to watch when they unfurl the sails. It's probably quite a sight. I've only seen ships like this at a distance."

I eased myself onto the bed—more difficult than I originally thought, as it swayed like a hammock. I lay on my right side. Fiona climbed up next to me and pillowed my head on her chest. This was new, and I decided I liked it a great deal.

I don't know how long it was—I think I dozed briefly—but I heard shouting from above.

"Cast off fore! Loose the headsail and the spanker! Look alive, men!"

"Let's go up," I suggested.

We emerged onto the main deck just as the sails caught the wind with a deep snap. Fiona headed up the ladder to the quarterdeck, and I followed. Looking over the main deck, it must have seemed like confusion at first to Fiona, with the different members of the crew pulling on different lines and the mates barking orders all at the same time. I tried to explain what the different groups were doing.

"They're not setting the big sails," she commented.

"We're in the harbor, and there are a lot of ships around, so we want to proceed carefully. In addition, the wind direction isn't good to help us reach the mouth of the harbor with the square sails. The headsail, up there, and the spanker, the one that is right over our heads, can use the wind as it is, and will be enough to get us to the open sea. Once we're free of the harbor, you'll see the captain unfurl the mainsails. The wind is generally from the south, which is good considering that we're intending to travel to the east-northeast. It puts the wind on our stern quarter, which should be a good point of sail for this ship."

"Aye, he's got the lay of it, missy," the captain interjected. "Anythin' ya wanna know 'bout the Pelican, jes' ask. I love talkin' bout 'er."

"Ya see, the main channel what takes us past the headland means a so'easterly course," he continued, pointing as he spoke. "That's against the wind from the south. Headsail 'n spanker ken use that wind, 'cause they're angled, ya see?"

"They're pointed nearly in line with the ship," Fiona said.

"Aye," Cole responded when he figured out Fiona's accent. "See how the wind hits' em and spills out of 'em?"

"Yes."

"So, e'en though we're sailin' toward the wind, the way it hits 'em, it shoves us forward. If we had the mainsails up, the wind would be blowin' us backward."

"I understand."

We continued threading our way through the harbor. When we neared the mouth of the harbor, the crew started to scamper up the rigging like monkeys.

As we reached the headland, Cole turned the wheel, and the ship's bow swung to the east.

A couple of men adjusted the angle of the headsail and spanker, while the bo'sun shouted, "Loose mains'ls!"

The men on the yards untied the robans, and the huge sheets of canvas flowed down. They flapped twice, three times. The men on the deck hauled on the braces to swing the yard to the proper angle, then, with a dull snap, the huge sails filled with wind. The *Pelican* canted over slightly, and you could sense the increased power through your feet.

"It's almost like wings," Fiona muttered to herself.

"Aye, missy. We'll get the tops'ls set, and then we'll start to fly."

The men in the rigging climbed up to do just that. A few minutes later, the topsails were set and trimmed. The increase in the ship's speed from when we'd left the harbor was noticeable.

"Feel that, missy? We are flyin'!" Cole said with a broad grin.

The ship did feel alive under my feet. The bow sliced through the waves, sending spray up with each one it hit. Fiona held the rail with her right hand.

"It's much steadier than the *Hazel Olivia*," she said. "I don't think this will bother me nearly as much."

22

Fiona's seasickness did not return. Though the *Pelican* was not immune to the action of the waves, the rise and fall was milder. She also stayed on the quarterdeck in the fresh air and sunshine.

Dinner was a rowdy affair, with Cole and two other men, the first and second mates, Jethro and Samuel. They were most appreciative of the wine I'd bought, and between them drank a bottle and a half. Fiona and I each had a single glass.

My appearance spurred the conversation at first, with the two mates wanting to know how I received two black eyes. When I told them I engaged in a practice bout with Varak, Jethro and Samuel agreed that I was lucky to have survived. Then they questioned my sanity for deciding to take part.

"There's a story behind it," I said, and then I mentioned how I needed the help of Varak and his disciples to recapture the three ships taken under Taggart's orders.

"That was you?" Jethro asked.

"Yes."

"Story's all over the docks, Mr. Falk," Cole stated. "Din't know that was you. But how'd that come to you and Varak squarin' off?"

"He insulted my companion. I chastised him in return. Varak suggested we engage in a practice match to decide which of us needed to apologize."

"Didja get yer apology? Samuel inquired.

"We both apologized when we finished."

"Cor! You got an apology outta Varak? And he left you lookin' like this? What'd you do to him?" Jethro asked.

"I'd really rather change the subject," I said.

"He cracked at least one of Varak's ribs and loosened his teeth," Fiona blurted.

"Most people who go inta the arena with him only last a coupla minutes," Cole said, "and they don't often manage to touch Varak with even a glancin' blow. Cheers to you, Mr. Falk."

Cole then steered the subject to other topics. Jethro told a story of how, when he first shipped out, the other members of the crew convinced him there was a mermaid. It turned out to be a seal.

Samuel told a story about a ship he was on, getting hit by a storm, wrecking on one of the unpopulated Kryyder Islands, and how they survived until help arrived. This led to a discussion of weather, and what they endured together on the Pelican. The conversation lasted until the second bottle of wine was gone.

That was the cue for everyone to leave the table. Fiona and I went back to our cabin. She forced me to chew some more willow bark. When I'd ground it up, she gave me some water to rinse the taste from my mouth.

"Tomorrow, we remove the gauze from your nose," she said. "I will ask the cook to boil some saltwater and, when it cools, we will rinse the inside of your nose with it."

"Why? It sounds unpleasant."

"Saltwater will aid in healing. I imagine it will not be enjoyable, but it will speed the process."

I'll spare you the details of what happened the next day. There was plenty of blood, and Fiona poured warm seawater (cooled off the boil, thank heavens!) up my nostrils. Eventually, the blood stopped flowing, and I was able to breathe through my nose again. We repeated the process all the way to Jenestra.

There were a couple of moments that stuck in my memory. The one I'll share happened on the third day. Fiona had just woken up when there was a knock on the cabin door.

"Cap'n's compliments, there are dolphins ridin' the bow wave," one of the men said.

We dressed hurriedly and rushed forward. Jethro showed Fiona the best place to look. It required leaning well over the rail, so I held her waist.

"They're playing!" she exclaimed. "Look how they leap!"

She watched for nearly an hour before they decided to leave. Her face bore a continual look of utter joy the whole time. Several of them leapt out of the water not far away as they departed.

"Good omen, dolphins," Cole said as we returned aft. "Marivelle's most beautiful handmaidens."

We faced a couple of squalls that came and went, but the weather stayed fair otherwise. The wind blew steadily from the south, and our crossing took only eight days. My leg and shoulder were still achy but now serviceable. The bruises under my eyes had faded enough so I would not scare children in the street. When we arrived near midday, Captain Cole recommended an inn to us.

It was no problem for me to carry our bags now. Before leaving the waterfront, I found a moneychanger who would convert my Thetlarian guilders and florins into the local currency. That done, we walked a couple of blocks to the city center and found the Tawny Lion on a large market square.

Fiona was at a disadvantage, as the local language, Lutetian, was something she'd never heard or seen before. I spoke it fluently, having visited Jenestra years before. It was a warm early summer day, and the streets and the square were bustling with people: shopkeepers selling their wares, food carts with all sorts of offerings, children darting underfoot playing games. We stepped inside the inn, and the noise quieted immediately.

"Welcome to the Tawny Lion," a roly-poly woman said, her voice lilting up and down in what I knew was a Jenestrian accent. "Room? Meal? Both?"

"A room, please, for one night, with dinner and breakfast."

"Four piasters—five if you require a hot bath."

"We do require a bath. We just sailed from Lenoa and would like to wash the salt off."

"Your Lutetian is excellent, but you have an accent. What ship?"

"*Pelican's Piety*. Captain Custer recommended you."

"Ah, Cole. A good sailor and a better man."

"If we could arrange for that bath now," I said, sliding the coins across the counter to her.

"The maids will bring the tub up shortly. Up the stairs, double back to the corridor, go right, and the third door on the left. You'll have a view of the square and should be able to see the tops of the masts in the harbor."

We found the door, and I unlocked it, revealing a cozy room with a four-poster bed and a small writing desk. The windows looked over the market square as promised. We had just opened our bags when there was a knock on the door.

Two giggling maids stood in the hall. They wrestled a long copper tub into the room, chattering between themselves. Once they set it down, one of them pulled two sachets from her pocket and put them on the washbasin, telling me what they were for. The other brought in two thick towels. They curtsied and left, giggling again.

"What did they say?" Fiona asked.

"They were surprised someone as beautiful as you would be with someone as beat-up as me."

"Wait until your bruises fade. Then they'll understand better."

"Sadly, we won't be here that long."

"What about the sachets?"

"One is some form of bath salts. The other is to wash milady's hair."

"I'm glad you understood. To me, it just sounded like birds chirping."

"Lutetian does have a musical quality to it," I acknowledged. "Once we wash the salt off, I intend to find the temple of Sylvaris and begin arranging how to get to Dorul. I've never been there, but from the map it looked like a ride of at least four days. Dorul is a town of good size, and I imagine there is a fair amount of traffic between there and Jenestra, so I hope there are inns along the way. Otherwise, I will need to arrange a tent and other equipment for us."

"I hope there are inns," Fiona said. "The ride from Tallesin to Lenoa was painful enough on my poor behind without needing to sleep on the ground. That just made it worse."

Another knock at the door revealed two boys, each carrying buckets of water. The first they brought were cold. They would bring the hot once they were ready. We sat and waited. The boys made four more trips, with water that got hotter each time. When they finished, I gave each of them a copper coin.

"This tub is huge," Fiona commented as she knelt to mix in the bath salts, which produced a pleasant scent. "And just hot enough. You go first this time."

I quickly stripped and eased myself into the water. It felt marvelous, particularly on my thigh, which was no longer purple, having faded to green and yellow. I had just put my head back to issue a lovely sigh when I snapped my eyes open to see Fiona climbing in as well, easing herself down between my legs.

"I decided I didn't wish to wait," she said. "It's big enough for two, and I like how your hands caress me when you wash me. If you wash my hair, I imagine it will feel sinfully luxurious."

She handed me the small sachet, then slid forward until her head fully submerged, then scooched back up to my chest. I pulled the ribbon, opening the small bag and dumped the powder into my palms. When I began rubbing it into her hair, it produced a thick lather that smelled of rosemary and mint.

"This is even better than I thought," she murmured. "Your fingers feel so good—strong, yet gentle. And it smells wonderful."

Fiona allowed me to minister to her, sighing occasionally. When I finished with her hair, my hands strayed to other parts to help rinse away the sweat and salt. She guided my hands where she wanted them, not necessarily for the purpose of cleanliness.

Eventually, she ducked down again, and I worked my fingers in her hair to remove the suds. It took a couple of dips. When her hair was finished, I pulled it back, exposing her long, elegant neck, and placed a kiss in a special spot I'd found.

"If you do that again, I may not allow you to leave until the water is ice-cold. Get up and trade places with me."

I stood and stepped over her as she scooted back. Now I sat between her legs, and she ran her hands over me. She pushed me down to wet my hair and worked my scalp with her fingers. I understood now why she had been sighing so deeply a few minutes before. She hugged me to her chest, and I could have spent the afternoon right there.

Somehow, I found the strength, will, and purpose to stand eventually. I offered her my hand and helped her up. We dried one another, trading small kisses in different spots. Fiona took my towel and wrapped it around her head like a turban.

"You get dressed and go to the temple. I'll wait for my hair to dry out a bit, then comb it. Please don't be long. I can't speak the language, but I would like to explore the city while we're here."

23

Once I dressed, I headed downstairs and let the woman know we had finished our bath. I asked if she knew where the temple of Sylvaris was. She gave me directions, and I set off, feeling much refreshed from the bath.

Jenestra was an interesting blend of the energetic chaos of Lenoa and the orderly bustle of Tallesin. People moved with purpose, but the undercurrent of conversations in lilting Lutetian lent an almost musical tone. The temple of Sylvaris was only two blocks away, well kept and seemingly prosperous. As I approached, I felt the numinal presence of Sylvaris in addition to the slight tingle that had not left my neck since Fiona arrived on my doorstep. A young acolyte was sweeping the steps—unnecessary, as they were already clean—when I approached.

"Hello? How may Sylvaris serve you today?" he asked politely.

"My name is Dexter Falk. I would like to speak with the head priest. I have pressing temple business to discuss."

"Father Lucien is within," he said. "Please follow me."

In the main sanctuary, I saw a couple of merchants meeting with priests. No doubt they were discussing donatives. We entered a corridor to the right rear and stopped at a door marked with the crossed-keys sigil of Sylvaris.

"Please wait," he said, then knocked softly, entering when he was invited in.

The door opened a minute later to reveal a man with salt-and-pepper hair and a neatly trimmed dagger beard. If it were not for the gray robes of the order, he would have looked like a prosperous trader. His eyes sparkled with restrained amusement. The acolyte slipped out at the same time.

"Dexter Falk," he said, "a name of some renown in the last few months. What business brings you to Jenestra? Come in, come in. May I offer you some tea?"

"No, thank you," I said.

His office was organized clutter. There were stacks of documents on his desk and a table behind it, and a map on the wall. I suspected, however, that Father Lucien knew where every piece of paper was in that room and could lay hands on it immediately.

"And what has made you aware of my name?" I inquired.

"Something to do with Marivelle, is my understanding."

"Ah. Nothing more recent?"

"No. Why?"

"Sylvaris saw fit to present me with another challenge," I said. "The next step is to travel to Dorul to find someone. I've never been there, so I'm here to learn more about the road. Is it well-trafficked? Are there inns? I will need to contact a livery to obtain mounts for my companion and me."

"The road to Dorul is excellent. There is even a royal post coach, though I would not recommend it—no springs—and it takes a day longer. They also try to steer you to the inns that they favor, which are of lesser quality. As far as mounts, we have a couple we can lend you if you promise to return them."

"An easy pledge to make and keep."

"May I ask the specific nature of your business here?"

"You may, but before I answer, let me ask you if you are familiar with the fate of a man named Oderic who usurped the temple in Lenoa?"

"I am," Lucien said, making a warding symbol with his fingers almost unconsciously.

"If I tell you my business, and you violate my trust, Azar will exact the same punishment. He is looking over my shoulder on this one."

"Understood," Lucien said with a sober nod. "It will not leave this room."

I then proceeded to relate to him the tale of what had taken place so far. He listened attentively, nodding in places. He waited patiently for me to finish.

"First," he said, "we have observed no unusual activity at the temples of Kravyna or Eldryne here in Jenestra."

"Good. I was going to ask."

"Second, the man you are looking for, Valerian Wouk, is a Calithran adept—god-touched. Finally, if he does not know of an astronomer who can help you, I do. We can have the horses ready for you first thing in the morning. If you get an early start, you can make Littleford tomorrow, then Harbrook the next day, and Sauga's Mill for your third and final waypoint. I will give you the names of the best inn in each town. You say Azar himself is involved?"

"We have a letter from Azar for Wouk. Even more interesting, Azar intercepted Miss Magellan while she was walking from Harkiss and had an acolyte give her a note for me, instructing me to assist her in every way. It would not surprise me at all if you received a letter from him telling you to help us. It's just that I made it here before his message did."

"Kravyna's spear, Korath's hammer, and Calithra's lute," Lucien mused. "Where do Korath's and Calithra's people stand on this?"

"I was under the assumption that they were on our side," I said.

"I wouldn't count on them for much," Lucien said. "If you get to the Hoard first, they'll claim they always supported you. If Kravyna's people win…"

"Will it be a risk, going to a Calithran for help with this ancient language?"

"Yes and no, but this is only a hunch. What little I know of the man, he lives for this kind of challenge. Translating a passage of ancient Mykenan, and a praise poem to Torsten? He'll be so excited he'll wet himself. But he is god-touched. Calithra may instruct him to give the same information to the other side."

"Then I may not ask him to recommend an astronomer. You said you know one?"

"Yes. Sister Elissa at the temple of Zoryn here in Jenestra. She's brilliant, and she owes me a favor. If we ask her to keep the knowledge to herself, she will. Any idea where the major gods stand regarding this matter?"

"Given that the Marivelles politely declined to offer us passage on a temple schooner returning to Namo, I would say that they're adopting a position of non-interference."

"That makes sense," he said as he stood. The only temple of the minor gods you'll find in Dorul is Vyran's. For that matter, only Zoryn and Teryssa of the majors have a presence there. The town's not big enough to support more. Come back here in the early morning. The horses will be ready, and we'll feed you before you go."

I left the temple and headed back to the inn. When I returned to the room, she was at the desk, reviewing her notes. She'd combed out her hair, and it lay loose on her back. In the afternoon light, it seemed to have a soft glow. She turned to me when I was halfway across the room.

"We leave in the morning," I said, and recounted my meeting with Lucien.

"Then I would like to explore the city before dinner," she said.

Hand-in-hand, we did just that. At a silversmith's shop, we saw a collection of jewelry with the sigils of the gods, major and minor. I bought a pin with Eldryne's sigil of an open book and fastened it to the lapel of the short jacket Fiona was wearing. She rewarded me with a brief kiss.

She kept hold of my hand almost the entire time we were out. Her expressive brown eyes were taking everything in. We returned to the inn for dinner.

"Thank you," she said when we sat down.

"For the pin? My pleasure."

"No. For showing me the world," she said, reaching over and clasping my hand.

As always, Fiona was up with the sun. She woke me, and I dressed and took our bags. We walked to the temple of Sylvaris. An acolyte was alerted to our arrival and immediately took us inside.

"You only mentioned you had a companion," Lucien said when we saw us. "You did not mention that she is so beautiful, only that she is brilliant."

He took Fiona's hand, bent, and kissed the back of it. She blushed slightly. He straightened and gave her a warm, conspiratorial smile, one that made him look like a favorite uncle who'd just slipped you a sweet behind your parents' backs.

"Father Lucien," Fiona replied, dipping into a slight curtsy.

"Enough of that, Miss Magellan. Just Lucien, please."

He led us to the table. The fare was simple—porridge with fresh raspberries, cheese and bread if we desired, and strong, dark tea. We ate quickly and when we finished, Lucien led us through the temple to the courtyard behind.

Two geldings were already saddled, waiting for us. I chose the larger of the two—a chestnut with white stockings—and tied our bags behind my saddle with a set of leather thongs. By the time I finished, Fiona was already astride her mount, a dappled gray. I'd planned to assist her, but she proved it unnecessary.

"Between the priests-militant and the local baron's men, the road should be trouble-free," Lucien said. "Dorul is of fair size, a gathering point for grain that ships downriver. If you had more time, I would recommend making the trip by barge, but the road is nearly a straight line and will take two days less than traveling upstream."

"Thank you for your assistance, Lucien," I said. "We'll see you when we return."

Fiona and I left, and I led us out of the city to the road to Dorul. She was wearing a gray green cortaderia skirt with a matching jacket, her hat on, and her new silver pin on her lapel. For someone who had never ridden before leaving Tallesin, she seemed quite comfortable in the saddle.

Once past the city walls, we entered broad fields, green with growing crops. The road was flat and straight as an arrow. We passed people working the fields, weeding, it seemed, for the most part.

The journey was rather dull. The landscape remained unchanged except for the occasional village we passed through. We passed numerous travelers heading to Jenestra and overtook several who were heading our way on foot. Each night we stopped at the inn Lucien recommended, and found them all satisfactory, but nothing special.

We saw Dorul on the fourth day, hours before we reached it. It was much more substantial than the villages we'd passed, but I would hesitate to call it a city. Lucien had explained that it was a trading hub for the surrounding countryside. Farmers delivered their grain here for shipment downriver and bought the goods here that they couldn't make themselves.

We arrived at the inn, the Golden Pheasant, just before dinner. After turning our horses over to the inn's groom, I booked the room for four days and asked the innkeeper if we could have a bath prepared while we ate. He agreed, and after dropping our bags in the room, Fiona and I headed to the dining room.

"Are you sore from the ride?" I asked Fiona while we were waiting to be served.

"No. Why?"

"You seem to be squirming in your chair."

"I'm excited," she said. "Tomorrow, we meet with Valerian Wouk, and I hope he can translate the parchment."

"I'm reasonably confident he can," I said. "My archpriest Azar *knows* things, and his letter for Wouk—"

"All the more reason for my excitement," Fiona said. "We will be a giant step closer to solving a mystery that has stood since before the twilight. As a scholar, detached from my personal involvement in this matter, that is thrilling enough. Given that Eldryne gave me this task and the challenges we have already faced just to get here, I have a deep personal interest as well."

24

Fiona did not sleep well that night. She tossed and turned, keeping me awake. Before sunrise, she was up and dressed.

"Mr. Wouk will probably not be ready to receive visitors for several hours," I remarked.

"I can't help it," Fiona said.

"You kept me awake for most of the night with your tossing and turning, and you are driving me crazy, pacing back and forth like a caged tiger. I've half a mind to punish you."

"Punish me?" she replied, her eyebrows lifted as she looked at me, her cheeks flushing golden pink as she gave me a coy smile.

"Yes," I growled, tossing the bedclothes aside and leaping up.

She squeaked in mock terror as I threw her over my shoulder and tossed her on the bed. She pretended to resist until my lips reached the spot on her long neck just below her ear. When I kissed her there, she let out a small moan.

"You're trying to distract me, aren't you?" she breathed.

"I am. How is it working?"

"Well. I was hoping you would do this last night. It would have calmed me down."

The sun was up when we dressed. We headed down to eat. When we finished, I asked the innkeeper if he knew Valerian Wouk.

"The old scholar? Aye."

He was able to give us directions, and Fiona and I headed out with the leather tube that held the palimpsest and her notes. Wouk's house—cottage, really—was just inside the town walls. The small yard outside was unkempt, with the grass knee-high on either side of the narrow path to the door.

Fiona knocked gently on the door. There was no response. I then knocked much harder.

"I'm coming, I'm coming," we heard a reedy voice call out.

A tiny man, shorter than Fiona by a couple of inches, opened the door. His white hair looked as though birds had nested in it. He was wearing a tunic covered with food stains and ink-smudges.

"Valerian Wouk?" Fiona asked.

"Well, aren't you a vision!" he said in Lutetian, focusing entirely on her. "Yes, I am. What brings you here?"

Fiona understood not a word he said, so I offered, "We need your help. We have a text in ancient Mykenan, and we—"

"Thetlarian, are you?" he said in our native tongue with a noticeable Lutetian accent.

"Yes, sir," Fiona replied.

"You're an Eldryne, aren't you? Why aren't you wearing the purple?"

"It's a long story," I said. "We have a letter for you from the archpriest of the Order of Sylvaris."

His bushy eyebrows twitched like a rabbit's ears. He held out his hand for the letter. Fiona retrieved it from her jacket and handed it to him. He tore it open and read it. Shortly after he started, he turned and went inside. When he finished reading, he turned and seemed surprised that we were still standing outside.

"Well, don't let the flies in. Watch your step. Some of those texts are … well, they were before the mouse got to the one … anyway, come in. This Azar— your archpriest, is he?"

I nodded.

"After he gets through the puffery of telling me I'm the only one with a requisite knowledge of ancient Mykenan to help you, he says that you have something truly amazing. What is it?"

"A palimpsest, sir."

"Sir? I'm no sir, just an old man who spends his life buried in literature. Call me Val. And you are?"

"Fiona," she answered with a small curtsy.

"And the prettiest thing ever to cross my threshold. By all that's holy, poets should fight among themselves for the honor of describing your loveliness. Give it to me."

Fiona opened the leather tube and withdrew both the vellum and her notes written on foolscap. Wouk took the parchment first, glanced at it briefly, and handed it back. He then seized Fiona's notes without asking.

"That's what I want," he said. "This is the scripto inferior?"

"Yes," Fiona replied.

He took the papers and sat down at a cluttered table, ignoring us. Fiona and I looked at one another, wondering what to do. Just as the silence grew uncomfortable, he muttered to himself.

"Oh, my, my."

"Yes?" Fiona asked tentatively.

"Torsten the Conqueror. These are Mykenan numbers," he said, waving at the figures Fiona had copied. "I can transcribe them for you, no problem. Below that is a forty-two-line poem in praise of Torsten the Conqueror. Most people think Torsten didn't really exist, you know. That the legends about him are an amalgamation of various warlords in the pre-twilight era. This might be proof that he was a real person after all."

"It's more important than that, Val," I said.

"More important than that? You don't understand, boy. Proving that Torsten was a real person is incredibly—"

"We think the numbers are astronomical calculations pointing to the location of his Hoard," Fiona said quietly. "And that the poem contains clues as to how to interpret the numbers."

"Torsten's Hoard? It might actually exist?" Wouk said, tearing his eyes from the paper to look at Fiona.

"I believe it does, and that this tells us how to find it," she replied, holding his gaze.

"By all that's holy!" Wouk breathed, then turned his attention back to the papers Fiona had given him. "The two of you are welcome to stay, but I will be a very poor host. A challenge like this? Come back tomorrow. I won't be finished, but I can tell you what I've found so far. Bring food."

Fiona and I looked at one another. Wouk's entire attention was focused on the foolscap in front of him. Fiona returned the palimpsest to the tube, and we headed out the door. I shut it gently behind us.

"What did he mean, 'bring food'?" Fiona asked.

"I suspect he is one of those people who, when he is engaged in solving a puzzle like this, won't stop to eat."

"Ah. I have been guilty of that," she admitted. "Now what?"

"We come back tomorrow," I said with a shrug of my shoulders.

"Aargh!" she groaned in frustration.

We amused ourselves by walking the streets of Dorul, but we finished by lunchtime. After we ate, I found a book of Lutetian love poetry in the inn's common room and suggested to Fiona that we find a nice spot and I would read to her. We returned to a small park we'd passed. I sat up against a tree, and Fiona leaned against my chest as I read aloud.

"It sounds so beautiful and melodic," she commented after the first one. "What did it say?"

"It was a series of similes, where the author compared different parts of his lover's body to different beauties in nature."

"Which parts?"

"All of them."

"Even the private bits?"

"Especially those," I said. "It's quite … Lysmeran, actually."

"Read me another, but this time, tell me what it says as you go."

I started the next poem but only made it three lines before I stopped. The text became graphic and explicit. It surprised me that a book like this would be in the common room of an inn.

"Why did you stop?" Fiona asked.

"The author got extremely naughty."

"How naughty?"

"Imagine if I wrote a poem describing what we did before breakfast."

"Oh. Definitely Lysmeran then. Please continue."

"Are you sure?"

"I want to hear what the author feels."

I did as she asked.

"You may stop now," she said, only four lines later. "Take me to our room. I would rather be doing than listening."

We returned to Wouk's cottage the next morning, bearing a bowl of porridge I'd convinced the innkeeper to allow us to take. It was only after I pounded on the door that we heard any response. Wouk opened it a moment later, wearing the same tunic from the day before and blinking sleep from his eyes.

"You brought food! Thank you!" said, snatching the bowl from my hands and scurrying inside.

We followed him in. Somewhere in the cluttered mess, he found a spoon. He ate with ravenous hunger, and when he finished, he belched loudly.

"Ah," he sighed. "Thank you. I did not eat after you left yesterday. The translation took my complete attention. Fascinating. Simply fascinating."

He set the bowl aside heedlessly, knocking papers to the floor. He wiped his mouth with the back of his hand, unconcerned with manners or decorum. His attention was once again focused on Fiona's notes in front of him."

"Have you translated it?" she asked.

"The first third," he said. "It took some time to reacquaint myself with the language. There were several dialects of ancient Mykenan, not just one. This is the dialect from the north-central area of South Gaugan, where Torsten is said to have lived, according to most of the legends."

"What does it say?" Fiona asked.

"I translated it into Thetlarian. It sounds much better in Lutetian, but then nearly everything does. It even sounds better in Gwael, which is unusual, because Gwael usually hurts my ears—sounds like dogs barking."

"What does it say?" Fiona repeated.

"Oh. Yes. Ahem. 'All praise to Torsten/The relentless storm/Foe-blood slakes/The thirst of his blade/Across seas of sand/And rivers of water/He extends his sway/His enemies he smote/With implacable fury/He seized crowns in eagle talons/Gates shattered/Fourteen cities are his/The gods themselves/Envy his treasure.' There are two stanzas remaining. If you come back tomorrow, I will have them finished. Bring food."

"Would you like us to bring dinner?" Fiona asked.

"Yes. Yes. Now go. Come back later."

He waved us away with a distracted wave of his hand. I took the empty bowl and then tugged Fiona gently to the door before she could protest. If she had her way, she would look over his shoulder the whole time, which would probably slow him down. Wouk didn't even notice our departure; he'd already returned to the text.

When we returned that evening with a bowl of the inn's stew, Wouk didn't even come to the door. He hollered that we should just leave it. With a shrug, I put it on the threshold.

The next morning, the bowl was still there, untouched. It had congealed into a cold, unappetizing mass, with flies buzzing around it. I knocked on the door—twice, three times, the last hurting my knuckles. There was no answer. Fiona gave me a look of alarm.

I tried the latch. It was unlocked. Wouk was at the table where we'd left him, slumped over. Before I became concerned, I saw fresh drool at the corner of his mouth and the slight rise and fall of his chest.

"Val?" I said, giving his shoulder a gentle shake.

"Huh? What?"

He sat up with a snort. His hair was even more unkempt than before, and he was clearly in the same tunic. He blinked sleep from his eyes as he turned to look at us.

"Oh! You're back. Did you bring food?"

"Yes," Fiona said. "We brought dinner yesterday, but you told us to leave it. You never touched it."

"You did? Ha! I suppose you did at that. I was right in the middle of a tricky passage. A borrowed word from the eastern dialect had me stumped, but I got it. Food?"

Fiona handed him the bowl. Wouk scattered papers around, searching for his spoon. Fiona spotted it first and handed it to him before he made more of a mess.

Wouk ate like a starving dog. I wondered if he even tasted the porridge laced with honey and fresh raspberries that we'd brought. When he finished, he wiped his mouth with his sleeve and belched again.

"Did you finish?" Fiona asked.

"No. One stanza left. Some borrowed words slowed me down. Come back later. Bring food."

25

Fiona actually stamped her foot as we left his cottage. She followed that by kicking at a clump of grass next to the overgrown path. I tried to take her hand, but she yanked it away.

"That man is impossible!" she hissed. "He treats us like servants. 'Bring food!' And his house is a mess!"

"Fiona," I said calmly, hoping not to stir her up even more, "he's an eccentric old man—a scholar. You said that you yourself would forget to eat when you were in the middle of something engrossing. He's just … more so."

"I know," she said with a sigh a couple of minutes later when she calmed down. "It's just frustrating. Eldryne, or some other god, put that piece of vellum in my hands. Even though we were just cataloging old junk, I noticed it was a palimpsest, and then Eldryne told me to find you. I've been excited ever since I noticed the scripto inferior, and now that we're on the verge of learning what it contains, I can't stand the suspense."

I stopped and pulled her close, wrapping my arms around her waist. Fiona was almost trembling with frustration. Waiting was not something I did well, and when you were so close to the goal, it could be excruciating.

"Fiona, love, Azar would not have sent us to Wouk only to be denied. I imagine we could count the number of scholars who can translate pre-twilight Mykenan, let alone distinguish between dialects, on one hand and have fingers left over. It will take however long it takes, and there is nothing we can do about it."

"I *know* that!" she spat. "It doesn't make it any easier to bear! I'm also mindful that Sister Wanda copied my notes. That means they have the numbers if they can find someone who can read them. We don't know whether there are hidden clues in the text or if they represent a significant adjustment. The archpriestess and her people might even now be in the general vicinity of the Hoard, and they might stumble across it."

"I don't think they're that close, love. My guess is that all they know is that it would be somewhere in South Gaugan. That's an entire continent, Fiona. If they're really clever, and really lucky, perhaps they'll figure out that we came to Wouk, and show up here after we've left."

"He'll tell them everything, won't he?"

"I think even if Valerian swore to keep the secret until death, he'll be so excited about the prospect of actually finding Torsten's Hoard that he'll forget and won't be able to resist talking about it."

"You're right," she admitted, then giggled. "Only after he tells everything he knows will he recall that he wasn't supposed to. I can almost see his face."

We returned that evening with a bowl of chowder and some bread. When we knocked, Wouk came to the door, a huge grin on his face. He snatched the bowl and the bread from me and retreated inside.

"Come in, come in," he urged. "I've finished. Thank you for the food."

He shoveled the chowder into his mouth at an unbelievable pace. When he could no longer pick any up with the spoon, he started mopping up the remainder with the bread. He finished and picked up a piece of foolscap and cleared his throat.

"All praise to Torsten/The relentless storm/Foe-blood slakes/The thirst of his blade/Across seas of sand/And rivers of water/He extends his sway/His enemies he smote/With implacable fury/He seized crowns in eagle talons/Gates shattered/Fourteen cities are his/The gods themselves/Envy his treasure.

"Torsten the conqueror/Razer of walls/Slayer of foes/Conqueror of lands/From high mountain/To valleys low/Guarded by stars/Where the eagle nests/His shadow drapes/Hidden treasures deep/Whispered by winds/Fourteen paths converge/The gods bow low/Before his Hoard.

"Eternal Torsten/Defier of fate/His legacy endures/Beyond mortal span/In crypts of stone/He rewards the wise/And punishes the fool/Fourteen keys/unlock the vault of treasure/Where divine sparks gleam/In endless night/The gods weep/At Torsten's might.

"That's in Thetlarian, of course," he said. "It sounds better in Lutetian. In Midonese, it would hurt your ears."

"You have it written down?" I asked.

"Yes. Here," he said, handing me the paper. "I included the translation in Lutetian as well."

"May we take it?"

"Of course. I have no use for it. I have no great collection of pre-twilight Mykenan texts. You're an Eldryne, young lady. It should go back to Harkiss with you."

"One important question for you, Val," I said. "How old is the text?"

"Excellent question! I was wondering the same thing myself. The use of borrowed words from the eastern dialect is the key."

"How old is it?"

"Oh, yes. Between nine hundred and fifty and one thousand years old," he said. "Older than that, they would not have borrowed words from the east, and newer, they would have had more, particularly the word—"

"May I have my notes back?" Fiona asked.

"Of course, of course," he said, gathering them up from the table.

"Valerian, we would appreciate it if you kept your silence about this," I said. "Others may approach you, seeking to know what the poem said. Please don't tell them."

"Don't tell them? But this is a monumental discovery."

"Please don't," Fiona pleaded. "Eldryne herself sent me on this quest."

"But I thought Eldryne always wants to share knowledge," he protested.

"There are others, with less noble intent, seeking the same goal," I said. "Our desire is to return whatever the Hoard contains to its rightful owners. If it contains Calithra's lute, we will give it to her order. We fear that our rivals would not be so generous."

"Ah. Keep it for themselves? Blackmail the order somehow?"

I nodded.

"Then my lips shall be sealed," Wouk said.

"Thank you, Valerian," Fiona said, stepping forward and giving the smelly old man a hug.

"Thank you, m'dear," he replied, blushing furiously. "Most interesting challenge I've had come my way in years. The pleasure has been mine."

I gathered the empty chowder bowl and shook his hand. He saw us to the door, shutting it softly after we stepped onto the path. Fiona was clutching the papers in her hand and looked as though she wanted to skip.

"Right away," she whispered urgently as we headed back to the inn, "I can tell that the number fourteen is significant. Otherwise, why would it be repeated? Fourteen cities, fourteen paths, fourteen keys?"

"And three stanzas of fourteen lines each," I added.

"Arrgh!" she growled, stopping suddenly. "And now we need to wait until we return to Jenestra to try to figure out what this means!"

"Have I told you that you look especially fetching when you're frustrated?"

"No," she replied, then three heartbeats later, asked, "You're teasing me, aren't you?"

"Perhaps."

"You realize I shall have to punish you for that when we return to the inn?"

"I certainly hope so!" I said with a grin.

She laced her fingers in mine, and we resumed walking to the Golden Pheasant. The late sun of a summer evening gave a special glow to her skin and brown hair. The streets of the town were much quieter.

"You know, punishment implies wrongdoing," she said. "But the form of 'punishment' for teasing is better construed as a reward."

"Ah, you're on to me now," I said with mock dismay. "You figured out my secret code."

She laughed, a sound like wind chimes on a gentle breeze. Tugging my hand, she pulled me to her. Raising on her tiptoes, she draped her arms around my neck and kissed me quite thoroughly.

"That's just a foretaste of the punishment that awaits you, Dexter Falk," she said.

We woke early, or should I say, Fiona did, and her stirring roused me from sleep. After dressing, we packed our bags, and I carried them down. The innkeeper's wife was there.

"Leaving? You're still paid for another day."

"Quite all right, madam," I said magnanimously. "No need to make an adjustment. We have pressing business in Jenestra, which we just learned of. Is there something ready for us to break our fast?"

"Porridge should be ready. Fresh raspberries, too. Shall I have the groom saddle your mounts?"

"That would be splendid."

We headed to the dining room and helped ourselves. In addition to the porridge, there was the robust black tea they favored locally. One cup would really open your eyes for the day. By the time we finished eating, our horses were waiting. I tied our bags behind my saddle and checked the girths on both horses.

"You look like you've been riding all your life," I said to Fiona after watching her swing herself onto the saddle gracefully.

"Fourteen is important," Fiona said a couple of miles after we left Dorul, "but so is the number three, I think. Three divine relics, three stanzas of fourteen lines each, with the number fourteen repeated in each stanza."

"There's no sense in letting it bounce around in your brain, dear," I said. "We have a ride of four days to reach Jenestra, and only an astronomer can tell us whether the fourteen or the three, or both, are important."

"You're right. I'll make myself crazy if I dwell on it."

"That would be bad," I agreed.

"Dexter?" she asked hours later. "This is what you do, isn't it?"

"What is?"

"This," she said, sweeping her arm around her head. "Going on adventures all over the world, wherever Sylvaris demands."

"To be honest, Fiona, the scope and nature of my adventures were fairly pedestrian until a year ago. Something has changed. I don't know why, and I doubt I would figure it out if I tried to, but what has happened in the last twelve months is a whole order of magnitude more involved than everything that went before."

"Such as?"

"Chasing down petty thieves, recovering stolen heirlooms, finding runaway sons or apprentices, forged bills of sale, and other mundane requests filled my days. I made good money and was generally busy, but there was no divine involvement. That is all new."

"And love," she added, her tone carrying the note of wonder that one feels when flipping over a puzzle piece reveals that it will fit.

"Yes, love. Unexpected. Exhilarating. And…" I trailed off.

"And sad, ultimately," Fiona finished my thought.

"Not in the sense of regret for what was," I said.

"But sad for what could not be. And you don't want to say it because you fear the same thing will happen to us, and you don't want me to be hurt. Some of those Eldryne has touched are granted glimpses of the future. I am not one of them, Dexter, but I have a sense of my own direction. When this is over, I hope to return to the order, but I will not stay in Harkiss. There is too much for me to learn in the world. Perhaps how to speak Lutetian. And you? You will go where Sylvaris directs. Our paths may cross, and I hope they do, but I cannot predict that. I know that I am with you now, and that is enough. When Eldryne sent me those dreams, I had no idea what was in store for me. Now that we have embarked on this grand quest, I cannot imagine doing it with anyone but you."

26

We arrived in Jenestra and the Tawny Lion. After taking our bags up, I suggested to Fiona that she make a copy of the translation Valerian Wouk gave us since we had not done so yet. I returned our horses to the temple of Sylvaris. When I returned to the inn, I asked for a bath to be prepared after dinner.

Once again, the tub was delivered by the giggling maids. This time, with the bruises under my eyes gone, they deemed that I might barely be handsome enough for a woman as beautiful as Fiona. I shared that information with her when they left.

"Perhaps," Fiona replied.

In the morning, Fiona was eager to get started. I needed to slow her down, pointing out that the rest of the world might not begin before sunrise. Impatience radiated from her all the way through breakfast.

We walked to the temple of Zoryn, with Fiona clutching the leather tube containing the palimpsest, her notes, and Wouk's translation of the praise poem. Zoryn's temple was a grand edifice, with a single spire reaching to the heavens— easily the tallest structure in the city. A novice in sky-blue robes greeted us at the entrance.

"How may Zoryn help you today?"

"We would like to see Sister Elissa."

"Please wait. I will see if she is available."

We stood on the front steps for several minutes. There was a fair amount of traffic in and out, even at this early hour, and other novices guided those arriving.

Our novice reappeared, followed by a striking woman with white-blonde hair. She locked eyes on Fiona as though she recognized her.

"I am Sister Elissa," she said in heavily accented Thetlarian. "You are the two Lucien warned me to expect. Please come in."

The interior of the temple was no less magnificent than its outward appearance. The main sanctuary space was a huge, vaulted room. Its ceiling was at least sixty feet above the marble floor. The feeling I had in crossing through it was one of awe, which I suspected was the designer's intent.

"Lucien told me you would be coming and what you would bring me," Elissa said as she sat behind a desk. "It is good that he did. I needed to check with the head priest to make sure I could assist you. He, in turn, contacted his superiors."

"How was he able to do that in such a short time?" Fiona asked.

"Our head priest is an adept—god-touched," Elissa explained. "Those so favored by Zoryn are able to communicate on the celestial plane, but many are not strong enough of mind to withstand the experience."

"Mad priests of Zoryn," I muttered to myself.

"Yes," Elissa said, "the mad priests. Zoryn alone of all the gods offers his favorites access to the celestial, but it makes many of them lose their grip on reality. Those who come into their power without years of training often become quite addled. Regardless, our head priest contacted his superiors about this puzzle you have. You are not the only ones in pursuit of the answer."

"Really? Have there been other inquiries?" I asked.

"Yes. Two priestesses of Eldryne and a priestess of Kravyna approached a sister in Timboli, on South Gaugan, a few days ago, asking for help interpreting a set of astronomical coordinates. They claimed it would reveal the location of Torsten's Hoard. Their search was fruitless. The coordinates pointed to a spot in the southern Entassa Ocean."

Fiona and I shared a look of interest and concern.

"We have information that may help your interpretation," Fiona said. "First, we have a reasonably accurate date of when the numbers were recorded— nine hundred and fifty to one thousand years ago."

"Pre-twilight," Elissa said. "That much was known to my sister in Timboli. A more precise date will refine the equations, but it will still probably end up being in the sea."

"There is also a praise poem in archaic Mykenan that accompanied the numbers," Fiona said. We just returned from having it translated."

"Valerian Wouk?" Elissa asked.

"Yes."

"There are few people alive who could accomplish it. He is one of them."

"In the poem, the numbers three and fourteen seem to have some prominence," Fiona said.

"You have this translation?"

"Yes. Both in Thetlarian and Lutetian."

"I will need to examine both," Elissa said. "And the numbers?"

'We have those as well."

Elissa held out her hand. Fiona extracted the sheets of foolscap from the leather tube, sorting through them, and then handing them to the priestess, while explaining what each contained. Elissa was most interested in the numbers first, then the translation. She arranged the sheets containing the numbers centrally.

"These are azimuthal coordinates," she said, her finger tracing over them. "Altitude and azimuth readings, paired with what I think are declination values. But they do not account for precession."

"*Precession?*" Fiona asked.

"The wobble of the earth on its axis," Elisa explained. "That's why knowing the figures date to a pre-twilight era is important, and being able to narrow it down to a more specific time is beneficial. Right now, those coordinates point to a spot, but what used to be there has moved."

Elissa moved the pages with numbers to the side and pulled the translation to the center. She read it more than once. I noticed her eyes moved more quickly while reading the Lutetian version.

"This is more than a praise poem," she said.

"As we guessed," Fiona said.

"The repetition of fourteen and the motif of three are important. Then, if you look at the center of the poem, the two lines right in the middle are, 'Guarded by stars/Where the eagle nests.' I'm willing to bet that those two lines provide a reference point for the numbers. Once I perform the precession calculations, I'll know where Aquila, the eagle constellation, was. Of course, betting put me in Lucien's debt, so you may want to temper your enthusiasm. It will take me a day to establish the proper base point. Once I have that, we can start to play with how three and fourteen will alter things."

"A day?" Fiona said, clearly crestfallen.

"These aren't simple sums and debits, Miss Magellan," Elissa said. "Spherical trigonometry, precession, and sideral time all need to be taken into account. Even with Zoryn's guidance, it will take time."

"I understand the value of precision," Fiona admitted grudgingly.

"I would hope so. Eldrynes like you value precision over—"

"I was cast out of the order," Fiona said.

"Not for lack of precision," Elissa said. "And once you have found Torsten's Hoard, how can they deny you your rightful place?"

"Lucien told you a great deal, didn't he?" I observed.

"He and I have few secrets. I know everything about both of you that Lucien knows. For instance, I know you, Dexter, were in it up to your neck with the Marivelles not too long ago."

"Fat lot of good it did," I muttered. "They wouldn't give us passage."

"Things have changed in recent weeks," Elissa commented. "The major gods have decided that they will not take sides in this affair, but they will help anyone who asks. That is why my sister in Timboli aided the Eldrynes and Kravynan who sought her assistance. They did not have the praise poem or a more precise date. Come back tomorrow afternoon—late. I should have the preliminary work done, and we can fiddle around with how the poem changes things."

Elissa rose, indicating our meeting was over. Fiona returned the palimpsest to the leather tube but left her pages of numbers and the translation on the desk. Elissa led us back to the front steps.

"I understand your excitement, Miss Magellan. You have made an incredible discovery. I'm sure you want to see it through, but I must be accurate."

"Thank you, Sister Elissa," Fiona said. "We have come so far, and my life has changed so much, that knowing we are closer to solving this puzzle makes me impatient for the next step."

"That makes you perfectly normal, Sister Fiona."

Fiona started slightly, hearing Elissa address her as "Sister." I suspected that Elissa did it to remind Fiona that her expulsion had been undeserved and would be rectified in the future. It was also a nice way of giving Fiona some of the respect she'd earned by her intelligence and hard work, not to mention the lengths to which she'd gone already. After Elissa turned away, Fiona tucked the leather tube under one arm and took my hand with the other.

"Why do you look troubled, Dex? I'm the impatient one," she said.

"Knowing that two Eldryne priestesses and a Kravynan are on the continent of South Gaugan worries me," I said.

"But they failed to determine the location of the Hoard."

"But they know, as you did before you ever set off to find me, that the Hoard is located somewhere on the continent. That's not much help—South Gaugan is huge—but the Kravynans have probably already sent pigeons to the temple in every coastal city, warning them to keep an eye out for our arrival."

"They'll follow us."

I laughed darkly—very darkly.

"Maybe that's what Sister Wanda and Sister Deirdre would do," I said, "but the Kravynans tend to be much more direct about such things. They would snatch us off the street and force us to give them the information. Once they had it, they would no longer need the assistance of your order. Septima Thoran's plan to have the Kravynans in her debt would come to nothing."

"They would … torture us?" Fiona said quietly, her grip on my hand tightening.

"Most assuredly," I said. "And we would be wise to tell them everything they want to know, sooner rather than later."

"What would they do?" Fiona asked with horrified curiosity.

"They would put both of us in the same room—tied up, of course. They would threaten to have a procession of disciples begin raping you until I told them everything. I would not delay, and I would hold nothing back, hoping that they would not follow through on their threat."

"You say that in such a way as to indicate that they might abuse me anyway?"

"They might, if only to see if what I told them changed."

"That's horrid!"

"That's Kravyna."

"And they would betray the Eldrynes?"

"If they are able to obtain the information regarding the location of the Hoard without Eldryne's assistance, what debt do they owe? Septima Thoran might think they are an ally, but to them, she's just a tool to be used and discarded. There is no respect there. They'll cast her and your order aside."

"Are the Kravynans so faithless?"

"Not by their definition," I said. "If Thoran offered them a contract and paid for their assistance, they would honor the agreement. When someone hires Kravynan mercenaries, the buyer can trust that the terms of the contract will be fulfilled. But I doubt Thoran has a contract with them. She enlisted their help, and they agreed, but if their self-interest leads to breaking the alliance, they are not bound by any contract."

"So, when we reach South Gaugan—?"

"We'll be hunted like mice in a house full of cats."

"We're doomed then."

"Not necessarily," I said.

27

"What do you mean? It sounds hopeless."

"Remember the god I serve?" I asked. "Other than recovering the palimpsest from the temple in Harkiss, I haven't needed Sylvaris's help at all. And, now that I recall, I don't think he gave me a bit of assistance then. It was a pretty easy job. We'll need his help to get past whatever screen the Kravynans set up to watch for our arrival, but if he aids us, we'll get through."

The ever-present tickle on my neck changed when I said that. It was almost like I was a dog who'd fetched a stick, and he was patting my head as a reward. Involuntarily, I jerked my head away as though to duck under it. I felt his strong amusement then.

"What was that?" Fiona asked.

"Sylvaris," I said. "Telling me we should go speak with Lucien."

"Why? Elissa is the one working on the calculations."

"Elissa can't get us into the interior of South Gaugan without being spotted," I said. "Sylvaris probably has some ideas for us on how to do that."

"Oh. Tricks," she said, with an Eldryne's disdain.

"Cleverness," I replied. "Intelligence without cleverness is like being given a wonderful set of lockpicks but not knowing how to use them. You've supplied the intelligence so far. Now it's time for me to be clever."

"Like you were with Varak? That wasn't very clever. That was stupid, if you ask me."

I couldn't help but laugh. Fiona's directness was refreshing, but her view was formed by the years spent in Harkiss. She was comfortable in the world of books and ancient scrolls. The world was new to her. Her education in that had just begun.

"Stupid, but necessary," I said. "I've explained why I needed to do it. From the standpoint of logic, it doesn't make much sense. When you look at it through the lens of human nature, and the ethos of the Order of Kravyna, however, it becomes unavoidable."

"So you've said. And now, Lucien?"

"Yes. We cannot sail to any of the major ports in South Gaugan as we are. In order to slip through without notice, we will need to change the way we look and present a different appearance."

"Didn't you just say the same thing?"

"Physical disguises are only part of a successful deception," I said. "We also need to show those watching for us a different relationship between us. There is also the problem of you not speaking either of the local languages where we will most likely land. Whatever we show the world needs to provide a ready explanation for that."

"Such as?"

"I have some ideas, but I would like to hear what Lucian has to say."

We made it to the temple quickly. Its modest size contrasted with the temple of Zoryn. The same acolyte was sweeping the front steps, and they needed it no more than the last time.

"Ah! You've returned, Mr. Falk, Miss Magellan. Here to see Father Lucien?"

"We are."

"He should be in his study. You remember the way?"

"We do."

We entered the temple, and again its moderate size and simple design presented a contrast from the soaring interior of Zoryn's sanctuary. It was no problem to find Lucien's study. We knocked on the open door, causing him to start. He had been engrossed in something he'd been reading.

"Dexter! Sister Fiona! From the looks on your faces, you've solved one set of problems, only to encounter new ones. How may I help?"

We explained how Elissa told us there had been an inquiry about the astronomical figures in Timboli. When I told him that I suspected the Kravynans would be keeping a sharp lookout for us, he nodded. He then frowned as he thought.

"You don't know yet where you will be heading, do you?"

"Not until Elissa tells us what she's found out."

"What South Gaugan languages do you speak?"

"Molutian, Bour, and some Pichenese," I said.

"Molutian will be the key. It might solve the other problem."

"What other problem?" Fiona asked.

"You, my lady, are entirely too pretty. I imagine you turn heads wherever you go, especially now that you're no longer in Eldryne's rags. We need to make you a drudge. The Kravynans will be like hounds on a scent, looking for a Thetlarian accompanied by a beautiful woman with golden skin and light brown hair. Every major port—Timboli, Rhavella, even smaller ones like Port Puzo—will be full of eyes. Traveling as you look now, you would be spotted immediately, like a golden coin in a beggar's bowl."

"What do you mean, make me a drudge?"

"Dexter can pass for a Molutian, but not in Molutia itself, I imagine."

"That is probably true," I agreed.

"The Molutians still practice slavery. We can use walnut juice to darken your skin, dye your hair black, dress you in homespun, and you will look like a typical example of Molutian chattel."

"She doesn't speak any of the languages, Lucien," I cautioned.

"Then you will need to be mute, Sister Fiona: mute and simple-minded," Lucien said, rubbing his hands together with a smile. "An even better disguise for someone as brilliant as you are. And it means that Dexter will need to present himself as none too prosperous, or he would be able to afford a better piece of property."

Fiona clearly didn't like Lucien's idea. Her cheeks were flushed red, and I could see she was about to protest. Lucien noticed as well and held up his hand in a calming gesture, his eyes twinkling with amusement.

"Do not take offense, my dear. It is not a reflection on your importance to this adventure—far from it. It's a way to hide your radiance of both appearance and intellect. They will not look closely at a scruffy Molutian trader hauling around a dim-witted mute slave girl. And for the southern continent, such a sight would not be too unusual. Not to say they have any great number of simple-minded slaves, but you get what you pay for, and it would reflect that Dexter was no one special, if all he could afford was—"

"Are you teasing me?" Fiona asked suddenly.

"No, although there is a delicious element of humor in what Lucien suggests," I said. "The Kravynans are not known for their perspicacity. If they see someone who looks like a scruffy, none-too-successful Molutian trader—me—accompanied by his slave, an unkempt, black-haired, olive-skinned drudge—you—their eyes will sweep over us without stopping. We only need to maintain the act until we are past them—a day at most. The stain on our skin will last longer, but that cannot be helped."

"You are dying your skin as well?" she asked.

"And my hair. I don't look Molutian as I am now. It means we will need to enter through Timboli or Rhavella, outside of Molutia. With darker skin and black hair, I can pass for a Molutian. Inside of Molutia, my non-native accent would betray us."

"So, I'm to be a drooling idiot?"

"Not quite drooling," Lucien said. "That would be carrying things too far. All you need to do is adopt a humble posture—shoulders stooped, slumping, dirty hands, feet, and cheeks, keeping your eyes cast downward. As far as the idiocy, you would be more vacant than imbecilic—the kind of person who needs to be told everything twice. And be prepared for your exasperated owner to tug you around a bit. He won't be mannerly."

"We'll keep your nice clothes packed away in our bags, which, unfortunately, you will need to carry briefly," I said. "You'll be dressed in a shapeless piece of homespun that hides your magnificent figure, with rope sandals on your feet."

"And then?"

"The Kravynans won't be stopping everyone and interrogating them. They'll just be observing, looking for the two of us as we appear now," I said. "Lucien, one thing that would help us a great deal—we dare not approach the temple of Sylvaris. The Kravynans will be watching. But it would be nice if we could somehow arrange for horses or mules so we can collect them after we leave the city. If you could have someone travel on the same ship to arrange that. And please tell them not to leave the stable leading two empty mounts! The Kravynans might not be terribly smart, but they would pick up on that. Whoever delivers the animals will need to walk back to the temple. If they can include a tent, bedrolls, food, and waterskins, please have them do so."

"Easily arranged. I'll send a priest or priestess with a letter. They'll separate from you at the dockside and meet again outside the city. We have a few captains we've worked with in the past who should be able to deliver you discreetly. I'll find out who is available and have them stand by. Do you have money?"

"I have a letter of credit—two thousand Thetlarian guilders."

"It seems likely that you'll be headed to either Rhavella or Timboli. I'll have someone go to the bank and exchange it for bour-marks. You have a means of carrying that much?"

"Yes."

"Unless you need to head to the southern half of the continent, bour-marks will be accepted just about everywhere. I suspect that Elissa will tell you that the Hoard is somewhere in the northern part of the central highlands."

"How do you know?" Fiona asked.

"Of the area Torsten was said to have held sway over, the north central highlands would be the place to hide something. One more thing you'll need—papers. Molutians either brand their slaves or the owners carry title to them if they're recently purchased. The idea of branding you, Sister Fiona, is abhorrent to me. It would be like defacing an artistic masterpiece. The documents would show that your parents recently sold you into slavery."

"My parents?" Fiona exclaimed in shock.

"Unfortunately, it happens there. Farmers get into debt. Sometimes they sell their children to raise cash. In your case, presenting you as someone not quite right, it would be easy to understand that your parents could no longer carry the burden you represent. At least as a slave, they would be assured that you would be clothed and fed, which would be a concern, especially if they are older."

"That's horrible!"

"Unquestionably," Lucien agreed. "But life sometimes forces terrible choices on people."

"Won't the Kravynans have people watching the roads?" Fiona asked. "If you think we will most likely sail to one of those two ports, wouldn't they post people on the roads leading south?"

"It's possible," I said, "but they only have so many disciples. Between watching the port and the main road south, they will be fully extended. That's why we will pick up our horses or mules well outside of the city."

"The more I think about it," Lucien said, "mules would be better. The north central highlands are reputed to be rough country. Mules would be more sure-footed."

"One more thing," I said. "After we change our appearance, we need to make it to the harbor unseen. If the Kravynans are watching the ports on South Gaugan, they're probably watching here as well. We'll move from the inn and stay here at the temple for the duration of our time in Jenestra. Expect us tomorrow morning."

"We'll have a suitable guest chamber prepared," Lucien said.

28

On our way back to the inn, in addition to the tingle from Sylvaris on my neck, I also had the creepy feeling that we were being watched. I took us on a roundabout path, stopping randomly to look in shop windows, but I was unable to spot anyone following us. The feeling persisted even so.

Fiona walked by my side, her hand in mine, oblivious to the odd feelings I had. We wove through the streets of Jenestra, with the melodic sound of the Lutetian language everywhere. It was a beautiful summer day, and I tried to dispel the unsettling sense that I was being watched.

"Fiona, my dear, I think we should leave the inn this afternoon and not wait until tomorrow," I said.

"Why?"

"I just have a funny feeling we're being watched. When we return to the inn. It would not surprise me if someone has been in our room and pawed through our things."

"The Kravynans?"

"Yes."

Fiona shuddered and clasped my hand tighter.

"As long as they're just spying on us, that's one thing," I said, "but they tend not to do things in moderation. They might act rashly."

"Well, I do have the palimpsest and the copies of the translation with me."

"Then we're turning around right now," I said. "We'll get you back to the temple, and I'll return and get our things."

"No, Dexter. If they're watching us, it's too dangerous for you to go alone."

"Fiona, you have the information they want. If they grab me, I can talk my way out or, if I have to, fight my way free. You don't have the same options. Let's go."

We hurried back to the temple of Sylvaris. My feeling of being watched did not lessen. When we reached the temple steps, I spotted two obvious Kravynans standing across the street. The same acolyte was still sweeping the steps.

"You notice our friends across the way?" I asked.

"I did," he said. "They showed up a minute or two after you left."

"Is that why you sweep the steps?"

"It is, Mr. Falk."

"You're not an acolyte, are you?"

"No, sir. Brother Keb, priest-militant."

"Nice to meet you, Brother."

"They're not even trying to hide," Fiona noted.

"Subtlety isn't one of their strengths, my lady," Keb replied. "You'll be safe inside. I'm good with a broom, but better with a sword."

"Back so soon?" Lucien said with a twinkle in his eye when we returned to his study.

"I had the feeling we were being followed and decided to return before they proved me right," I said.

"Keb told me we have watchers outside. You probably made the right play, Dexter. Want me to send some people to the inn to collect your things?"

"I'll go, but I wouldn't mind some company," I said.

"Let my people do it, Dexter. If they're bold enough to put watchers right across the street, they're bold enough to nab you and ask you some questions in an uncomfortable way."

"Fine. Tawny Lion, room seven," I said, handing him the key.

"I'll get some people over there right away. We'll need to send word to Elissa to come here whenever she finds something. No sense in leaving the temple until you're ready to sail."

"Will Elissa need to worry about the Kravynans?" Fiona asked.

"Interfering with a priestess of Zoryn would be the nearest thing to suicide," Lucien said with a chuckle. "And not just for those involved—the whole order might be punished. There's a reason why we call the major gods by that appellation. They are far more powerful than the lessers, like our *Sylvaris* or your *Eldryne*. And if Kravyna's people attempted to enter our temple without being invited, the four majors would step in to punish the offending party quickly."

"Then why do we need to fear the Kravynans when we arrive in South Gaugan?" Fiona asked.

"Because taking us from a public square or on the open road is not the same as entering another god's sanctuary," I said.

"But it would still be a conflict between the orders," she protested.

"Small in scale and not violating anyone's temple," Lucien pointed out. "I realize it's a fine point, but that is where the line is drawn."

"So, if they had snatched us from the street—?"

"The Order of Sylvaris would be upset and would work to get you back as quickly as possible as soon as we learned of it."

"And if they refused?"

"Well, to be honest, I don't know what would happen then," Lucien said, scratching his head. "Since the twilight, this is probably the closest to open conflict that the orders have come."

"I'm sorry to say, Mr. Falk," Keb said when he returned, bearing our valises, "but someone went through your things while you were out. The clothes were scattered all over the place. And there were two of them watching the inn."

"Thank you, Brother Keb," I said.

I dumped my valise out onto the bed in the chamber we'd been assigned. With a sigh of relief, I saw that the false bottom was undisturbed. I opened it and withdrew the letter of credit I had from the bank in Tallesin.

"They went through our things?" Fiona asked. "That's … disgusting, to think they pawed—"

"Just as a precaution, we'll have everything washed, my dear."

"Still, just knowing that…" she said with a shudder. "As we get closer to the end, things are getting more … serious."

"That's often the way of it, Fiona.

I stepped up to her and wrapped my arms around her. She melted into my embrace, resting her head on my shoulder. I didn't want to tell her that things would get much more serious before we finished our search. We would take it step by step and deal with the problems we encountered as we reached them. The precautions we were taking now would, I hoped, make the future obstacles we would run into a little easier to deal with.

I found Lucien and handed the letter of credit to him. He arranged to have someone launder our clothes. It was a minor precaution. The Kravynans might have treated them with something that would cause irritation to the skin. It was an old tactic of theirs.

They delivered our things, clean and dry, late in the afternoon. We packed them away. At dinner, Lucien handed me back the letter of credit, along with a weighty money pouch.

"I doubt you'll need that much money," he said. "The pouch has five hundred bour-marks from temple funds. That should be enough to see you safely there and back again. We've also arranged transport for you. For the next few days, the tides are perfect for a middle-of-the-night departure. You'll be on the *Fleur Amelie*, owned by Rita Osgood, but I've also paid two other boats to leave Jenestra harbor the same night."

"In case the Kravynans are paying attention to ships coming and going," I noted.

"I didn't see any of them down by the docks," Lucien said, "but that's because they know you are still in the city. By having three leave on the same night, they won't know which one you're on. All three will travel to different ports."

"Is all this necessary?" Fiona asked, holding my hand tightly under the table.

"Perhaps not," Lucien said with a grin. "It might be much more than is required, but if I can confuse the Kravynans, it makes me happy. Tomorrow, we start changing your appearance, Sister Fiona. We will transform you from a golden jewel to a dirty drab. We already have everything we need on the premises. I suggest you bathe this evening. It will be the last time you feel clean for a couple of weeks, I'm guessing."

"This walnut juice—you said it will darken my skin? Will it be permanent?"

"Gracious, no, child. Within a week—two weeks at most—it will fade away. The same thing with the hair dye. A couple of baths will see it return to its usual color. If it's any consolation to you, Dexter gets the same treatment."

"Oh."

"Dexter, my one concern with your appearance is your rapier," Lucien said. "It is entirely too fine a blade for someone like the scruffy trader disguise we plan to use."

"I can't leave it behind, Lucien," I said. "Chances are good I will need it. What about baggy pantaloons instead of breeches? I think I'll only need to cover it up until we're away from the docks. With a loose enough tunic, we can cover the hilt and hide the rest down the leg."

"That should work."

"Sister Mira will travel with you and arrange for temple mules. She will meet you at the first village outside the city, heading south. They'll be loaded with all the equipment you'll need if you have to sleep rough."

"About the disguises?" Fiona asked. "How long will it take?"

"No time at all, my dear," Lucien said. "The walnut juice works instantly, as does the hair dye. You'll be ready to travel as soon as Elissa finishes her calculations. You'll both pass muster as a none-too-successful Molutian trader and his unfortunate property."

"And papers?"

"I started someone working on those earlier," Lucien said. "They'll be finished tomorrow."

Fiona was quiet for the rest of the meal. When we finished, Lucien again suggested that we bathe. He showed us that the temple was equipped with a rather decadent tiled tub, large enough to hold several people at once.

"One of my predecessors had this built," Lucien explained. "The Lutetians, and particularly the Jenestrans, love their creature comforts. I'll make sure the two of you are undisturbed for an hour. After that, expect company."

He showed how to open the spigots that fed hot and cold water into the bath, then left us, closing the door behind him. I adjusted the flow of water to reach a nice, hot temperature without scalding us. Fiona found some sachets of the bath salts we'd enjoyed at the inn and poured them in.

We'd bathed together before, and it was delightful, but here we had much more room. Fiona made sure I was clean, and I did the same to her. When I ran my fingers over her scalp, she sighed deeply and relaxed against me.

Eventually, the tips of our fingers started to wrinkle. We dragged ourselves out reluctantly and put on the robes Lucien told us we could wear. While Fiona gathered our clothes, I twisted the stopcock that would empty the water.

Returning to our chamber, I made sure the door was latched behind us. When I turned around, Fiona had shed her robe. She stood in all her glory.

"Dexter, I need you to make all the danger seem far away. Please?"

We came together gently, our lips meeting as she embraced me. There was a quiet urgency in Fiona, and I did my best to try to slow things down and give her the reassurance I felt she wanted. We managed to forget the rest of the world for a time.

29

The following morning, after a quick breakfast, Lucien directed us to a room next to the bath. A priestess, Sister Carmina, was waiting for us. She directed us to strip and handed us each a bowl of dark liquid and a piece of rag.

"This is the walnut juice. Apply it to yourself all over. Help each other with the hard-to-reach spots. Don't be bashful, dearie," she said when Fiona blushed at her comment. "I know you're intimate with one another. Just pretend I'm not here and have fun."

Fiona blushed deeply but dipped her rag into the bowl and started wiping it over my shoulders. She moved around and worked her way down my back. I managed to turn around and started to wipe the liquid on her.

It quickly darkened her skin from the radiant golden glow to a rich olive. She lifted her hair from her neck so I could get that. I then daubed it gently onto her face.

We took turns covering one another, and almost forgot Carmina was there. When we finished, we inspected ourselves to make sure we hadn't missed any spots. Carmina came over and double-checked.

"Time to do your hair," she said.

Carmina took charge of this step in the process, working with Fiona first. She even used a small pad to apply it to her eyebrows. Then it was my turn.

"Now just sit until I tell you," Carmina said. "We need to let the dye set. In about half an hour, I'll send you into the bath for a quick rinse. Then we'll make sure you both look plenty grubby—especially you, dear."

After our dip in the bath, Carmina drizzled some oil into Fiona's hair and worked her fingers through it. When she finished, Fiona's tresses were coal black and in uneven clumps. It looked as though she might never have washed her hair.

Carmina did the same to my hair, but not to the same degree. I looked badly in need of a bath but might have had one a few months back. I thought we could easily pass for Molutians.

"Put on the clothes I left on the bench," Carmina said. "I'll be waiting outside."

"This will wash out, right?" Fiona asked, after the door shut.

"I'm tempted to tease you and say no, but that would be cruel. Yes. In two weeks or less, you will look like your normal self."

We put on the clothing they'd picked for us. Fiona had a dress made of homespun, with numerous patches. It was as shapeless a garment as you could have imagined, completely obscuring her figure and hanging down to her shins.

I had a pair of pantaloons that were baggy, with a rope belt. My tunic was a dirty gray color and also very loose. I felt I could easily conceal my rapier for the brief journey through whichever city we landed in.

"How do I look?" Fiona asked, but not in a happy way.

"I'm sorry to say that you are still far too pretty," I replied. "Come here."

With my fingers, I raked some of her clumps of hair forward so they obscured her face. That helped hide her features. Posture would also be critical.

"Look down at your feet, as though you are ashamed of yourself, and slump your shoulders," I instructed. "Now walk to the mirror just like that. Don't straighten up. Just shuffle your feet."

With the hair in front of her face and her downcast attitude, the beautiful and brilliant priestess of Eldryne was gone. In her place was a human being who looked like a member of the lowest class. Fiona peered through her hair into the mirror.

"It's effective," she said quietly. "I hardly recognize myself."

"You sound so sad," I commented.

"I'm just now realizing something. I never considered myself vain. You know that when we met, I did not put much effort into my appearance. But now that I look so different, so … plain … I feel sad."

"This is just a mask, Fiona. Its purpose is to get us past those who would try to stop us. Underneath the mask is the same person who walked a month to find me, who finds ancient secrets in old pieces of vellum. And part of this mask, this deception, is humility in your bearing. Shortly after we reach South Gaugan, you'll be able to take this mask off."

"I know it's foolish to worry about it. But since we met, I've been seeing myself more and more through your eyes—the way you stare at me sometimes. At first, it bothered me, but now I find I enjoy the way you look at me—as though I am something precious. But how can you look at *this*," she gestured to the mirror, "the same way?"

"You'll find that I do," I said with a smile. "Because I realize that it is a temporary disguise that does not reflect the passionate scholar you still are and the bold adventurer you've become."

"You always seem to know what to say to make me feel better," she commented. "Is that Sylvaris speaking through you?"

"If I relied on him, he would make me say the most awkward and outlandish things just to amuse himself. I'm afraid it's all me."

"And you're telling the truth. That relieves me."

"Aren't you dressed yet?" Carmina asked as she entered.

"Sorry, Sister Carmina," I said. "We're ready."

"Remember to slouch, Fiona," Carmina said as she adjusted the homespun dress on Fiona's shoulders. "Shuffle to me and back to the mirror. Don't lift your feet. Drag them on the ground because you are in no hurry to get anywhere. Turn now, keep your head down, but try to look through your hair and see how you present yourself to the world."

"I don't know who that is," Fiona said with slight wonderment, "but it's not me. I've seen people who look like this in Lenoa and here in Jenestra, and my eyes went right past them."

"Unworthy of your attention," Carmina said. "Don't feel guilty. It's human nature."

"Can you do anything about how itchy the dress is?"

"No. People in your position are lucky to have clothes. If it helps, Dexter's are just as uncomfortable."

"And he looks almost as disreputable as I do," Fiona smirked. "Do you do this often?"

"Are you asking me, or Dexter?" Carmina asked.

"Both."

"We find a need to put someone in disguise two or three times a year, Carmina answered.

"I've only made a change this drastic a few times before," I said. "Generally, I do what you saw in Harkiss—more of an adjustment of attire and bearing than dying my hair and skin. The way that you carry yourself is incredibly important."

"That's why you keep reminding me to shuffle and slouch."

"Exactly," I said.

"I'll try. I want us to succeed. We've done so much already, I would hate to ruin things as we approach the end. It helps to think of it as a mask that I will take off when the need passes. I will say, Sister Carmina, you are good at this."

"Pshaw," Carmina scoffed. "This was easy. If we needed to make you into a cripple, that would have been a challenge."

Fiona reacted with horror at first. Then she saw the glint in Carmina's eye. After a moment, Fiona started to laugh, realizing that Carmina was joking.

"Would you saw my leg off? Or just bind it up behind my rear?" Fiona asked when she stopped chuckling.

"Depends on whether you felt you might need it in the future," Carmina said with a wink. "Sawing it off would be easier, but you'd need to really commit to the deception."

"I'll say," Fiona replied with a smile. "Skin color, hair dye, and a scratchy dress seem much more tolerable all of a sudden."

"Excuse me," an acolyte said, poking her head through the door. "Lucien's looking for Mr. Falk and Miss Magellan. A priestess of Zoryn just arrived."

"Sister Elissa?" I asked.

"I don't know her name. Lucien just asked me to fetch you to his study."

"She must have finished her calculations earlier than anticipated," Fiona said.

"Use this opportunity to practice," I said. "You're excited to see what she has found. Can you shuffle slowly and slump your shoulders? See if you can confuse her for a moment."

It was clear that Fiona would rather have dashed to Lucien's study, but she nodded, after a moment, and set off slowly and seemingly reluctant to go anywhere. Her head was down, and her hair covered most of her face. I was delighted that she was making such a good attempt.

"I'm going to play my part as well," I whispered to her. "Try to go along with it."

When we reached the door of Lucien's study, I clasped Fiona by the wrist and tugged her forward, causing her to stumble slightly.

"C'mon, you!" I said in a frustrated tone, as though I had needed to do this many times before.

"Mmph!" she whined.

Elissa looked confused as I pulled Fiona in. She looked at Lucien, wondering what the heck these two scruffy people were doing, entering his office without knocking. Lucien kept his face blank as Fiona shuffled in, her head down and face obscured.

"Falk?" Elissa asked after a moment.

"Yes, sister," I replied.

"Sister Fiona?" Elissa asked, incredulous.

Fiona straightened her shoulders, lifted her head, and pulled the hair out of her face, then said, "Yes, sister."

"By all that's holy!" Elissa gasped.

"Well done, Fiona," I said.

"It was," Lucien agreed.

"I absolutely did not recognize you, Sister Fiona," Elissa said. "It was only because of Mr. Falk's presence, and you holding the scroll tube that I was able to guess."

Elissa's astonishment was genuine. Her white-blonde eyebrows arched high as she stared at Fiona. The priestess shook her head slowly, her face a mixture of admiration and amusement. Lucien betrayed his love of mischief, chuckling behind his desk.

"Come," he said. "Sister Elissa finished sooner than expected. Take a look at the map."

"What did you find?" Fiona asked.

"Well, the poem is crucial, as is having a tighter range of dates. I'll spare you all the computations and calculations I performed. The threes and fourteens play an important part. But what is left is this," she said, pointing to a particular spot on a map of South Gaugan. "This is the location—in this valley, roughly fifty leagues south of Rhavella."

"Lucien, do you have a more detailed map?"

"I do."

We waited while he left the study in search of the map. Elissa kept stealing glances at Fiona. Fiona, for her part, stood up straight and allowed her to gawk.

30

Lucien returned with an armful of maps. He dropped them on his desk, then quickly started unfurling them enough to see what section of the continent they covered, then shoving them aside onto the floor. When he reached one that covered the right territory, he weighted the corners down and smoothed it out.

Elissa read the notations on the margins and consulted her notes. With her finger, she traced a line across until she reached a point and stopped. Just above her finger was a hill of higher elevation than those nearby.

"Somewhere in this area," she said. "Look for a cave. Clues in the poem all indicate one: 'Hidden treasures deep … crypts of stone … vault of treasure … endless night.' I suspect you'll find it somewhere on this hill."

"I don't see any settlements marked on this map," Fiona commented.

"Not surprising," Lucien replied. "As I recall, the north central highlands are inhospitable territory—a rocky desert."

"How do we get there?" I asked.

Lucien searched through the maps he'd swept to the floor. When he found the one he wanted, he unfurled it atop the one we'd just been examining. With his finger, he traced our route.

"You'll sail to Rhavella. From there, you'll take the main trade road south. Just past the town of Hella, here, you'll leave the road and make your way west along this valley. It's more than a week to Hella, and then another three or four days of rugged travel."

"It looks like there are towns along the way," I said. "That means we can probably stay at inns. We'll get a bath, wash the grease out of your hair, and you can resume wearing comfortable clothes again, Fiona."

"I'll look forward to that," she said.

"Sister Mira will meet you with the mules here," Lucien said, pointing to a town named Bidde. "It looks sizeable enough to have an inn, and it's about a day's journey from Rhavella, so chances are good that it does."

Having said that, Lucien rolled up the map showing the road and handed it to me. He then examined the one showing the possible location of the Hoard. "According to this, there should be a stream in the center of this valley. You'll need at least a week's worth of food. I'll make sure Sister Mira arranges that. It will probably need to be jerky. Firewood will be scarce, so I fear that cooking will not be an option."

"When can we sail?" I asked.

"Tonight. The *Fleur Amelie* is standing by. Tide goes out just after midnight. We'll move the two of you after it's dark."

"Is there anything else we should be aware of, Sister Elissa?" Fiona asked.

"It would not surprise me at all if there are multiple caves. I doubt there would be fourteen, so figure on three. There might be other clues to decipher in order to reach the Hoard safely. They might relate to the praise poem, or they might be something you find at the site," Elissa said as she rolled up her notes and handed them to Fiona.

"Thank you, Sister Elissa. This information is critical."

"Zoryn guides the stars, Sister Fiona, but you control your steps. Best of luck to you both."

As Elissa departed, Fiona took the notes and slid them into the leather tube. I took the two maps. Before folding them, I paused.

"Do you have copies?" I asked Lucien.

"No, but the cartographer from whom we purchased them does. Go ahead. That reminds me … your papers."

I folded the maps into a more convenient size to carry, then examined the papers. One was a crumpled bill of sale for "Fauna," noting that she was mute and sold by her parents voluntarily. Even more rumpled and aged was a Molutian trading license, identifying me as "Amil Daro." It even had a stain and blurred ink from spilled wine.

"These are excellent," I said.

"Our forger, Brother Joss, is quite good. You have the remainder of the day. Rest and relax. We'll collect you once it's dark and head to the harbor. A two-day sail to Rhavella, and a day of walking until you catch up with Sister Mira."

Sister Mira introduced herself to us at dinner. We discussed what we would need for our journey. She confirmed that there was a decent inn in Bidde and she would meet us there with three mules—two for us to ride and a third to carry the equipment.

"You have valises," she commented. "Make sure they're scuffed properly and show signs of hard use. I'll bring saddlebags with the mules. It will be easier to put your things in them once you're mounted."

Her comment about the appearance of the valises was an excellent point. Fiona's looked entirely too nice for a down-on-his-luck trader's belongings, let alone a slave's. I asked Lucien if they had something more suitable. He sent an acolyte into a storeroom, and he returned with two large jute sacks.

"Those will be perfect," Mira said. "They fit the image you're trying to present, and you can discard them in Bidde with no one noticing. Leaving two leather valises behind would be a question mark."

After dinner, we returned to our chamber and moved everything into the two jute sacks. When we finished, Fiona looked at me with an uncertain expression. I stepped two paces toward her, and she reached out for me.

"All these precautions," she said. "It makes me nervous. Do we really have that much to fear from the Kravynans? After all, if we find the Hoard, and Kravyna's spear is part of it, won't we just return it to them?"

"That is an excellent question, and I have wondered the same thing," I said, holding her in my arms.

"Have you figured anything out?"

"I think I have. The three legendary items that might be a part of the Hoard are Calithra's lute, Korath's hammer, and Kravyna's spear. From what little I know, the lute and hammer are somewhat benign. The spear is not. I believe the reason that you and I are working together is to prevent the Kravynans from regaining the spear."

When I said this, Sylvaris again gave me the feeling he was patting me on the head like a good dog. I flinched. Fiona noticed.

"Sylvaris?" she asked.

"Yes. I think I guessed correctly. He, at least, does not want the spear to fall into their hands. I suspect Eldryne feels the same."

I felt another psychic pat on my head. Not for the first time, I wondered why Sylvaris didn't just send me these signals in the beginning. Then I considered that he might be amused by watching me stumble along until I figured out what the game was. Oof—another pat. I couldn't help but laugh this time.

"What's so funny?" Fiona asked.

"Me, I think," I replied, then explained my thinking.

"What if you headed in the wrong direction?"

"I have a feeling he would let me know, along with him sending a feeling of disappointment that I was too thick-headed to suss it out."

"The gods work their wonders in mysterious ways," Fiona said. "That's what my mother always told me."

"She was right."

Lucien and Mira came to collect us a few hours later. We were given dark cloaks and told to pull the hoods over our heads. The Kravynans might be watching, but we wanted to make it difficult for them.

We left the temple from a gate in the rear of the complex. Keb and another man, Brother Adrian, were with us, also cloaked. When we stepped onto the street, I could not see anyone watching. When we were three blocks from the waterfront, the tingle on the back of my neck changed to a burning sensation.

"Keb," I whispered as I pulled my cloak to the side and put my hand on the hilt of my rapier, "look alive. There's trouble."

Three paces later, a group of four men stepped out of the shadow of a doorway and into the middle of the street. All of them were carrying the short sword the Kravynans favored. In the dim light of the moon, the blades of their swords and their shaved heads gleamed dully. I drew my rapier, as Keb and

Adrian unsheathed their weapons. The three of us stepped in front of Fiona, who had stopped in her tracks.

"Stand aside, and no one gets hurt," one of the Kravynans said. "Give us the Eldryne and what she has in that tube, and the three of you can live."

"If you turn around and run back to your temple, perhaps I'll let *you* live," I said with a smirk, trying to goad them.

It worked. The leader charged toward Keb who was in the center of our little group. Another went toward Adrian. That left two for me.

"Go to the doorway on the right," I told Fiona.

I heard her feet moving as I shuffled to the side to put myself between the Kravynans and her. The one closer to me matched my movement, but his partner stood still. That was a critical mistake, as the one in front blocked his partner briefly. I took advantage of the brief opportunity and darted forward, burying the tip of my blade into the nearer one's shoulder.

With a curse, he dropped his weapon. A backhanded flick, and my rapier gave him a new grin, three inches below his mouth. His hands flew to his throat as the blood spurted between his fingers. I had no time to admire my handiwork, as his partner was upon me with a shout.

The man's blade slashed down, aiming to carve me in two. I managed to deflect his blow, but the impact sent a shock up my arm. His following move, a short jab toward my groin, almost caught me, but I skipped aside just in time.

I heard the clash of steel on steel. Keb and Adrian were engaged. Fiona was no longer in my line of sight. That was good. She was behind me.

My opponent lunged forward again, feinting high but sweeping low. I gave ground, once again deflecting his blade. He was strong and quick, reminding me of Varak. He kept up his assault, forcing me back, step by step. I was waiting for, hoping for, that one misstep that would leave him just a bit off-balance. In the meantime, he continued hammering away. My wrist was aching from the force of his blows.

Finally, he moved a half-foot too far on a lunge. I skipped to the side and slammed the sole of my left shoe into the side of his knee. The crunch was audible, and he went down. I stabbed down, inside his collarbone, piercing heart and lungs with one thrust, then jumped back.

Keb had just finished his opponent and went to help Adrian. While Adrian and his opponent glared at one another over crossed blades, Keb stabbed the Kravynan in the back. He slumped to his knees with a gurgle.

"They'll hate that, Brother Keb," I said. "Kravynans like to die with all their wounds in the front."

"Too bad," Keb replied as he wiped his blade on the fallen man's tunic.

I cleaned my rapier off and sheathed it. Turning my head, I saw Fiona in the shadowy doorway she'd run to. I beckoned her to come out. She stepped out, clutching the leather tube and the sack with her things. I picked up my sack from where I'd dropped it.

"Let's not linger," Keb said. "There might be others, and I don't want to be standing here when the city watch comes along."

"You're just going to leave them there?" Fiona asked.

"Fiona, we have places to go and things to do. Waiting to report this properly would cost us a couple of days. In addition, the Kravynans would see what we look like now and send a pigeon south."

"Is that why you killed them, too? Because they'd seen us?"

"We killed them because they gave us no choice," I said. "They would have killed the three of us and then taken you. Please. Come."

We resumed heading for the waterfront. Fiona cast several glances over her shoulder at the bodies as we strode away. I noticed that she also kept her distance from me.

Keb knew exactly where the *Fleur Amelie* was tied up and took us straight to her. When I tried to assist Fiona over the side of the boat, she flinched at my touch. I realized it was one thing for her to see my scars, even trace them with her fingers, but she had only ever considered in the abstract how I received them. Before we reached Rhavella, I figured she would process what she'd just seen and come to me with questions.

Rita Osgood and Sister Mira were waiting for us. Osgood had her crew cast us off immediately. Clear of the pier, they broke out long oars to get us some maneuvering room, as the wind was directly against us. When she judged we were out of traffic, they shipped the oars and raised the mainsail on the sloop.

31

Fiona kept her distance from me until we went below to sleep. When we woke in the morning, she found Sister Mira. The two of them talked all the way through breakfast.

I kept my distance, eating my porridge. The cook had added some fresh fruit to it, but I barely tasted it. I know Fiona was upset by what she saw the previous night.

When they finished eating, Fiona excused herself from Mira and approached me. She did not stand as close to me as she had been accustomed to. For a time, we stood in silence, watching the waves roll by the *Fleur Amelie*.

"Dexter," she said finally, "I want to talk about what happened last night."

"I guessed as much. What would you like to know?"

"I've read books," she began, then hesitated.

The delay was long enough that I had to laugh. "You certainly have."

"Don't make fun of me," she said gently. "I've read books, and in many of them the author describes scenes of battle, of armed combat, of death. What I saw last night was nothing like the descriptions I'd read. It was faster, more violent, more brutal, more ... final. Those men did not die heroic deaths. One second, they were alive, trying to kill you, and the next, they were dead. The transformation is sudden and shocking, and there is nothing heroic or poetic about it."

"That's true."

"Does it bother you?"

"Yes, for a variety of different reasons," I answered. "Fiona, I have never set out deliberately to try to kill anyone. When I am attacked, I will defend myself. Most often, my opponents do not give me a choice. They will continue to try to kill me as long as they can. The only way to end those fights is by ending their lives. You've seen the scars I bear. I did not receive a new one last night. That is unusual. Those Kravynans would not have hesitated to kill me, Keb, or Adrian in order to capture you and the information you carry."

"You're saying it was justified?"

"That is for Thalorix to decide," I said. "Given the choice between allowing them to take you or opposing them, I would not let them snatch you away. When it was clear that we would oppose them, they could have withdrawn, but they did not. It would have been much better if they had."

"They bear part of the blame for their own deaths?"

"They do, even though that sounds like a weak excuse."

"You said there were a variety of reasons it bothers you."

"Yes. One of those reasons is how much it troubled you to see it. I would spare you that sight if I could. Once seen, you cannot unsee it."

"That is true. Let's set that aside for now. What else?"

"The Kravynans will know that their people did not fall at the hands of street thugs. In addition, the last one bears a wound in his back. I was only half joking when I told Keb that Kravynans like all their wounds to be in the front. One reason is that it means the person died bravely. The other is that he did not fall victim to treachery. Given how they think about the Order of Sylvaris, they will immediately assume treachery. This view will spread. It might even be important enough to them to include it in whatever message they send by pigeon to the southern continent. If that happens, it makes the next encounter more dangerous."

"I was not there to see you fight Varak," she said. "Until last night, I had only seen the kinder side of you—with me, but also with people like Billy Rodhe and Johnny Greer. I have seen your scars. They've been a source of some fascination for me, but I've pictured you receiving them in the sort of heroic clashes I've read about in books. Last night, what I saw … that lethal person who inhabits the same soul and body as the man who was so kind to Billy and Johnny, and so gentle and loving with me, and whose touch can make me quiver. It is difficult to reconcile."

"What did Sister Mira say?"

"Distilling it into its simplest form, that violence and death are parts of the world as much as kindness and life. We strive to avoid the darker and seek the lighter—at least, most people do—but sometimes the dark is brought upon us and, when it is, we depend on good people to oppose it."

"And where do I fit?"

"On the side of good. It's just that what I saw was so very disturbing. How do you bear it?" she asked, reaching over and taking my hand, bridging the physical gap between us.

"Sometimes better than others. I always regret the necessity. That's especially true when it marks an escalation of hostility instead of an end to it."

"And you feel that is what took place?"

"Yes."

"I'm sorry it had to happen, but I believe you when you say that those men would have killed you without compunction. I'm sorry I pulled away from you afterward," she said as she stepped to me, wrapping an arm around my waist and leaning against me. "It was shocking to witness."

"I understand."

She tilted her face up to me. I bent down to meet her lips. She relaxed as our kiss continued, finally pulling her head back with a sigh.

We reached Rhavella two days later. The journey across the Middle Sea between North and South Gaugan was easy. Early in the morning, we rode the tide in.

The *Fleur Amelie* slipped in with the grace of a dancer, riding the light breeze. The city spread out before us—red tiled roofs above whitewashed walls. Tall warehouses hugged the docks, and the city rose gradually behind them.

Rita Osgood guided us through the harbor traffic—everything from fishing boats to a galleon that must have lumbered in from the southern tip of the continent. We approached the third pier of the seven largest.

"We'll drop you here," she said. "Then it's back to Jenestra for us. Good luck with whatever it is you're doing."

"Who says we're doing anything?" I asked.

"I've known Lucien a long time," she said with a grin, putting her finger beside her nose.

She brought us alongside, staying just long enough for Sister Mira to hop out, followed by Fiona and me. Fiona was carrying both jute sacks and was in character from the time we entered the harbor. Head down, hair obscuring her face, shoulders slumped, she shuffled along listlessly, despite my attempts to get her to pick up the pace.

My rapier was tucked into my pantaloons, and my tunic covered the hilt. The homespun I was wearing was itchy and uncomfortable, but I reminded myself that, at the end of the day, once we reached the inn at Bidde, we could discard the irritating garb.

I spotted the Kravynans standing in the shade of a warehouse, as they were watching people arriving. They paid us no special attention. We trudged past them and into the city.

Fiona kept up her act, moving slowly and shuffling along. It was hot and uncomfortable. Before we reached the southern gate, I stopped to fill our waterskins at a public fountain. Fiona bent over and drank sloppily from cupped hands. From her initial reluctance, she was now leaning into her role as a drudge. It made me want to smile.

At the gate, the guards demanded to see my papers. The guards were Bour, and the documents were written in Molutian. They had no idea what they said, but they inspected them carefully nonetheless before passing us through.

We continued south, with a fair amount of traffic heading both ways along the road. There were enough people close to us that we dared not talk. After all, Fiona was supposed to be mute, and conversing in Thetlarian would have drawn attention.

There were three smaller villages we passed through before we reached Bidde. I refilled our waterskins in the first and the third. The dry heat wicked our sweat away before it had the opportunity to bead, making us feel grimy and dusty.

At last, we saw the buildings of Bidde. The inn, the Naughty Goat, was in the main square. Following Mira's instructions, we did not go through the front door. Instead, we headed for the stable behind. She was waiting for us, dressed in normal clothing and not the robes of the order.

"You made good time," she said. "Any problems?"

"None. The Kravynans watching the harbor paid no attention to us, just as we hoped. No one followed us, as far as I could tell, and I checked regularly."

"Good. Room eleven," she said, handing me the key. "Two baths are waiting. The water will be tepid, which should be refreshing after the heat of the day. I would suggest letting Dexter wash your hair, Sister Fiona. Carmina put so much oil in your hair that it might take a couple of attempts to get it all out. I'll meet you for dinner in an hour."

We entered the inn through the back door and climbed the stairs, finding our room. We saw no one in passing. When I closed the door behind us, Fiona dropped the jute sacks and immediately pulled the homespun dress over her head with a sigh of relief.

By the time I stripped off my things, she'd already slid into one of the two copper tubs. On a stool in between them were two sachets. I waited to open them until I'd immersed myself fully. The water felt divine, rinsing away the dried sweat and road dust.

Both sachets smelled the same. I picked one up and emptied half of it into my palm, setting the rest aside. Recognizing by the feel that it was the gentle soap used for hair, I worked it into my scalp quickly, raising a substantial lather. I cleaned myself quickly, noticing that Fiona was just sitting and relaxing.

When I judged I was as clean as I would be, I stood and went behind her. With a gentle push from my hand, she slid under the water and got her hair wet. Upon surfacing, I took her full sachet, poured it into my palms, and began working on her hair.

Carmina had poured a lot of oil on it to make it look so dirty and stringy. Fiona was perfectly content to let my fingers do the work. As a result of the oil, it did not create much foam. When I felt I'd completed the first pass, I told Fiona to submerge again and stay under as long as she could while I tried to get the suds out. She held her nose and went under.

When she resurfaced, I took what was left of my sachet and used it on her hair again. This time, with less oil to contend with, it lathered up more richly. I finished with her hair and my hands wandered over the other parts of her body that I could reach. While I would have told her that I was just trying to help her get clean, that wasn't exactly the truth.

Eventually, with my help, she rinsed her hair out and stood. I was mostly dry, and I took a towel and patted her down all over. Again, I was just trying to help. She wrapped the towel around her head like a turban, and we dressed in clean clothing—not itchy homespun.

After a time, she unwrapped the towel from her hair. We'd removed a great deal of the oil Carmina had put in, but not all of it. What remained made Fiona's now-black hair look glossy and sleek. With her olive skin, she was an exotic beauty, no longer a mute slave. Her eyes caught mine in the mirror.

"You're staring again, just the way I've come to like," she said.

32

We headed downstairs to the dining room shortly after. Mira, along with a young man, had already claimed a table. When she saw us, she gestured for us to join them, but before we sat, she rose and crossed to the innkeeper.

"I just told him to have the maids empty and remove the baths," she explained when she returned. "Hassan is a friend of the order. We helped him a few years ago when he was in a jam, and he returns the favor by being conveniently forgetful when we need him to be. This is Lares. He rode with me from the temple. We'll walk back tomorrow."

In the morning, Fiona woke first, as usual. I roused myself and dressed, and we transferred our things from the jute sacks to the saddlebags Mira gave us. At breakfast, we saw Mira and Lares leaving the dining room.

When we finished eating, we went back to the stable. Mira had our mounts saddled. A third mule was loaded with the tent, bedrolls, and food for the animals and us.

"It will take you nine more days to reach Hella. Once you leave the road there, grazing is likely to become thin within a day. As long as you stay near the streambed, water shouldn't be an issue, but keep your skins full anyway," Lares said.

We said our farewells and set off. Fiona's straw hat had not survived the journey so far intact. The crown was dented, and the brim was creased and rumpled in different spots. It was remarkable to note the change in her appearance. Coupled with her now olive skin and black hair, the battered hat gave Fiona a look that was less elegant and more worldly.

"You're staring again," she commented.

I told her why. She tilted her head as she considered my words. Then she smiled.

"I am considerably more worldly than when I set off from Harkiss to find you, though I still have much to learn. It has already become difficult for me to remember how naïve and inexperienced I was. When this adventure ends, I don't see myself returning to life in the cloister."

"What will you do?"

"I'm still trying to determine that. Assuming the order accepts me back—"

"Which they will," I said. "They would be idiots not to, and the Eldrynes are not idiots."

"Assuming they accept me back, I might engage in mission work—like the woman who came to my village and found me. I would like to learn to speak Lutetian—such a pretty language. Being with you, traveling with you, has opened my eyes to life outside of books. I will still love books, of course, and the pursuit of knowledge, but returning to the libraries of Harkiss is something I may postpone for a few years."

We continued south. The weather grew hotter and drier, and the road took us gradually higher in elevation. After Bidde, fields of grain gave way to vineyards, and then to olive groves, as the terrain changed from plains to rolling hills. The towns we passed grew smaller and less affluent. Traffic dwindled in both directions, except for caravans making the long trek between Rhavella and Togranes, a sizeable city at the confluence of two rivers that marked the southern border of the kingdom of Bour.

Although the inns grew rougher and smaller as we went, the kindness and hospitality of the innkeepers did not. With fewer travelers, each customer was treasured. They delighted in taking care of us and the few other guests.

Leaving Hella, we continued south for a couple of hours. I had examined the maps the night before and knew where we would encounter the streambed that we would follow west. When it was time to leave the road, I checked and made sure no other travelers were visible ahead or behind. Venturing into open country, with no settlements in the direction we were headed, would be sure to draw attention.

With no one in sight, I turned my mule off the road, leading the pack animal with me. Fiona followed. For someone who had never ridden until we set off from Tallesin to Lenoa, she now seemed at home in the saddle.

The streambed was dry, but Lares had said that as we went further west, we would find water in it. About midday, he was proven correct when we encountered a patch of mud. A little bit further on, and there was a trickle of water. When we reached a point where I felt there was enough that the mules could drink without lapping up as much mud as water, we stopped to let them slake their thirst.

Fiona slid from her saddle gracefully and led her mule to the stream. The animal lowered his head and began to drink. I dismounted, and my mount and the pack mule followed suit. Fiona walked a bit upstream from them and knelt down, cupping water in her hands and splashing it on her face.

The terrain was rocky and jumbled. There were a few scrubby bushes and the occasional stunted tree marking the course of the stream. The sun beat down on us from a cloudless sky.

"This heat is relentless," Fiona said as she stood. "How far until we reach the hill Elissa indicated?"

"Two more days after today," I said.

"Do you think anyone is following us?"

"An excellent question," I mused. "I suppose we'll find out eventually."

"Sylvaris hasn't given you any indication?"

"He has not. He's still paying attention, that much I can tell you. It seems he's never left me alone since you arrived at my door."

"What is his motivation?" Fiona asked. "None of the relics rumored to be part of the Hoard are his."

"He let me know back in Jenestra that he does not want Kravyna's people to regain her spear. While his only motive might be to tweak Kravyna's nose, I suspect others of the minor gods feel the same way about the spear. If we find Calithra's lute and Korath's hammer, and return them to their orders, then those two gods will owe a huge debt to Sylvaris, as will Eldryne. What I haven't been able to figure out is where the major gods stand on this."

"Non-interference, assistance to both sides," Fiona said. "They're staying neutral."

"For now. But if several of the minor gods are opposed to Kravyna's order regaining the spear, I wonder if the major gods may weigh in if we find it."

"Meaning?"

"I don't know," I said. "If you look at it as a game of chess, with Sylvaris on one side and Kravyna on the other, you and I are just two of the pieces on the board. Calithra and Korath, and Lysmera, I think, are on Sylvaris's side. Eldryne is sitting and watching, dismayed at the trouble she's caused and not knowing what to do about it. The other minor gods and the majors are paying attention as well, but not openly declaring a preference. That may change as the game plays out."

Feeling hungry, I retrieved some jerky for us to gnaw on. Fiona looked at it skeptically. She'd never eaten jerky before.

"Break off a piece and start chewing," I suggested. "It will take a few minutes to soften up, but it's nourishing."

We remounted after the mules had their fill and continued heading west. Fiona worked her way through the piece of jerky I'd given her. She didn't complain, so I took that as a good sign.

The landscape around us grew rougher. We ran into the occasional boulder or rocky outcropping that forced us to dismount and pick our way around carefully. As we continued, the trickle of the stream grew ever so slightly. As the sun dipped lower ahead of us and started to paint the rocks in orange and red, I stopped at the next open space we encountered.

"We'll make camp here tonight," I said.

On our journey over the pass from Tallesin to Lenoa, the priests-militant had set up our tent. Fiona had been paying attention, though, and was ready to offer assistance to me as I needed it. We managed to pitch camp and get the mules watered and fed in a reasonably efficient manner.

Dinner for us was more jerky with a dessert of dried fruit. I sat on the ground, and Fiona placed herself between my legs, leaning back against my chest. Darkness fell, and the night grew chilly quickly. Fiona shivered.

"I find it difficult to believe that, as hot as it was today, it is now cold," she said.

"That's the way of things in the desert," I said, wrapping my arms around her chest. "No clouds to hold the heat. When the sun goes down, it cools quickly. I'm sorry we can't have a fire, but there isn't enough wood around to keep one going."

"Then I suppose you will need to warm me up," she said as she stood, tugging me gently with her hand toward the tent.

The next day was hot, dry, and difficult. The terrain grew more inhospitable even as the stream we were following became slightly more robust. More and more often, we needed to thread our way through the rocks before being able to follow the watercourse.

The sun beat down on us like Korath's hammer. The dry air evaporated our sweat the instant it appeared. In the places where we stopped for water, Fiona and I splashed as much on ourselves as we drank, soaking our shirts to provide a cooling respite until they dried.

"This land feels as though it was forsaken by the gods," Fiona said at one point. "No farms, no villages, not much is able to grow away from the streambed—it's all just rocks and dust. Perhaps that is why Torsten chose this area as the resting place of his Hoard. The ground we've covered has convinced me that we will not find chests of gold and jewels. It would be too difficult to carry them through this wilderness."

"I agree. There's no way a wagon train made it through here. The stream provides just enough to keep us watered, but it would not support a large group. They'd drink it dry."

"What if we reach the hill Elissa indicated and find nothing?" she asked.

"It's possible," I admitted. "A thousand years have passed. A rockslide could have completely covered the entrance. I suppose we'll find out, though…"

"Though, what?"

"Sylvaris delights in pranks. From the very beginning, I have wondered if he jumped into this solely for the purpose of getting the minor gods stirred up for what would turn out to be no reason."

"Is he that cruel?"

"Cruel? No. Mischievous, yes."

"It would be cruel to toy with the two of us in this way. And how does that explain the palimpsest? And Elissa's calculations?"

"It doesn't," I admitted. "And as far as his cruelty, he's left me in the lurch a few times, but only when he judged I could extricate myself without his assistance. He's never been that mean-spirited, just … playful."

When we reached a small ledge blocking our way late in the day, I noticed the stream flowed over the center of it. If it had been a sheer drop, it would have been a tiny waterfall. As it was, the water had carved a shallow declivity. I had a good feeling we might find a small pool on the other side.

We dismounted and picked our way up and around. When we reached the top, I was delighted to learn I had been correct in my guess. It was about ten feet across. When I reached the edge and looked down, it seemed about five feet deep. The water was completely clear.

"Let's pitch camp here," I said. "When we finish, we can take a swim as a reward."

It was the quickest we'd ever set things up. In less than a half-hour, the tent was up, the mules were fed and watered, and Fiona and I were stripping off our clothes. I found a place where we could enter and exit the water and pointed it out to her. She stepped in, sighing as she felt the cool water embrace her.

"It's perfect," she said with a sort of moan. "Cool, but not cold. Refreshing."

I followed her in and learned her assessment was correct. It was just right. Of course, I couldn't resist the temptation to assist Fiona in helping wash away the dried sweat from her body, and she was happy to provide the same service for me. I couldn't help but notice that the olive tint to her skin was diminished, and it was returning to its previous golden glow.

Before things escalated, however, she climbed out of the water. Ever practical, she pulled out dirty clothing from our saddlebags and started tossing it to me. Together, we rinsed all of our things out and set them on the rocks to dry. By the time the air turned chilly, we were able to dress again.

33

Well past midday, we reached the hill Elissa had indicated. Hill might have worked for map nomenclature, but it was not an accurate description. It was a rocky crag nearly two hundred feet higher than everything else surrounding it.

We set up the tent next to the stream at the closest point to it. A part of me wanted to run over immediately and begin looking for the cave, but the day was fading. Tomorrow would give us more time and better light.

"Dexter, I am not god-touched the way you are, but, in the past, I believe Eldryne has communicated with me, sending me a feeling of certainty," Fiona said that night when we retired to our bedrolls. "I have that feeling now. It's a quiet, deep sense of knowing I have found the answer."

Her chin was on my chest, her fingers idly tracing the paths of some of my scars. My hand was on her back, stroking her gently. I could feel every inch of where our bodies touched.

"We still need to find it," I said.

"We will. It's what happens afterward that concerns me. I doubt the Kravynans have given up."

"I suspect you're right. At some point, word will arrive that the *Fleur Amelie* and two other boats left Jenestra. They will realize that we slipped past them at one of the ports and will send riders south to find us. Our disguises won't help us. All they will ask about is a man and a woman heading south. They'll pick up our trail. I doubt they'd be able to track us after we left the road, but they won't need to. We will need to head for either Rhavella or Togranes, and they'll be waiting to intercept us."

"You told me that Catherine once advised you not to borrow trouble from tomorrow, Dex. I think that is sound counsel right now."

"You're right. Tomorrow will bring what it brings. For now, we're here."

"And here is a good place to be," she said, pressing her lips to mine.

We managed to tire one another out to the point where sleep took us despite our excitement over what we might find the next day. Morning came, and Fiona woke with the first of the sun's rays. Her movement roused me from sleep.

"Eat," she commanded. "We have a Hoard to find."

We left the mules at our camp and headed over to the crag on foot. We brought the notes and waterskins. It was a steep climb. We'd decided to begin at the top and work our way down, going level by level as much as the ground would allow us.

We zigzagged up the eastern side, the morning sun at our backs. There was no trail, and there were parts where I needed to help Fiona. Loose rock underfoot was always a concern. When we reached the top, we celebrated by catching our breath and having a drink of water.

"Now what?" Fiona asked.

"I think the smartest thing will be for me to descend about ten feet or so and work my way around. If I find an entrance, I'll holler, and you find a way of marking it up here. Once we're confident I've found all the possible cave entrances, we can take the next step."

"I feel left out," she said.

"I'm sorry. I just think it will be quicker for me to do the scouting."

"You're probably right, but I don't like doing my fair share."

"Your moment will come, Fiona."

I headed down the slope and started traversing. After one full circuit, I'd seen nothing, so I dropped down another ten feet. This time, on the north face, I found a cave entrance just below me. It had not been visible from above as there was a slight overhang. I climbed down and found I was able to crouch in the entrance. The whole time, I was shouting up to Fiona and telling her what I saw.

By the time I'd reached the bottom, I'd found two more entrances. One was big enough for me to stand. The other would require crawling on hands and knees. I climbed back up to consult with Fiona.

"Aren't you a mess?" she commented when I appeared.

It was true. I was covered with dust and dirt. All I could do was shrug my shoulders.

"I made a rough sketch of the three points where you found the entrances," she said. "It's late enough that we should wait to explore them tomorrow. Perhaps looking at the night sky will give us a better idea of which one to try first."

I agreed. The day's exertions had tired me out. Fortunately, I'd found an easier route to the bottom, and that was the path we followed to return to camp.

Fiona took charge of feeding and watering the animals while I rested. We ate a simple meal of jerky and dried fruit while we waited for the stars to appear. Fiona made us move so we were facing north and showed me her drawing—a circle with x's marking the cave entrances.

"Three caves, three relics," she muttered. "Did they split them up?"

"I don't think so, but that's just a hunch. Two of the entrances probably lead to nothing. But, and this is what worries me, I wonder if there are any traps."

"What sort of traps?"

"Physical and magical. The physical ones, like deadfalls or false floors, might not have survived all this time. Magical wards would. We'll also need a torch. I thought I saw some creosote bushes. Before we head out tomorrow, we'll need to cut some branches."

When the stars appeared, we tried to match the location of the constellations, particularly Aquila—the eagle—against the three compass points. Even factoring in precession, nothing lined up.

We gave up and retired into the tent. Fiona folded herself against me and drew my arm over her chest. She fell asleep quickly. I did not.

When the sun came up, I went to the shrubs I'd spotted earlier. They were indeed creosote bushes. I cut several lengths of branches. They would burn despite being green, but they would not last long. I brought the armful back to camp and tied the bundle with a leather thong. When we headed out, I brought my tinder pouch. Fiona brought the two jute sacks we'd used as our luggage earlier on the journey.

"I knew they would come in handy, so I kept them," she said. "We can carry the relics back with them."

"Brilliant," I said.

We climbed up the easier path I'd found the day before. When we reached the top we had a decision to make. I turned to Fiona.

"Which one?" I asked.

"I was hoping the constellations would give us a clue, but they did not," Fiona said. "The only thing I can think of is the line from the poem: 'The gods bow low/Before his Hoard.' You said the first cave would require you to walk in a stoop. That's bowing low. The poem didn't mention walking or crawling."

"That's as good a reason as any," I said cheerfully.

We reached the entrance. Once there, I took a branch from the bundle and arranged a small pile of tinder. I caught a park in it, blew gently, and a flame rose up. The tiny fire lasted just long enough for the tip of the branch to light with a sputter.

I took the flaming branch and went forward, bent in half. In the sputtering light, I looked carefully for any signs of traps. As I progressed slowly, I could sense the presence of divine numen ahead.

After fifteen feet, the ceiling rose, and I was able to stand. Fiona came when I told her the way was clear. When she arrived next to me, I handed the flaming branch to her.

"I'm pretty sure we guessed correctly. I can feel the presence of asomatous energy. It's getting stronger with every step."

"I don't feel anything."

"Perhaps you will when we're closer. Stay behind me—close but not too close. I need to be able to see, but if I trigger anything, I don't want you to be in danger."

"We're in this together, Dex."

"Yes, but I don't want us both to die," I retorted.

We moved through the cave slowly. The branch was getting close to the end, so I lit another from the bundle I'd brought. Fiona dropped the stub of the first, and we resumed moving forward. The presence of divine energy grew with each step.

"Dex!" she gasped. "Mykenan lettering!"

I stopped and allowed her to bring the torch closer. Sure enough, there were runes carved into what looked like blocks inserted into the rock wall. There were thirty-two, in four columns of eight.

"Does it say, 'Watch your head' or 'Beware of dog' or anything useful like that?" I joked.

"I think it's the alphabet," she replied, "or most of it. Mykenan had thirty-six letters, if I recall correctly."

"Oh."

I took two steps forward. Suddenly, I felt as though I was caught in a spider web. When I tried moving my arms and legs to free them, the bonds of whatever held them grew tighter.

"Fiona, stop!" I said calmly.

"What's wrong?"

"I can't move. I think I just found out the answer to my question about whether there are any traps."

"I can't see anything holding you," she said.

"Some sort of magical ward. I'll bet the letters you saw provide a way to release it."

Fiona's eyes widened in the torchlight. She glanced back at the runes. I wanted to urge her not to panic but knew that I'd be better off keeping my mouth shut.

"A puzzle," she said. "If we get the answer, it should set you free."

"That would be good."

"Well, the poem mentioned fourteens and threes. The three probably relates to the number of caves and the relics. Fourteen must play a part. Maybe select every fourteenth letter."

She moved to the runes and started counting quickly. She pressed the fourteenth, the twenty-eighth, then counted another fourteen, and so on, until she pressed the sixth rune. When she did, I felt as though my clothes were burning.

"Aie!" I yelped.

I looked and saw no evidence of fire, but I sure felt it. My clothing was untouched, and my skin appeared no different, but the pain was awful. In addition, the jerk of my head caused the bonds around it to tighten further.

"What's wrong?"

"When you pressed the sixth stone, it triggered something. I feel like I am being burned alive," I said through gritted teeth.

"I'm sorry," she said in a distressed tone.

"Don't be sorry," I said, my teeth clenched against the searing pain that enveloped my skin. "Be calm and intelligent. You'll figure this out."

I could see the lines of concentration on her forehead. She was muttering to herself. I was doing my best not to move, despite the agony. Every twitch caused the bonds around me to tighten. I was beginning to feel my chest becoming constricted.

"Fourteen, and three," she said. "Three, then fourteen. That must be it."

She started counting, pressing the runes. As she did, she kept looking over her shoulder toward me. When she reached the sixth, a new torture began.

"Arrgh!" I groaned, although I tried my best to suppress it.

"What now?" she cried out.

"I've never been flayed, but I'm pretty sure this is what it would feel like," I grunted.

It indeed felt as though my skin was being peeled off, strip by strip, beginning with my extremities. The peeling hurt tremendously, but the residual effect was excruciating. I tried my best not to move, but it was impossible. My body started to tremble, and each movement tightened my bonds. It was becoming increasingly difficult to breathe.

34

The branch she was holding was nearing its end. If it went out, Fiona would need to get the tinder pouch from me, which might snag her in the trap. On top of that, I doubted she would be able to kindle a flame.

"Fiona, light a new branch," I grunted. "Quickly."

"Right," she said, and fumbled, extracting a new branch from the bundle she'd dropped on the floor of the cave.

She managed to light it before the flames of the old one reached her hand. She dropped the stub, and it guttered out on the floor a minute later. I could see the distress on her face. She kept glancing over at me.

"Numbers didn't work, Fiona. Try something else," I suggested, each word a gasp.

"Eagle? No. Not enough letters. Hoard? Not enough," she said, then paused as a thought came to her. "Could it be that simple?"

She searched the runes, then pressed six of them as she identified the letters she sought. When she touched the sixth, the pain stopped, and I was released. I fell to my hands and knees. Fiona laughed with delight but stopped suddenly and rushed to me.

"What was the answer?" I croaked.

"Torsten," she said.

"That's seven letters."

"The Mykenans had a letter for 'st.' There were a couple of other combined consonants and diphthongs," she explained.

"Well, it worked," I said, rising slowly to my feet with her help.

The phantom pain of the magical ward still echoed in my limbs. My skin felt raw, like I'd scrubbed vigorously with sand. Fiona looked at me with deep concern, the torch sputtering in her hand.

"Are you all right?" she asked.

"I will be," I said, forcing myself to smile, though from Fiona's reaction, it probably looked more like a grimace. "Torsten, eh? So much for brilliance. I think even I could have figured out that one."

"Then why didn't you?"

"I was a bit tied up," I said, then realized, "Are you teasing me? Remind me to punish you later."

"Promises, promises," she said.

"Give me the branch. I'll take the lead again. I hope there aren't any other traps, but better for me to be caught than you."

I took the flame and continued forward cautiously. The numen I'd felt earlier was stronger now. It was almost like an inaudible hum.

"The hair on my arms is standing up," Fiona whispered.

"Divine energy," I said. "We're getting closer."

I was in no hurry, inspecting the walls, floor, and ceiling for any sign of another trap. The only sounds were our breathing, the movement of our feet, and the occasional sputter from the oily wood of the burning branch I held.

We were heading slightly downward, and the air grew cooler. Fiona was right behind me now, her fingers resting lightly on my back. In addition, I could feel Sylvaris's excitement.

"Hand me a new branch," I asked.

Fiona pulled one from the bundle and placed it in my left hand. I lit it from the other one, and in the combined light of both, we could see a small chamber ahead. It appeared roughly circular, not much smaller than the living room of my flat.

We could not see what it held. The temptation was to rush forward, but something warned me against it. Here, close to the goal, would be an excellent spot for another trap.

I found it a half-step later. The stone under the forward half of my left foot gave way, bringing down with it an entire section of the floor. Fiona grabbed my shirt and tugged backward as I teetered briefly on the edge.

"Thank you," I gasped when I recovered some of my breath.

A gap of nearly six feet faced us. We would need to jump across. For me, it would be no problem, but I worried about Fiona.

"Give me another branch," I said.

She did, and I lit it. I tossed the first one across to make sure there was no obstacle that might prevent us from making the leap. It landed safely. In its light, we could see three pedestals. I knew those held the divine relics.

"I think I should go first," I suggested.

"Please," Fiona said, her voice betraying nervousness she was trying to suppress.

"I'm going to take a running start. Hold the torch. If the floor holds on the other side, toss me the rest of the branches, then make a running jump yourself. If it falls away underneath me, well … at least you'll know to turn back."

I handed her the torch, then took the two jute sacks from her and tucked them into my belt. I backed up three paces. Dashing forward, I leaped over the gap, landing on my feet. I staggered forward for two steps and stopped.

"Easy," I said, and bent over to pick up the still burning branch. "Toss me what's left of the sticks. You can jump holding the torch or drop it. Your choice."

Fiona dropped it and tossed the rest of the sticks over to me. They landed next to me and skittered past. I let them slide. I could see that Fiona was terrified.

"Fiona, dear, think of all you've been through to get to this point. The gods will not let you fail now. Take a running start and jump across."

She nodded nervously, turned and walked back four paces. With a visibly deep breath, she started toward the gap. She jumped, clearing it easily, and staggered into my free arm.

I caught her with a grunt, swinging my hand with the torch away. Fiona's fingers clutched at my shirt like talons, and her breath came in short gasps. For a heartbeat, we just stood there.

"I did it," she said quietly, amazed and triumphant at the same time. "Nothing in my life has ever been so scary."

"But you made it," I said. "And it's time to see what we came for."

I bent and picked up another branch and lit it from the one in my hand. The light blazed forth, and I handed it to Fiona. We could see the three pedestals, each waist-high and carved with Mykenan runes.

"I need to write these down," Fiona said suddenly. "We'll have Wouk translate them."

She pulled a scrap of foolscap from the pocket of her jacket and a pencil from her hair. I hadn't seen the pencil there in a long time and must have missed it earlier in my excitement. She handed her torch back to me and dropped to one knee in front of the nearest pedestal.

I stood right behind her, and I could feel the numen of the three objects in my chest. It was almost a vibration.

The pedestal in front of Fiona held a hammer; its head forged from a metal that gleamed like obsidian. The handle was wrapped in sweat-stained leather, seemingly untouched by the passage of time. On the next, in the center, lay a lute of exquisite craftsmanship, its wood gleaming with an ethereal glow. The third held a spear. It was shorter—a throwing spear, like a javelin. The wood of its shaft seemed blood red, and it had a leaf-bladed tip of what I guessed was razor sharpness. There was no dust on any of them.

Fiona moved from one pedestal to the next, copying the runes. Before moving, she double-checked to make sure she made no errors. When she finished, she tucked the paper back into her pocket and stuck the pencil in her hair.

"I find myself short of breath," she said. "This is amazing! We did it, Dex. We found Torsten's Hoard!"

"We did," I said. "Thanks to you finding hidden script on an otherwise unremarkable piece of vellum."

"Eldryne guided me. What now?"

"We take them to Rhavella," I said. "The lute and the hammer we deliver to the temples of Calithra and Korath. I'm not sure what to do about the spear. My guess is that Sylvaris will let me know what he wants me to do later."

"I'll lift the objects and put them in the bags," I said, pulling the two jute sacks from my belt and handing them to Fiona. "Just in case there are other magical wards protecting them."

"Do you think there will be?"

"Only one way to find out," I said as I reached for the lute.

The wood felt warm to my touch. It was clearly imbued with divine essence, which I could sense throughout my body. As I lifted it from the pedestal, nothing happened. I slid it carefully into the sack Fiona was holding open.

"That's one."

I then picked up the hammer. The asomatous energy felt different, but just as strong. It was not as heavy as it looked. I slid it into the second bag.

"The spear won't fit into the sacks," I said. "I'll just have to carry it and the hammer. Tuck the remaining branches under the arm you're using to carry the lute and hold the torch with the other."

"How will we get back?"

"We'll need to jump again. This time, you go first, then I'll toss you the lute and the hammer. I'll jump with the spear."

Fiona nodded nervously, and we headed back down the passage to the edge where it dropped away. I had her pull one of the few remaining branches from our bundle. After lighting it, I tossed it to the other side and dropped the nearly spent one on the floor next to me. I threw the other branches across also—well away from the flame.

"You've done this before," I encouraged Fiona. "Running start, then jump."

Fiona backed up two steps, took a deep breath, and charged forward. She cleared the gap easily, stumbling only slightly upon landing. She turned and came back toward the edge.

"I'm going to send the hammer over first. Don't worry if you don't catch it. I doubt it can be damaged."

Fiona nodded. I lobbed the bag with the hammer over. It landed with a dull thud.

"Now the lute," I said.

"Don't worry. I'll catch it," she said.

She did, snagging the sack cleanly out of the air. She moved everything out of the way. It was time for me to jump. I took three paces back and ran for the gap, making it across without difficulty. I picked up the bag with the hammer, and we headed back the way we came.

The magical ward was no longer active, and we walked past the spot without incident. We had only one unburnt branch remaining when we reached the point in the cavern where we could see light from the entrance. Bending over double, we returned to the outside air.

It was not yet midday. We worked our way down the side of the crag and returned to our little camp. Working together, we packed everything up and began heading back toward the road. We could get five hours or more behind us before stopping for the day.

"Tell me more about what we recovered," I asked that night.

"The lute and the hammer are inspirational in nature," Fiona explained. "It is said that when a gifted musician plays the lute, his or her skill is enhanced beyond their normal bounds, and that those who listen to its music are stimulated with new ideas. A painter who worked while hearing it being played would create a masterpiece. The hammer allows its user to shape metal as if it were soft, wet clay. Items forged by the hammer were said to be unbreakable. It cannot be used to create weapons; however, only tools."

"And the spear?"

"The spear is rumored to be aggressive and corrupting in its influence. It makes the user nearly unconquerable in battle, granting the one who wields it increased strength and quickness, but it comes with a physical and psychic toll. The legends vary. Some say that one who uses it will suffer lash-like wounds on their back, similar to being flogged. Others talk of physical disfigurement or premature aging. All are in agreement that repeated wielding of the spear infects the user with unquenchable blood lust."

"I can see why Sylvaris and the other gods might want it destroyed."

"You've been carrying it," she said. "What have you felt?"

"That sense of increased strength and speed is evident," I said. "I have not used it as a weapon, so the other things remain to be seen."

"I would urge you not to use it," she said.

35

"I can't believe we did it," Fiona said.

"Well, we're not finished yet, my dear," I cautioned. "We need to reach with Rhavella or Togranes, and I suspect the Kravynans will be waiting outside both."

"That's tomorrow's problem," she said as she rolled over on top of me. "Besides, you promised to punish me later. It's later."

"I did promise that, didn't I?" I said, then rolled over so I was on top.

I moved my hands quickly to her ribs. Earlier, I'd learned exactly where Fiona was ticklish, and I now exploited that knowledge without mercy. She shrieked and laughed and tried to squirm away until I finally relented.

Fiona lay there, gasping for breath, her face flushed, and her eyes sparkling with a mix of pretended outrage and delight. Our bedrolls were now a tangled mess, and our clothes were askew. She swatted at my arm.

"Unfair!" she protested.

"Well, you've gotten so much better at teasing me, I felt I needed to escalate your penalty."

"I couldn't breathe."

"I thought you liked it when I made you breathless."

"I do, but the usual way, please," she said, wrapping her arms around my neck and pulling me down into a kiss.

Fiona's stirring at sunrise woke me. She was already dressed, and I hurried to catch up. We sat on the ground and ate some more jerky and dried fruit before breaking camp.

For the next day and a half, we crossed that broken country until we reached the road. It seemed easier than it had when we headed out. Perhaps that was because we weren't going to be searching for an unknown hill. We did not stop where we found the pool. I think we were both eager to return to civilization, even with the threat that was undoubtedly waiting for us.

"Decision time," I said when we reached the road. "North to Rhavella, or south to Togranes?"

"Which do you think is safer?"

"I have a feeling the Kravynans will be waiting outside either city. The Order of Sylvaris presumably has a larger presence in Rhavella because it's a port, but I'm not counting on their help. I would love to have it, but we can't rely on it."

"Perhaps Sister Mira alerted the temple to keep a watch on the Kravynans?"

"That's a nice thought, but I suspect that even with all the priests-militant gathered, there would be more disciples of Kravyna. And the priests-militant have caravans to shepherd between Rhavella and Togranes and other towns."

"Rhavella is in the direction we want to go. Let's head north."

We reached Hella not long after. The innkeeper welcomed us and was delighted to prepare a bath. After we were clean, we headed down to a delicious spicy lamb dinner.

"I was getting tired of jerky," Fiona admitted. "It was not awful, but it isn't real food. Warm, fresh bread, meat that I can chew without gnawing it to softness first, a few vegetables, wine—I missed this."

"It makes you appreciate it more, doesn't it?"

"In Harkiss, food was … a necessity—a sometimes unwelcome interruption to work, attending to the needs of the body. People did not linger over meals. They ate and left. Of course, the food was not very good. There was no reason to savor it. Since leaving the temple, I've discovered that there are many different and enjoyable aspects to meals: the way the right wine can complement the flavors of a dish, how good company can make even a simple offering more enjoyable, and how dining can help build anticipation for the rest of the evening."

"And what do you anticipate?"

"A comfortable bed instead of the hard ground, and your arms around me."

We continued north from Hella. Every mile increased my anticipation of trouble. The lute and hammer were in our saddlebags. The spear was tucked under the fender of my saddle. I scanned ahead of us continually for signs of a waiting group of Kravyna's disciples.

By the time we reached Bidde, Fiona's skin and hair had returned to their normal appearance. The hair dye had washed out gradually, and the last bath two stops before had dismissed the last of it. She hadn't said anything, but I caught her looking in the mirror with a smile.

Over dinner in Bidde, I noticed she was on edge. We hadn't seen any sign of the Kravynans. Tomorrow, we would, unless they'd given up hope of regaining the spear, which I thought incredibly unlikely. I guessed they would intercept us out of sight of the city gates, not wanting the city watch to interfere. Fiona and I had avoided talking about it, but we were both well aware that every mile brought us closer.

"Is there anything I can say to help you calm down?" I asked after we returned to the room.

"Nothing you can say," she replied as her emerald dress slid to the floor, "but something you can do."

I was out of bed before Fiona, for perhaps the first time. I could tell she was awake, but lingering in the sheets, which she'd never done before. Sitting next to her on the mattress, I reached over and stroked her hair.

"You'll have the lute and the hammer," I said. "When we encounter the Kravynans, you are to run for the city gates as fast as your mule will move. I'll have the spear, and I'll make sure they see it. They won't have any reason to detain you."

"I'm not leaving you," she protested, sitting up.

"Yes, you will. You must. I don't know what will happen, but I have a strange confidence. Get to the gates. Seek refuge in the temple of Sylvaris. Have them send word to the temples of Calithra and Korath. I will join you when I can."

"What if you can't?"

"That's up to the gods," I said, "and I don't think your assistance in what will happen will influence the outcome, unless you linger and the Kravynans gain control of the lute and hammer. That seems to me to be something to avoid."

"But we've done this together," she complained.

"I left you behind when I recovered the palimpsest, for much the same reason I want you to ride for the gates when we encounter the Kravynans. I have skills that you lack. By the same token, I would never have seen the scripto inferior on the vellum. Our talents are complementary; they don't mimic one another."

"I suppose you're right," she said with a sigh as she rose slowly. "I don't have to like it; I just need to do it."

"You've just described ninety percent of life, my dear," I said with a thin smile.

We dressed, packed our things, and headed down to eat. Fiona had no appetite. When we went to saddle the mules, she dragged her feet in the manner we'd coached her to do when playing the role of a drudge. I would have laughed except I was sure she would not see the humor. Perhaps I would tell her later.

Before we mounted, she darted over and threw her arms around my neck. She pulled my head down and gave me a ferocious kiss. When she released me, the golden skin of her face had a red tint.

We set off, heading north. Both of us were looking ahead, scanning for trouble. Just past midday, we spotted it. We had just crested a small rise. On the other side, a group of eight riders, mounted on horses, blocked the road. Their shaved heads gleamed in the sun.

"Fiona, stop right here for a moment," I said quietly, "I will pull them to the side. When I do, ride for the gates of the city. They want the spear more than anything."

"Dex—" she pleaded, tears welling in her eyes.

"It will be all right," I said. "When they clear the road to follow me, go."

I withdrew the spear from under the saddle's fender and held it up so the Kravynans would see it. Holding it up, I could feel the power inherent in the blood-red relic. If I were linked to Kravyna the way I was to Sylvaris, I imagined I would feel invincible.

Sylvaris let me know that he approved of my bravado. Nudging my mule, I left the road heading into a fallow field. The leader of the Kravynans directed his group to intercept me.

"Oy! Thief!" he shouted in rough Bour. "Give us what's ours, and we'll make your end quick. We might even go gentle on the woman."

"You want it? Come take it, if you can." I hollered back in his language.

The distance between his group and me closed rapidly. I wasn't trying to run away. I only wanted to give Fiona an opening to get past. She began moving toward the city, and none of the Kravynans noticed. I reined in and allowed the Kravynans to approach. They came in a semicircle, trying to surround me.

"Sylvaris," I prayed silently, "be with me. Help me drag this out to ensure Fiona's safety."

He sent a feeling of reassurance. This was an emotion I had not felt from him since the earliest days after my arrival in Meropan as an ignorant farm boy. He would lend me his eloquence, and I would use it to buy Fiona as much time as possible.

Beyond them, I could see Fiona racing toward the city walls under a clear blue sky. The Kravynans only had eyes for me, or, more accurately, the spear I brandished in my right hand. I just needed to maintain their focus for a few more minutes, until Fiona was closer to the gates and the city watch.

"Gentlemen," I called out, still speaking in Bour and noticing that my voice carried an unusual degree of resonance. "Or should I say, disciples of the ever-bellicose Kravyna?"

"Hand it over, thief," the leader growled. "It doesn't belong to you."

"It probably irritates you to no end that your sacred weapon is in the hands of a servant of the god of tricks. I'm god-touched, you know, and Sylvaris tells me that he can make good use of such a mighty weapon. Your simple minds cannot even begin to comprehend the power this spear holds. Did your master send you out like obedient hounds? They give you a scent, and you pursue it mindlessly until you capture and kill something, or drop dead from exhaustion?"

The leader's face twisted in a snarl. He didn't like being compared to a dog. I had plenty more, and worse, that I could give him.

"You're right to rein in, my friend, and keep your distance. I am no fox you're chasing. With this spear in my hand, I am the mightiest lion on the savannah, and jackals like you would do well to fear me."

"A mighty lion on a rented mule? I think not."

His men chuckled darkly behind him. Their swords were all drawn, glinting in the sun of this cloudless summer day. It was eight against one, and my brain was trying to tell me that I had no chance against these odds. The spear, however, and Sylvaris, were telling me a different story.

Sylvaris was enjoying my cheekiness, I could tell. Beyond the men, I could see Fiona receding in the distance. Even if they turned now and galloped toward her, she would make the gate.

"You're right," I said with a half-bow. "A mule is no mount for a lion such as I. But it is not the mule that makes me mighty. It is this treasure of treasures that I hold in my hand. You know I killed members of your order in Jenestra who tried to stop me from finding this spear, and I did it with an ordinary rapier. Sylvaris is itching for a chance to see what I could do with this instrument of lethality."

I twirled the spear experimentally. The thing was perfectly balanced. I hadn't worked with a spear like this in over a decade, but I still knew how to handle one.

"Hand it over, thief, and I promise to kill you quickly. That's the best offer you'll get from us. Your other choices involve a great deal of pain."

"Thief? Yes, I stole something, but not this spear. I think I stole the favor of your goddess. How she must despair right now, watching this! Eight of you, and one of me, and all we're doing is flapping our lips and not fighting."

Sylvaris sent me a warning then. I remembered Fiona telling me about the properties associated with these three relics. According to different legends, the Spear of Kravyna made its wielder near-unconquerable, but it exacted a physical toll on the user.

I had been goading these men to fight, but Sylvaris was letting me know that I might be better off easing the tension. Fiona was well away by now. The leader of the group facing me looked as though steam was about to pour from his ears.

"But Sylvaris is also the god of trade," I said, "of merchants and commerce. Surely we can reach an equitable arrangement, where you offer me something of value in exchange for this priceless relic?"

The eloquence Sylvaris lent me when I said this caused the thick-necked leader to actually ponder it for a moment. It was only a moment. Then the scowl returned to his face.

"You will not leave this field alive, trickster," he snarled. "Hand over the spear and kneel before me, and I will remove your head quickly and cleanly. That is the bargain I offer you."

"Or?"

"Or we have our sport with you, and leave you alive and suffering, hanging on the steps of our temple, a living testament to what happens to those who insult our goddess and our order."

"Utred?" one of his men spoke up.

"What?" the leader snapped.

"Riders coming. Woman's gone."

Utred whirled in the saddle, looking over his shoulder toward Rhavella, his shaved head gleaming in the sun. There was no sign of Fiona, but there was a cloud of dust. The city watch? Priests-militant? It didn't matter. Time was running out for the Kravynans, and that meant it was running out for me as well.

"Enough!" Utred shouted. "Now! For the goddess!"

He jammed his spurs into the flanks of his horse. With a squeal, it reared and bolted toward me. His men followed his lead a split-second later.

I was one against eight, on a rented mule against trained horses. My mount brayed in fright and tried to turn and run. I cringed. Eight blades would carve me to shreds. Instead, there was an instant of searing heat, then darkness.

36

The first thought I had was of being trapped underwater. I could see light above me, and a voice in my head told me to swim, swim as hard as I could before I drowned. My limbs felt as though they were made of lead, my lungs were burning, but I struggled, trying to reach the surface before I was overcome. My head broke through, and I gasped for air.

I was not in water. I was in a bed, sitting bolt upright. Fiona had grasped my wrists. What was she doing here? Where was I?

"Easy, Dex. Easy," she urged soothingly.

I blinked, trying to focus. It was dark except for the candles in the room. On the wall past my feet, I saw the crossed keys sigil of Sylvaris. From that, I reckoned we were in the temple.

My body ached as though I'd been rolled down a steep, bumpy hill in a barrel. There was a ringing in my ears. My memory returned in flashes … Utred's roar, the Kravynans charging, my mule braying, then … what?

"Fiona," I croaked, my throat raw and dry, "What happened?"

"I did not see," she said. "I rode for the gates as fast as I could. The city watch saw what was happening on the plain but would not interfere. They said that outside the walls was not their problem. After pleading with them to no avail, I decided to head to the temple of Sylvaris. I ran into Sister Mira before I'd traveled a block, and she had half a dozen armed men mounted behind her."

"Priests-militant," I said.

"Yes. When I told her what was happening, they galloped off. Sister Mira brought me here. They brought you in not long after."

"What happened? The Kravynans were about to attack me, and then … I don't know anything after that."

"They told me a bolt of lightning struck the spear out of a clear blue sky," she said. "I heard the crack of thunder. It killed your mule and knocked you and the Kravynans unconscious. The priests-militant arrived just as they were recovering. The Kravynans were in no condition to fight, so they ran."

"A bolt of lightning?"

"Out of a cloudless sky," Fiona confirmed. "Seems pretty obvious who sent it."

"Zoryn."

"Clearly. The priests picked your body up and brought you back. That was three days ago."

"Three days?"

"Yes. I have been waiting here for you to wake up … if you would. The sisters and brothers of Vionelle who attended you were not certain you would."

"Three days? I've been asleep that long?"

"If you were sleeping, it would have been less frightening," she said. "You were near death. Your pulse was weak and slow, your skin was ashen and clammy, and your breathing was labored. How do you feel?"

"Weak. Battered. My ears are ringing."

"You were very pale, but the color is returning to your face now. You look almost normal."

"Almost?"

"You have a streak of white hair on your right temple, about as big around as your thumb. It's white from the root to the tip."

I reached up to feel. It felt like the rest of my hair. There was no difference in the texture.

"A souvenir, I reckon," I said. "At least it's not a scar."

"You joke," she complained, "but it's not funny. I have been by your side for three days, not knowing whether you would wake."

"Thank you. I don't mean to make light of—"

"Yes, you do, Dex. It's your way. Don't worry. I will punish you for your cheekiness later when you are more recovered."

"I'll look forward to it. What happened to the spear?"

"The priests-militant found only one fragment—the metal tip. It is bent and twisted, but they brought it back."

"Does it still radiate with divine energy?"

"The priests who retrieved it say it does. Whether it is diminished from before, they would not know. You would be able to tell."

"It is still dangerous, then. And the Kravynans will remain a threat until it is destroyed."

"It is safe now, in the vault below the temple. Mother Robin, the head priestess here, has assured me of that. She doubts the Kravynans would be so foolhardy as to attempt to assault the temple, especially after witnessing Zoryn's intervention."

"That does not mean they've given up entirely. And the lute? The hammer?"

"The heads of the temples of Calithra and Korath came to retrieve them. They are thrilled, as you can imagine. They have already thanked me profusely and will probably be here soon to thank you as well, now that you are back among the living. They plan to send them to the seats of their orders, probably with great ceremony. I imagine that if you and I accompanied them, we would be feted quite grandly."

"All the more reason not to," I said.

"I would agree. I have no desire to be the focus of a public spectacle."

"I wonder what we're supposed to do with the tip of the spear?" I mused.

"Today? Nothing," Fiona said firmly. "You must recover your strength. Right now, I doubt you can even get out of bed without help."

"I wasn't planning on addressing the issue immediately."

"It might not even be your problem to solve," Fiona continued. "Zoryn seems to have a direct interest. Perhaps his people will handle it."

"You're right," I said.

It was then that I realized how drawn Fiona's face was. Her golden complexion was marred by deep circles under her eyes. I had been concentrating on how I felt, but this had also taken a toll on her.

"How long has it been since you slept?" I asked gently.

"I've slept."

"Where? In that chair?"

"I could not bear to leave you."

"The danger is passed, I think. Come. Let me hold you," I said as I wiggled to make room for her next to me.

Fiona lifted her legs onto the mattress and lowered her head to my chest. She threw her right arm and leg over mine, and I folded my arms around her. Her hair smelled of jasmine and sandalwood. She relaxed with a sigh that I felt but did not hear.

"I was not ready to say goodbye yet," she murmured.

Within minutes, her breathing was deep and regular. I continued to hold her, pondering what had happened. That the tip of the spear remained troubled me. I wondered how it survived Zoryn's lightning. Sylvaris was silent on the matter.

For the first time since Fiona had appeared at my door in Tallesin, I did not feel the tingle on the back of my neck that indicated his interest. I immediately worried that Zoryn's bolt had severed my connection with the clever god. If that were the case, would I be free to live my life on my own terms instead of at his whims? Perhaps it was merely an indication that this task he'd set for me was complete. Either way, the absence troubled me.

I did my best to put it out of my mind and simply enjoy the feel of Fiona in my arms. My body still ached, and my ears still heard a sound like a chorus of cicadas on a hot summer night.

I wondered what might have happened if I had surrendered the spear to Utred and his disciples. Would Zoryn have acted? And how much would the Order of Kravyna blame me for the spear's destruction? Would I need to fear them everywhere I went for the rest of my life?

These and other troubling thoughts plagued me as I held Fiona. Eventually, my mind grew too tired to continue finding new things about which to worry. At some point, I fell asleep as well.

37

Fiona's stirring from where she'd slept on me woke me. Through the window, I could see that the sun must have just risen. She certainly had an uncanny ability to rise at the break of day.

She was still on my chest but looking up at me. Her long-lashed eyes gave me one of her slow owl-blinks. I had to smile. She had not done that in weeks. Her face wrinkled slightly.

"We should try to get you out of bed today, Dex. While I ordinarily enjoy the smell of you, you have grown a bit pungent. I will ask Mother Robin about a bath for you. Stay here. Don't try to get up."

Fiona hustled out of the room. After she left, I realized that I hoped she thought about food. I was starving all of a sudden.

With daylight available, I could see the room's interior more clearly. It was a simple chamber, not unlike those in other temples of Sylvaris. On the whole, I'd prefer a nice inn, but that might be an issue if the order of Kravyna was still looking for me.

I felt as though I'd been dragged behind a horse, but without the scrapes and cuts. My ears were still ringing, and I had a headache, but I guessed I should consider myself lucky to be alive. Surviving being hit by a bolt of lightning was something for which I should feel grateful.

Fiona returned in a few minutes, followed by a stout woman in the gray robes of the order. A silver pin with the crossed key sigil was on her chest, marking her as the head priestess of this temple. Behind her came a novice bearing a tray with a mug and bowl, both steaming.

"Good morning," Robin said. "Sister Fiona told us you were awake and reasonably coherent. Quite amazing."

"I was just reminding myself that I should be grateful."

"We brought some porridge and a cup of willow bark tea with honey and lemon," Robin continued. "Willow bark tastes nasty, but it does help with aches and pains. The honey and lemon should make it less unpleasant to drink. We mixed some peaches in with the porridge. They're in season right now. My recommendation would be to choke the tea down and then hope the taste of the peaches makes you forget how horrid the tea was."

"Thank you. That sounds wonderful."

"We're also preparing water for a bath. You'll find that it gets hot later in the day, so I thought tepid rather than warm. Sister Fiona said that she will assist you."

"That will be fine."

"From what Vionelle's people said, you should not push yourself too hard, too quickly. Not many people survive being hit by lightning, and they don't have a good idea of how long it will take you to recover. All I can say is that Zoryn spared your life for some reason."

"I was thinking the same thing."

"The heads of the local temples of Korath and Calithra would like to visit you. Do you think you will be able to entertain visitors later this morning?"

"If I can eat, bathe, and change clothes, I think that will be perfectly fine. Fresh air and sunshine will probably help as well, even if it is hot out."

"Very well. Sister Fiona, you're in charge. Let us know what you need."

Mother Robin and the novice left. Fiona took the mug of tea and offered it to me. I gave it a sniff first, then took an exploratory sip to see how hot it was. Finding that it wouldn't scald my tongue, I decided to drink it as quickly as I could. Robin had been correct. The lemon and honey helped some but could not counter the bitter taste of the willow bark.

As soon as I handed the mug back, Fiona offered me the bowl and a spoon. The bowl held thick oat porridge with large chunks of peaches. I scooped some up and made sure I included some of the fruit. I decided a few more bites would effectively banish the taste of the tea.

While I was shoveling breakfast into my mouth, some acolytes brought in a small round tub and began filling it with water. They finished with that chore about the same time I ate my last bite. I handed the bowl back to Fiona and swung my legs over the edge of the bed.

Fiona offered me her arm to steady myself. I was pleased to learn that I felt no dizziness as I pulled myself up to a standing position. My body ached, but I was not wobbly. Keeping my hand on Fiona's arm, I walked slowly to the tub. I stopped there, and Fiona quickly set about stripping my clothes off, then helped me step into the water.

The tub was too small to sit in. Fiona thought quickly and retrieved the mug that had held the tea. She dipped it into the water and began dumping it on my head and over my body. When I was thoroughly wet, she took a cloth and applied some soap, then started washing me.

"Nothing for your hair," she said. "We'll just try to rinse it out as best we can."

I just stood still, enjoying the feel of her hands on my body. The willow bark was starting to take effect, and my head, especially, was getting clearer. When she finished washing, she used the mug to rinse me off. Offering her hand to steady me, she allowed me to step out of the tub where she dried me and combed my hair. She then assisted me into clean clothes.

"Bed? Or chair?" she asked when we finished.

"Chair," I said, "but are there more comfortable ones to be found?"

"There are. Come with me."

She led me slowly through the residential portion of the temple outbuilding to a veranda. It was situated so that it would remain in the shade all day. Wicker chairs were arranged along it.

"Perfect," I said, and sank carefully into one.

Fiona took the seat next to me. She clasped my hand and intertwined her fingers with mine. We sat and looked over the small courtyard in front of us.

"You look better," she said. "The color is back in your face. When they first carried you in, I thought … well, never mind what I thought."

"Ah! But no scars," I said.

"Your hair."

"Now that you mention it, I'd like to see it. Would you please get a mirror? I want to make sure it enhances my peculiar style of beauty."

She returned a minute later with a small hand mirror. I held it up and saw what had changed. From my right temple, starting from my scalp, in a swath about an inch wide, the hair was white down to the tip. My hair was on the long side for me. I tucked both sides back behind my ears.

"Remind me to get something to tie this mess back. What do you think?" I asked. "Does it enhance or detract?"

"It makes you look even more like a rogue," she said. "As though someone cracked you there with a wine bottle in a tavern brawl and that caused your hair to change color."

"That's certainly a much more believable story than what actually happened. It will certainly serve as a reminder not to play with toys that don't belong to me."

"Mister Falk? Sister Fiona?" a novice said as she approached.

"Yes?" Fiona replied.

"The heads of the temples of Korath and Calithra would like to speak with you, sir, and the head priest of the temple of Eldryne wishes to meet with you, Sister Fiona. If you'll come with me, sister."

Fiona flashed a look of concern and curiosity at me. I gave her what I hoped she would view as a reassuring smile. Fiona had done great service that reflected tremendous credit on the Eldrynes, and her reward had been to be cast out by the archpriestess. She followed the novice away into the main sanctuary.

When the novice returned, she brought two people in the robes of their orders. I struggled to my feet as they approached. One, a short, stocky woman, was wearing the dull gray of the order of Korath. The other, a tall, thin man, was in the teal of Calithra. They both bowed before me.

"Mr. Falk, my name is Gretchen Wilmer, and I am the head priestess of the temple of Korath here in Rhavella. I would also like to present Jacob Cerule, my counterpart in the temple of Calithra. We owe you and Miss Magellan a debt that can be repaid by neither coin nor craft."

"We knew of the legends," Cerule said, "but that is all we thought they were. The stories regarding Torsten were assumed to be amalgamations of the deeds of a variety of pre-twilight warlords, enhanced and embellished for dramatic effect. The tales of the sacred relics were considered to be just as much works of fiction. We knew of the myths but never dared to hope that such things ever existed. Thank you."

"You are welcome, of course," I said. "But it is Sister Fiona who noticed hidden script on an unremarkable piece of old vellum. She, spurred by Eldryne, started this quest."

"And we have already thanked her profusely," Wilmer said.

"We wished to ask you," Cerule continued, "what is Sylvaris's aim in this matter?"

"I cannot speak for the order," I said. "I have no office or rank within it."

"But Sister Fiona told us you are god-touched," Wilmer said. "Surely, Sylvaris has given you some indication—"

"As far as Korath and Calithra, I'm sure Sylvaris will enjoy them being in his debt," I replied, "and even more so in the case of Eldryne. He also gave me the impression that he and perhaps others of the gods would prefer that the Spear of Kravyna not fall into their hands. That is the limit of my understanding."

"That would certainly seem to be the case, based on Zoryn's actions," Cerule said.

"And yet Zoryn did not destroy the spear entirely," I said. "The metal tip still survives, although I am told it is warped and twisted. Do you have any idea what should be done with it?"

The two of them looked at one another, not expecting my question. After a moment, both shook their heads. I frowned.

"Sylvaris has not communicated with you regarding this?" Cerule asked.

"Not yet," I said. "But I just regained consciousness last evening. Perhaps he is allowing me to recover a bit before giving me more instructions."

I saw Fiona appear behind them. They noticed the shift of my gaze and turned themselves. Fiona approached, her steps quick and purposeful. There was excitement in her eyes, but I doubted it registered with our guests.

"Fiona, may I present—"

"We've had the pleasure," Wilmer said.

"You'll have to pardon me, Mother Wilmer, Father Cerule, but it is time for Mr. Falk to rest," Fiona said. "He only woke last night, and he needs to regain his strength."

"Of course, sister," Cerule said with a bow. "We merely wanted to express our gratitude."

"And that of our orders. We brought something for each of you, as a token of thanks," Wilmer said as she and Cerule each withdrew two small leather pouches from their robes and offered them to us.

I took one from each of them. Inside each little leather sack was a talisman, bearing the sigil of their order. They were made of pure gold.

"Those signify that you are friends of our orders," Cerule said. "If you ever find yourself in need of assistance, anywhere in the world, show your talisman at one of our temples, and our people will assist you in any way they can."

The two of them then bowed, first to me, then to Fiona, and departed. As I watched them go, I wondered what had happened with the Eldryne that caused Fiona to dismiss them. It would obviously wait as Fiona urged me to stand and return inside.

"What?" I whispered as we headed back to my chamber.

"I just met with Father Bartholomew," she said, after she closed the door to my chamber behind us.

38

"Father Bartholomew was a font of information," she continued. "He apologized on behalf of the order and declared on his own authority that I was reinstated."

"That's wonderful, and you certainly never deserved to be cast out," I said. "But does he have the authority to—"

"A consensus of Eldryne has been requested," she said. "Eldryne has communicated to the members who are god-touched that Septima Thoran has been rejected as archpriestess of the order. She also communicated that I was a true and loyal servant of the goddess and should be reinstated and treated with the utmost respect."

"As is only right," I said with a smile. "This is wonderful news."

"There's more. He offered me a place in his temple."

"Here in Rhavella?"

"Yes, but as we spoke, it seems the best opportunity for me is actually in Jenestra. He has been in communication with the head priestess of the temple there, and the brother who has been doing their mission work, traveling that area of North Gaugan and finding people—"

"Like the one who spotted your intelligence and ability," I said.

"Exactly. The brother who has been doing that from Jenestra is older and has developed rheumatism. She needs a replacement. When I mentioned my interest in mission work, Father Bartholomew became very excited. He left immediately to write Mother Erma. Apparently, it is difficult to find Eldrynes who would rather travel. Most prefer to stay in the cloister—"

"As you did," I pointed out.

"Yes. Most prefer the company of books and scrolls to people, but the order needs people to go out into the world and seek those with a thirst for knowledge. It's more than just recruiting new acolytes, though. It's about spreading the love of learning and keeping my eyes and ears open for any ancient texts that may exist."

"You would need to learn to speak Lutetian," I remarked.

"Which I am eager to do," she said.

For the first time since being struck by Zoryn's thunderbolt, I felt Sylvaris on the nape of my neck. I did not welcome it, for he was conveying the same sense of certainty I'd felt when I realized that Agatha's path led in a different direction from mine. Fiona and I would part. I would return to Tallesin alone.

The thought hit me with the force of one of Varak's blows with his waster. Fiona's excitement about her future—mission work, traveling, spreading knowledge—aligned on a path separate from mine. Our courses had converged for this quest, but we were nearing the end, and with it, the closing moments of our passionate journey approached.

"Fiona, that's wonderful," I said, more calmly than I felt. "You'll be brilliant at it, and you'll pick up Lutetian in no time."

"You are not lying to me," she said, holding my gaze, "but your voice carries a hint of melancholy. I feel the same sadness amid my excitement about my new role. I came to you to find a missing piece of parchment. What I found, what you showed me, was the world outside my dusty tomes. Passion, physical pleasure—even in such things as meals, excitement, terror, and also seasickness— were all new to me. I am richer for these months. The person I am today is not the one who knocked on your door."

She had changed, but I had learned from her as well. Agatha had opened my eyes to the fierce pull of love. Catherine had shown me the fire of passion. In showing Fiona the pleasures of love, I had shared in her joy of discovery.

"I do not look forward to our parting," I said, "but our quest is not quite finished. The remnant of the spear remains. We are meant to do something with it. Until then, we share the same path."

"I'm glad for every day with you, Dex, but I wish Zoryn had destroyed the entire thing at once. Father Bartholomew believes that Zoryn's intervention was an important sign. The major gods stay out of the squabbles between the minors, but the spear threatened to upset the balance of things. Father Bartholomew thinks we should dedicate the tip to Zoryn at his temple here in Rhavella, offered as tribute to the god who shattered it, and a reminder to all the gods, major and minor, that Zoryn remains the most powerful of them all, except for Thalorix."

"That makes sense," I said. "Dedicating it to him, I assume he will neutralize whatever power remains in it. But getting it there … the Kravynans will try to prevent it from happening."

"Father Bartholomew said the same. He met with Mother Robin after we finished speaking. Maybe she has some ideas."

"We'll speak with her."

"In the meantime, we both need to rest. You're looking pale again, and I'm feeling the lack of sleep from the previous three days."

We stretched out on the narrow bed in my chamber. Fiona nestled in my arms. I wondered how many more times I would get to hold her close.

A knock on the door woke us not too long after. A priest and priestess of Vionelle entered. We sat up quickly, Fiona blushing scarlet. They poked and prodded me, asking all sorts of questions about how I was feeling. In the end, they told me there was nothing wrong with me that rest wouldn't cure. I could have figured that out without interrupting my nap.

Still, it was time for lunch, and my stomach growled. After they left, Fiona took me to the dining room. Mother Robin was there and beckoned us over to her.

"I spoke with Father Bartholomew after he finished with you, Sister Fiona," she said. "He mentioned his idea of dedicating what is left of the spear to Zoryn. I agree that it makes sense. If you feel you will be strong enough to make the walk, we would like to do it tomorrow."

"What about the disciples of Kravyna?" I asked.

"They still want to get their hands on it," she said. "But we think we can prevent that."

"How?"

"Wait and see," Robin said with a grin. "I think you'll like his idea."

With that, she turned her attention to others. Fiona and I found seats at the table and enjoyed a hearty lunch of slices of cold roast fowl, greens, bread, and fresh fruit. When we finished, we returned to the veranda, where I fell asleep with Fiona sitting on my lap.

The next morning, Fiona was up with the sun, as was her custom. After doing little to nothing the day before, I felt significantly better. My aches had diminished, and the ringing in my ears was gone. I dressed without assistance, and we headed to the dining room hand in hand.

"Good," Robin said when she saw us. "In a couple of hours, I will come get you, Mr. Falk. We will retrieve what's left of the spear from the vault. Then we will walk to Zoryn's sanctuary."

"What about the Kravynans?" I asked.

"We've come up with a way to neutralize them. That's all I want to say for now."

Mother Robin had something up her sleeve. I didn't know what it was, but Sylvaris did, and he approved. In fact, he could hardly wait.

When Robin came to find me, Fiona headed toward the front entrance of the temple, saying she would be waiting there. Robin led me down into the cool, damp cellar. There was a heavy iron door, and she withdrew a key from inside her robe and unlocked it.

When the door swung open, I could feel the numinous energy of the spear fragment. Robin gestured for me to pick it up, and when I did, strength flowed into my limbs, banishing all residual aches and pains. We headed back up and to the front door.

Waiting for us outside were nearly four hundred people, all dressed in the robes of their orders. Priests and priestesses, novices, and acolytes filled the street. Even the temple of Thalorix was present in their black-hooded robes, and they never took part in public ceremonies. The orders of the minor gods were all there, save one—Kravyna.

It occurred to me that they would not dare oppose this act of solidarity. Attacking this group would bring upon them the wrath of all the gods. The best they could do was absent themselves in a form of protest.

Fiona took my arm, and together we followed Robin into the middle of the throng. As soon as we stood in the middle of the street, the entire assemblage started moving. The residents of Rhavella lined either side, and as we passed, they fell in behind us.

Sylvaris heartily approved of what Bartholomew had arranged. It occurred to me that he was enjoying a moment in the spotlight. Perhaps he had to share the moment with Eldryne, but she would not relish it with the same enthusiasm.

The procession moved like a multi-colored river through the streets. The sky-blue of Zoryn's attendants led us, the dread black of Thalorix brought up the rear. In between were the rich green of Vyran, the teal of Calithra, the charcoal gray of Korath, the white of Vionelle, the gold of Serethyn, the rosy pink of Lysmera, the deep blue of Marivelle, the earthy brown of Teryssa, and the purple of Eldryne. The only color lacking was the blood-red of Kravyna.

The citizens of the city murmured with awe as we passed. They had never seen all the orders in procession. Children clamored to see, and adults lifted many of them into the air as we passed.

I clutched the twisted remnant of the spear in my left hand. Fiona rested her hand on my right arm, her golden skin glowing in the bright sunlight. She squeezed my forearm gently.

"Do you feel it?" she whispered, leaning close enough that her breath tickled my ear.

"All I can feel is Kravyna's numen," I said.

"There's something else in the air," she said quietly. "It's the crowd, a feeling of unity and strength. It's amazing."

We rounded a corner not long after that, and everything changed. The procession stopped abruptly. The crowd fell silent. In that silence, a voice rang out.

"Where is the thief?" I heard Utred bellow.

I pushed my way through the crowd of our procession. People parted to allow me to pass. Fiona stayed by my side, her head held straight.

When we reached the front, I saw that the red-robed disciples of Kravyna blocked the road. Men and women, all stout and muscular, stood with drawn swords. They all had shaved heads or topknots. Utred stood front and center, his face a mask of fury.

"Thief!" he shouted when he saw me. "That belongs to us! Surrender it, or we'll take it by force!"

"Utred, I know you're not a fool," I answered calmly, my voice carrying with unnatural power and ease. "Have you already forgotten what happened the last time you tried to take this spear? Zoryn himself prevented it, as he will prevent you now. And look around. Every order save yours is marching with us. An attack on any member of this group would bring the wrath of all the others upon Kravyna. She would not survive. Your entire order would become outcasts, shunned by all good people. I'll make you a deal, Utred. When I lay what remains of the spear on Zoryn's altar, if he shuns my gift, you may take it with my blessing."

"It belongs to Kravyna," Utred replied, but his voice lacked the punch and anger from a minute earlier.

"Sister Fiona and I retrieved three holy relics from the Torsten's Hoard," I said. "The Hammer of Korath and the Lute of Calithra are already in the hands of their people. Those divine artifacts are benign in nature, imbued with the power to create and inspire. Your spear was different. It was created for destruction, and the only limit to its use was the physical toll it took on the one who wielded it. Zoryn sent the thunderbolt on the plain outside the city. I wondered why he did not destroy it entirely at that moment. Now that I see all the orders assembled, it becomes clear to me what he intended. Join us, Utred. If Zoryn shuns the gift, take it. If he does not, he does not mean for you to have it. Accept his will."

When I finished speaking, there was a grumble of thunder. Like everyone else, I looked up. There was not a cloud in the sky. I could almost see Sylvaris clapping his hands in delight.

"Stand down," Utred grumbled to his people. "The thief is right. I'm not a fool. Only an idiot would persist after hearing that."

39

The disciples of Kravyna withdrew to the sides of the road. With the others, Fiona and I started walking. The tall spire of Zoryn's temple was just ahead. It pierced the cloudless sky like a needle of white marble.

The crowd's murmurs had picked up again after the confrontation with Utred ended. Our multi-colored procession flowed forward, approaching the steps of the temple. Fiona's hand rested on my arm as she strode beside me. This was her triumph as much or more than mine. The shy, sheltered woman who had left Harkiss at her goddess's urging had become a confident, seasoned adventurer.

As we reached the steps, the few in front of us parted, revealing a gaunt-faced, white-haired man in the sky-blue robes of Zoryn. As Fiona and I started to climb, he smiled at us. When we were two steps below him, he raised his arms. We stopped, and the crowd around us fell silent.

"Brothers and sisters," he said, his voice booming out above the crowd with unnatural vigor, "you see before you a convergence of divine will. The Spear of Kravyna, a holy relic of perilous power, was shattered by Zoryn's bolt—shattered but not completely destroyed. Today, these two brave adventurers, Fiona Magellan and Dexter Falk, come to offer this dangerous fragment to Zoryn, honoring the sky-father who rules the heavens and the pantheon. Dexter Falk, Fiona Magellan, step forward with your offering."

The head priest moved aside, leaving the way clear to the black marble altar behind him. Fiona and I approached. I placed the remnant of the spear in the center of the altar and went down on one knee. Fiona kept her hand on my arm and did the same.

All around us, I could feel a powerful swirl of asomatous energy. It was not just Zoryn's, but a weave of divine presence from all the gods and goddesses. There was a feeling of richness, of robustness, that I had never experienced.

For the space of three heartbeats, nothing happened. From my knee on the ground, I felt a slight tremor, as though there was a rumble just outside the range of my hearing. In the clear blue sky, a small black cloud appeared directly overhead out of nowhere. A slender bolt lanced from it to the spear tip. One moment it was there, the next, it was gone.

When it vanished, the numen I felt all around us changed. It brought with it a surge of vitality—of life essence. The aches I still felt from being hit by Zoryn's bolt on the plain were washed away.

The crowd felt it, too. After a moment of silence, they began cheering raucously. Zoryn's priest gestured for Fiona and me to rise. He waited for the cheering to begin to subside, then raised his arms again.

"Behold! Zoryn has accepted the gift, and the gods approve. Harmonious balance is our reward. Let no order claim dominion over another. Let this be a day of celebration. Sacrifices have been prepared for us all to enjoy!"

"All the orders decided that today should be a public feast," he explained to us, his voice barely carrying over the renewed cheering from the crowd. "You'll be able to smell the meat cooking in a few minutes."

He led us to the side where a small awning had been erected to protect against the blazing sun. There were two cushioned wicker chairs there. He waved us to them.

"You are the guests of honor today," he said. "This is a celebration of your incredible accomplishment. Sit. Watch. Enjoy."

Zoryn's priest left to oversee the preparations underway. Fiona and I took our seats. She reached over and twined the fingers of her left hand in my right. We could now smell the meat cooking behind the temple.

Novices and acolytes in the robes of all the orders (except Kravyna's) scurried about, setting up long tables for the feast that was to come. A couple of wagons were drawn up with barrels of what I guessed was ale, and carts filled with cheap wooden cups were pulled next to them. People of all walks of life were milling around, and children were darting through the crowd, enjoying themselves.

"The feast days in my village were nothing like this," Fiona said. "And celebrations in Harkiss were subdued."

A group of musicians in the teal robes of Calithra appeared in the back of the throng, playing a lively tune. Hearing the music, the children broke off their games and went to listen, and then to dance. Seeing the children inspired some of the adults to cut a caper, to the cheers of their friends watching.

In a knot, toward the back of the assemblage, I saw Utred and his people. They were standing apart from the celebration, with arms crossed. At least they hadn't stormed off to plot more trouble. Of course, Kravyna's people held onto grudges the way misers cling to gold. Word of what had happened would spread throughout the order. They would undoubtedly make trouble for me in the future.

Jacob Cerule approached us, begging us to tell the full story of our adventure to one of his temple's scribes before we departed Rhavella. A priest of Teryssa delivered an armload of flowers that he arranged beside Fiona's chair. When the feast was prepared, acolytes of Zoryn brought us platters of roasted ox meat, fresh bread, and cups of ale. All we needed to do was sit and enjoy the spectacle.

"I wonder when they started planning this?" Fiona asked. "Something of this size doesn't just fall into place."

"We started to discuss it when we learned that Mr. Falk lived," the head priest of Zoryn said, having returned just in time to overhear her remark. "Zoryn sent me a vision in my sleep. Father Bartholomew of your order received a similar message from Eldryne. In fact, every god-touched priest and priestess in the city did. We all reached out to one another at the same time."

"Have you ever experienced anything like it before?" Fiona asked.

"No. And what strikes me as the most unusual thing is that Sylvaris and Eldryne served as the catalyst. Sylvaris likes to make mischief, and Eldryne tends to be reclusive, and yet they are responsible for this surge in unity between all the orders."

"Except for Kravyna's people," I commented.

"Did you ever wonder if the presence of her spear is the reason why the existence of the Hoard was allowed to remain hidden?" he asked.

"Interesting," I said, having not considered that. "But Fiona found the palimpsest."

"An accident, or a vagary of Serethyn's," he said. "Who knows? But, once found, it couldn't be unfound, so to speak."

"How much of a part do you think Zoryn played in all this? I thought the major gods stayed out of the squabbles of the minors."

"I think he declared himself on the plain outside the city. Until then, I'm sure he was watching what the two of you were doing with great interest. If you had not been successful, or had been thwarted in your quest, he might have stepped in earlier."

"That might explain…" I mused.

"Explain what?" Fiona asked.

"From the moment you arrived at my door, Sylvaris stayed closely connected with me—until the thunderbolt. Normally, he comes and goes. I had been thinking that his unusual interest was driven by wanting Eldryne in his debt. But now?"

"Those are thoughts best kept to yourself, Mr. Falk," the head priest said. "We are celebrating the unity of the orders today. Suggesting that Zoryn may have persuaded Sylvaris to assist in this matter might not serve either of their purposes."

As he said this, I could feel Sylvaris strongly confirming the wisdom of the priest's advice. I remembered Azar once told me, "Sometimes there are questions you want to ask out of curiosity, but you don't really want to know the answer." This seemed to be one of those times.

He excused himself once again, leaving to manage the proceedings. Fiona and I watched the happy gathering. A novice in the green robes of Vyran approached, carrying a goblet. She delivered it to Fiona.

"For the Golden Scholar, with Vyran's blessings," she said as she curtsied and departed.

"The Golden Scholar?" I asked as Fiona took a sip of the wine within the chalice.

"Calithra's people have been busy," she said with a smile. "You should hear how they refer to you."

"The Mule-Riding Fool?"

Fiona snickered. "No. The Thunder-Touched Trickster, although your idea has a better ring to it."

The group of musicians had been gradually wandering nearer to where we were. Their music was lively, and I found myself tapping my toes. It must have affected Fiona the same way, or perhaps the wine did, but she suddenly rose and tugged my hand.

"Dance with me, Dex. Let's make a memory."

I followed her down the steps and into the crowd of people dancing. The crowd folded in around us, and we joined in with them. Fiona was not a skilled dancer. The last time she probably tried was as a girl, before she went to Harkiss, but she laughed over her missteps, and her smile was radiant.

We danced until we were breathless, then returned to our seats overlooking the festivities. People kept bringing us refreshments throughout the day. Honey cakes, ale, wine, and much-welcomed water, given the heat of the day. As evening approached, more meat and bread were given to us. We danced when the spirit moved us, and I reveled in the look of Fiona's laughing face, her golden skin, her long-lashed brown eyes, her swirling hair, and her delightful figure.

As darkness crept up, things began to quiet and slow. The crowd, tired from a day of revelry, started to drift away. I took Fiona by the hand, and we returned to the temple of Sylvaris together. When I closed the door of our chamber, Fiona draped her arms around my neck and kissed me.

"No matter what happens, we have today," she said. "A memory to hold onto and treasure. I love you, Dexter Falk. You have changed me, and I will always be grateful."

"And I love you, Fiona Magellan," I said as I picked her up by the waist, "but the day has not yet ended, and there are still things we can do to make it even more memorable."

I tossed her onto the bed, eliciting a shriek and a giggle. She stretched her arms up to me, and I could not resist the invitation. It was some time later that sleep claimed us both.

<h1 style="text-align:center">40</h1>

When morning came, the pace of things in the temple was much slower than usual. Everyone was exhausted by the previous day's revel, and Fiona and I were no exception. She, for once, did not wake with the sun.

After breakfast, Jacob Cerule arrived with a Calithran priestess. She spent the morning interviewing us, extracting every detail of our story we could remember, as she scribbled notes frantically. Fiona showed her the palimpsest and all her notes, along with Valerian Wouk's translation of the praise poem, and Sister Elissa's astronomical calculations.

It was time for lunch when she finished. We joined the group in the dining room, and Mother Robin waved us over. After we served ourselves, we sat with her at the end of the long table.

"There is a ship bound for Jenestra leaving on the morning tide tomorrow. I booked passage for you both."

Her words dispelled the pleasant feeling that lingered after our conversation with the Calithrans, as we relived our adventure. We would travel to Jenestra. Fiona would take up her new role at the temple of Eldryne, and I would sail across the Tiburn to Lenoa, collect my horse, and return to Tallesin.

Fiona gave me a weak smile across the table. Robin noted the exchange. She offered a rueful smile of her own.

When we finished eating, I decided the best distraction would be to begin teaching Fiona the Lutetian language. We worked first on common phrases. Fiona's quick mind not only mastered them easily, but she also began figuring out the grammar and structure.

"You'll be speaking like a native in no time," I assured her. "If the crew of the boat is Lutetian, you can practice with them."

"I'd rather practice with you. I've always enjoyed it when you teach me things," she said with a naughty glint in her eye as she slid into my lap.

"I think I'm beginning to regret teaching you about teasing."

"Oh? Am I teasing you now?" she smirked with mock innocence as she squirmed devilishly. "Perhaps you should punish me."

I pulled her hair away, and my lips found the place under her ear that I knew was extremely sensitive. With a moan, she twisted away and pulled me to my feet. Our clothing disappeared, and we soon found that rhythm we'd discovered together.

During dinner, I taught her some more Lutetian. One of the priests overheard. He was fluent and joined in. When the meal ended, he took Fiona away, promising to return her in an hour or so.

"You'll be parting in Jenestra, won't you?" Robin observed.

"I'm afraid so."

"You look like you're carrying the weight of a thousand chains, Dexter."

"It feels that way right now."

"She seems excited about the work she'll be doing for the Eldrynes. Do you have anything to look forward to?"

"Not that I know of. People come to me with problems that can't be solved by the usual means. I never know when they'll knock on my door."

"You sound so sad. I understand your distress at parting from Miss Magellan, but you just accomplished something remarkable. Do you take no pleasure from that?"

"For the last year or so, my life has been a whirlwind, Mother Robin. Sylvaris has sent me three great challenges. With each one, there was a woman, a marvelous woman. I fell in love with each one—I still have love in my heart for them. But with all three, he let me know—sometimes gently, sometimes harshly—that my future does not include them. It is a bitter draught to swallow."

"Have you prayed to him about it?"

"He sends me vague reassurance that my time will come. Yet each of these women has been full of drive, passion, spirit, and intelligence. Each of them is different, but all are fabulous. I can see myself leading a blessed life with any of them, but he lets me know it is not to be. So, yes, I am sad."

"And yet I can tell you that you are favored by Sylvaris like none of his other servants," Robin said. "After your success here, there can be no other mortal, save Azar, whom Sylvaris treasures more. You view this as maltreatment at his hands, but I doubt that is his intent. Have you considered that he has put these women in your life as a reward for doing his will, and as helpmeets?"

"A reward? With each one I have tasted profound love—fierce and real— only to have it ripped away."

"But they have helped you, haven't they? Agatha, in bringing Oderic to justice, as horrible as it was, Catherine, with freeing Iliona and recapturing the ships, and Fiona? Without her, the Hoard of Torsten would have remained only a legend, but Eldryne sent her to find you."

"They were essential to my success, obviously. But why take them away?"

"Perhaps to make you hungry for the next? If Sylvaris didn't care for you, Dexter, he could have supplied you with some shriveled-up crone or a crippled dwarf to help you, and not a beautiful woman in each case."

I felt Sylvaris's equivalent of a cuff alongside my head as I listened to what Robin said. She saw me wince. She grinned.

"I'm right, aren't I?" she said. "Sylvaris has been listening, hasn't he?"

"Yes, and yes," I said with a sigh. "He just let me know that you are correct. He could have sent a crippled dwarf."

"Then I urge you to be grateful," Robin said with a smile, "and hope he doesn't change his mind the next time."

I could help but chuckle, even if it came somewhat ruefully. Sylvaris gave me a pat on the head. That made me laugh again, less ruefully.

"You're right, Robin. The pain of parting is so hard that I forget to consider my blessings. Agatha, Catherine, and Fiona were more than companions; they were gifts. Each of them made me better than I would have been without them."

"Celebrate what was and look forward to what comes next. Sylvaris seems to be relying on you rather heavily. I suspect that will continue. He probably intends to make more use of his god-touched wanderer."

"Thank you. This has helped," I said as I stood.

I looked around and spotted Fiona sitting in front of the empty fireplace, speaking earnestly with the priest who'd taken her away earlier. She caught my gaze. I jerked my head in the direction of the veranda and went and sat down, enjoying the relative coolness of the evening. Fiona joined me a few minutes later, kissing my cheek and curling up in my lap.

"Brother Michel was most helpful," she said.

"What did you learn?"

Fiona spent the next few minutes telling me, practicing her pronunciation. The priest had taught her a few tricks. She rolled her r's more smoothly and hit the right nasal tone on some of the vowels.

A knock on the door woke us in the morning. The sun was not yet up, but the tide called. We dressed, and I took our saddlebags over my shoulder. The *Margaret Clarisse* was waiting for us. As soon as we boarded, they cast off, and we headed north to Jenestra.

The crew of the boat was Lutetian, and Fiona spent the entire voyage chatting with them in their language. Heeding Robin's advice, I focused on what I'd been given, or lent, to put things in proper perspective, rather than on what I would lose. Fiona delighted in learning.

The voyage went smoothly. On the third day, we arrived in Jenestra in the morning. We headed to the Tawny Lion. Fiona had agreed to one more night before we went our separate ways.

The same two giggling maids brought up the tub for our bath. Fiona shocked them when she interrupted their comments with one of her own. The three of them engaged in a humorous conversation. I stayed out of earshot, figuring I was one of the topics of their discussion.

When the tub was ready, I climbed in first. Fiona slid in between my legs with a sigh. She gathered my hands in hers and placed them where she wanted them.

"And what did our silly maids have to say this time?" I asked.

"They like the white streak in your hair. They think it makes you look like a dangerous rogue, nothing like the man with two black eyes they saw when we first arrived. They wanted to know what sort of lover you are."

"Oh? And what did you tell them?"

"Not to tease you," she said as she burst into laughter.

We made the most of our last night together. The candles were spent before we were. After dressing and dining, I escorted Fiona to the temple of Eldryne. The novice at the door asked our business.

"I'm here to see Mother Erma," Fiona said.

A few minutes later, a sweet-looking older woman came bustling out. When she saw Fiona, her face creased in a smile.

"Sister Fiona?" she asked.

"Yes, Mother Erma," Fiona replied, dipping into a brief curtsy.

"We'll have no more of that, my dear. I received the most wonderful letter from Father Bartholomew. He sings your praises and informs me that you will soon become quite famous. We would be honored to have you join our temple. And is this the equally renowned Dexter Falk?"

"At your service," I said with a small bow.

"My, you're a handsome devil. Well, I'm afraid it's time for farewells, sister. We have work for you waiting."

Fiona turned to face me. Her eyes and mine were brimming with tears. Our kiss was gentle, almost chaste. She wiped her eyes and entered the temple with Erma.

I headed to the temple of Sylvaris to find Father Lucien. The sooner I could get on a ship to Lenoa, the happier I would be. With any luck, there might be one leaving on the evening tide. I certainly hoped so. There was no reason for me to linger in Jenestra. If Sylvaris had another adventure planned for me, I figured I might as well get to it. Besides, I'd left Rufus at the temple in Lenoa.

ABOUT THE AUTHOR

John Spearman has been a Fortune 500 sales and marketing executive, a Latin teacher and coach at a prestigious New England boarding school, and an award-winning author. He lives in coastal Maine with his wife and their dogs.

If you enjoyed reading this book, please consider leaving a positive review on Amazon.com or Goodreads.com. It will help other readers like you find books they might enjoy. To learn more about the author's different works, please visit www.johnjspearman.com.

www.ingramcontent.com/pod-product-compliance
Lightning Source LLC
Chambersburg PA
CBHW071736150726
47998CB00005B/1669